Finding Our Balance

Lauren Hopkins

Cover art by Sarah Hopkins

 Gymternet Productions

To my family for encouraging all of my dreams
no matter how crazy

Thursday, April 14, 2016
113 Days Left

"Team pressure sets! In your training groups! Everyone hits or no one hits! Repeat!"

I'm gulping down water after a warm-up that felt like a Navy SEAL boot camp. I would kill for an ice bath and ibuprofen right about now, but the day's not even close to over. When I glance over my shoulder, the other 29 girls at the U.S. Olympic Gymnastics Training Center are already lined up across the floor at attention. "Everyone hits or no one hits," they yell in unison. Lined up from smallest to tallest, arms at their sides, they look like soldiers ready to march into battle.

That's kind of how this place feels. Like a war zone. And we're about to tear each other to pieces.

Vera Malkina, the national team head coach, looks over at me disapprovingly. She's pushing 70, but is still athletic enough that I wouldn't be surprised to see her whip out a floor routine and kick my ass while doing it. I suck at floor.

Confession – I'm terrified of her. But I'm also obsessed. When I was in middle school I spent basically all of my free time looking up her old routines on YouTube. As a gymnast, Vera competed at four Olympic Games in a row – first with the Soviet Union and then with the United States – before retiring to become a coach. She opened a gym in Wisconsin with her husband, and they coached their own daughter Natasha – now my personal coach – to six Olympic medals of her own.

They are gymnastics royalty. I've been training at Natasha's gym, the Malkina Gold Medal Academy, for four years and this is my third invite to the training center, but I'll never stop feeling like a giggly six-year-old in Vera's presence.

"Hurry up, get in line!" Vera bellows as everyone scrambles out of their warm-ups and over to the six balance beams. The practice beams are regulation height, but one end of the row faces a big foam pit where we land dismounts, giving our ankles and knees a break.

The training rotation groups form, but I'm clueless, like I've just crawled out of a deep and drooly nap. I try to remember where I'm supposed to go, and when that doesn't work, I pretend to be busy with my hair, winding my honey brown ponytail into a neat bun at the top of my head while secretly eyeing the teams forming.

Finally, dead center, there's my group – three tiny juniors who look nauseous with fear and then Maddy Zhang, the 2015 world champion on vault.

"You're going last," Maddy says I as I jog over. "You better not fall, or we all have to go again."

I roll my eyes. I've only been at "the farm" – what everyone calls the training center, partly because it's a working Wisconsin dairy farm but mostly because the press likes to compare it to old Soviet collective farms where life was so brutal not everyone survived – for less than 72 hours but I'm pretty much over the attitudes.

The juniors steadily make their way through their routines. Not bad, but easy, I can't help thinking. Level 10 acro and basic leaps and turns, but hey, at least no one falls.

Maddy's older and her routine is a lot more difficult, though she has absolutely zero grace or flow to her movements, making her look like a drunk toddler as she goes from skill to skill. Still, her dismount is one of the hardest in the world – an arabian double front, same as mine. Even though she only lands it into the pit, I know her punch off the end of the beam and the quick rotation of her flips are more than good enough for her to land it on a hard surface.

Maddy actually squeals and claps for herself before climbing out of the pit. I make a face, but inside I'm freaking out. I know she's been working super hard on this routine and it's one of the most difficult sets in the country, but beam's *my* thing, so yeah, I'm anxious. If by some miracle I do make it to the Olympics, it'll be for this event.

As I wait for Maddy to get over herself so I can have my turn, I notice Vera's eyes are glued on me from across the gym. No pressure.

Natasha signals for me to start. I give the springboard a good bounce before going into my press handstand mount, biting the inside of my cheek because it focuses me. That, and repeating the name of each skill rhythmically in my head as I do them. Concentrating on a beat keeps my mind from wandering, and before long, I'm so zen, the world melts completely away and I can do anything.

"Back-hand-SPRING-back-hand-SPRING-lay-OUT," my brain punches out each piece, emphasizing the last syllable of each skill as I land them. "Dou-ble-TURN, side-aer-i-AL-o-no-DI, sheep-JUMP-Yang-BO…"

From start to finish, it's perfect – clean form, fluid connections, and most importantly, zero wobbles. I know the dismount won't be a problem, especially with the safety of landing in the pit, but I don't dare change my ritual. I close my eyes, inhale deeply, picture myself finishing perfectly, exhale, open my eyes, and then do it for real.

No one applauds, because that's not how things are done at the farm. But the gym is dead silent, and I know I've made an impression. I let myself sink into the foam blocks for a second to hide my smile before pulling myself out and dusting off the chalk.

Vera is staring at me, and she looks…angry? No. Inquisitive. Curious. Her eyes narrow, her lips purse, and she takes a second to gather her thoughts before slapping her hand on her clipboard.

"Every group except the team at beam D had falls," she announces in her Russian accent, still thick despite her thirty years in the U.S. "Terrible. Disastrous. Do you expect to win Olympic gold if you can't hit your events? What are you waiting for? Get started, full routines! Beam D, you can practice dismounts, ten each."

"What a great prize," Maddy scowls from the mat, where she sits casually in a split.

We line up again and do dismount after dismount. Vera's eyes are on me for every last one.

***

"Four full beam sets. *Four*. Because of that idiot junior Sarah Flannery. How did she even get an invite? Vera's on crack."

I pick out Emerson Bedford's voice from across the room. My eyes scan the dining hall until I spot the tall (shut up, 5'3" is tall in our world), rail-thin, 18-year-old blonde in front of the serving trays, wrinkling her nose at tonight's dinner of rubbery grilled chicken and soggy vegetables.

"Uhhh, Sarah didn't need an invite? She was the junior champion last year?"

That would be my best friend and training partner Ruby Spencer, who at 19 is a little older than your average elite gymnast. Ruby was a former junior star pegged to win the 2012 Olympic all-around gold medal until she tore her Achilles just months before the Games.

After three years of toying with a comeback, she returned to competition last summer, but she wasn't mentally ready. The press called her "tragic" and "washed-up" so naturally, she decided to get revenge by getting in the best shape of her life. Typical Ruby.

"It's so cute when Emerson bitches about girls who weren't even born when she was starting level four," Ruby, a dead-ringer for Misty Copeland with her mocha skin and long dark hair, says to me, but loudly enough for everyone in the state of Wisconsin to hear. "Oh, did I say *cute*? I meant mind-blowingly obnoxious."

I laugh, but stop when Emerson glances my way. Emerson is a spoiled, selfish, entitled snob, but she also won nationals four years in a row, is a back-to-back world all-around champion, has a Gatorade sponsorship, and went to her prom last year with the guy who quit One Direction. I can't stand her, but up until a year ago, I worshipped her. Like, posters from *Gymnastics Insider* magazine covered my bedroom wall from floor to ceiling. Bitch or not, I kind of want her approval.

"You were shockingly really good," Emerson says, making her way over to our table with Maddy, her sidekick.

It somehow sounds more like a threat than a compliment, but I'll take what I can get. I almost choke on my water, something Emerson definitely notices, smirking her trademark half-smile that somehow looks condescending and friendly at the same time.

"My coach said your start value on beam is like, a 6.9 or something. That's like, China-good. What's your name?"

"Amalia. Blanchard." I don't even bother asking Emerson's name, and Emerson doesn't bother offering. We both know I already know.

"You know we have the same beam dismount, right?"

"Actually," I start, and I take a split second to debate telling her, but my mouth is moving faster than my brain, "this is really funny but when I decided to go elite, we were trying to figure out what my upgrades would be and I said I didn't care as long as I got to do a Patterson dismount because that's what you did. That's why I also do the press mount, and the Onodi…my coach totally didn't think I'd be able to hit a routine that hard, but I wanted to because of you, so I worked really hard and it's finally coming together…"

Ruby snorts laughing, cutting my word vomit short. My face is 50 shades of hot pink, which I'm not embarrassed to know is Emerson's favorite color. I definitely went too far. Emerson smirks again, and I know she's totally unfazed by people losing their minds in her presence.

"That's so cute," she says, like she's talking to a three-year-old messing up the alphabet. "Can't wait to see your full routines in verification." Again, it sounds like a threat.

"Yeah, can't wait," Maddy echoes as the two head to the TV lounge to eat – forbidden, unless you're Emerson and can do whatever you want.

Ruby is still laughing.

"You literally freaked out," she spits out between giggles. "Look at me. I have tears coming out of my eyes!"

I want to stab myself with a fork. "Do you think she hates me?"

"Mal, I've known Emerson for like, six years. She definitely hates you. She hates everyone who's not her."

"Whatever, I don't care, but seriously, do you think I creeped her out?"

"You definitely creeped her out. You sounded like a rescue dog trying to get adopted."

"You're the worst." But I start to laugh because I know she's right.

"Whatever," she says, picking up our trays. "She probably forgot about your entire existence the second she walked away, so don't sweat it. And if she does hate you, you can always hang my posters on your walls and copy my routines and obsess over me. Now let's watch *Teen Moms* and be thankful our lives are at least somewhat under control."

***

My entire body melts into the mattress at lights out. It's springy and hard and probably a hundred years old, but it feels like a pool of feathers to my battered and exhausted muscles. Everything hurts and I'm dying. But as desperate as I am to relax, my mind is absolutely not letting me.

At 15, I should be spending my nights sneaking out of the house through my bedroom window, sexting my crush, cyber bullying my classmates...that's how teenagers behave, right? I'm secretly, like, forty. I seriously can't even picture what normal people my own age do with their lives.

I'm *not* a normal 15-year-old. I am an elite athlete who eats, breathes, and sleeps gymnastics, with every ounce of energy and focus spent trying to reach my goal of making it to the Olympics. I wake up, work out, go to school, work out, do homework, and go to bed. On the weekends, swap school with sitting in an ice bath and binge-watching entire TV seasons. What a life.

But aside from the whole "one of the best gymnasts in the country" thing, my life is painfully average. I have great parents with good jobs who own a three-bedroom house in a nice neighborhood just outside of Seattle. I get good grades, my friends are fantastic, I've never had a boyfriend, and no one has ever peer pressured me into doing drugs. Not even cigarettes! Fifth grade health class was a lie.

I started gymnastics when I was four. Back then my coaches at the YMCA didn't even want me to compete, because even though I picked up on skills quickly, the second I had to show my stuff in front of parents or other kids, I froze. So I was a rec kid, basically there to play on the trampoline a few times a week, something my parents loved because I'd pass out from exhaustion the second I got home.

Eventually, one of the coaches said they might as well add me to the level 4 competition roster. Chalk it up to a slow year. At seven, most of the kids starting out at that level were a year younger than me, but I had all of the required skills down, and my parents thought performing in front of a crowd would help me build confidence. I was terrible at first, falling at almost every meet, but I picked up on skills faster than anyone and moved up quickly through the levels.

I'm still a nervous wreck at competitions, but with my little mind games I can trick myself into hitting my routines even if my heart feels like it's being strangled to death. At ten, I won my division of level 9 national championships, and that's when my YMCA coaches told me to move on. I was the most advanced gymnast they'd ever had and they didn't want me to hold me back. They helped me find the Malkina Gold Medal Academy, aka MGMA, aka where I now spend 98% of my time.

It's been almost five years since the move, and Natasha has taken me to levels I never thought possible. When it came time to make the decision to go elite – the hella intense level that puts you on track to go to the Olympics – I didn't think I had what it took, but Natasha believed in me. Cheesy, but true.

Okay, so I failed at qualifying last year. Failed? More like fell apart entirely when tasked with performing insane levels of difficulty for the first time. But what can you do? Push it to the back of your mind. Work harder. Get better. Everyone here thinks I only got invited to the farm this year because my coach is Vera's daughter, but I've worked my butt off. I know I deserve to be here. And tomorrow's my time to prove it.

Friday, April 15, 2016
112 Days Left

It's verification day. I scream into my towel while waiting for the shower water to heat up.

Verification...it's like a competition, but in a training gym at the farm in front of the other gymnasts, their coaches, and the national team staff instead of in a giant arena in front of thousands of people and broadcast on network television.

Yet somehow, verification is scarier.

Vera watches us at competitions, but with so much going on at once, her focus isn't as laser-sharp as it is when we compete one at a time at the farm. Also, crowds cheering and the general noise in an arena is basically like white noise for gymnasts, helping us stay in the zone. The silence at the farm makes 90 seconds on beam feel endless.

It's all part of Vera's evil genius, I know. Vera uses the time at the farm to weed out those who can't hack it under the most intense pressure imaginable. What better way to do this than expect you to perform mistake-free with the best gymnasts and coaches in the country silently judging you?

After a hot shower and a breakfast of yogurt, granola, and fruit, Natasha brings me and Ruby into the gym for a little meeting before warm-ups.

"Trust me," she starts. "I know my mother. I know what she's looking for. If you want to make the Olympic team, you have to hit *today*. The Open, nationals, trials...none of them mean a thing if you lose your cool at verification. You have the skills. You have the talent. You have the mental game. If you're nervous, pretend you're not. Body language is key. Don't let the competition know you're nervous. Make them think this is just a preschool rec class to you. It's child's play. You're above it all. If you *do* decide to make a mistake, fight like hell. Even if you can't save it, show that you're a fighter. And yes, I get it. You're under a ton of pressure, everyone's watching...but think of it as practice. Your biggest enemy here is your own mind, so shut it off, focus on your rhythm, and hit your routines. And have fun."

"You have been reaped for the 2016 Hunger Games," Ruby jokes. "Be prepared to die, because you probably will, but have *fun!*"

Okay, so I've been calm through every workout and test up to this point, but once the realization that this one day could determine my future sets in, I can feel my heart do a double back.

"Don't listen to her," Natasha rubs my back to soothe me. "It's your first time, so I don't expect you to be perfect, but I do expect you to do your absolute best."

"I don't expect you to be perfect but I *do* expect you to be perfect," Ruby snarks. How is Ruby so relaxed? I am going to throw up, cry, and explode all at the same time.

"You know what I mean, brat. Okay, start jogging. Get warm. Whatever happens today, just please, don't suck."

***

When "Eye of the Tiger" finishes, I click off my iPod, twist the earbuds into a perfect coil, and secure them with a rubber band before slipping them into my gym bag. It's the most ridiculous song ever, but it's the one my dad used to play in the car on the way to my level 4 meets when I was just starting out.

I'm a creature of habit. I trust rules, tradition, patterns...the beat of a song or the texture of my favorite leo controls the chaos of the world outside my brain. I feel at home a thousand miles away, and nothing can break my focus.

Unlike at actual competitions, there are no announcers or emcees at the farm, no music pumping through a stereo system between events, and no scoreboards boasting results. The day is quiet and smooth without the distractions of an arena, though I can't help tensing a bit at the thought. Those "distractions" are all very much a part of my routine.

"I didn't fall on beam in practice the other day, and it was so quiet, I could hear my heartbeat," I reason, nibbling my thumbnail. "I'll be fine."

"Second breakfast?"

I look up to see Emerson standing over me. I suddenly make a resolution to stop biting my nails, and refocus my jittery hand's attention to adjusting my bobby pins.

"I'm before you in the lineup," Emerson says. "Like, right before you. Alphabetical."

"Cool." I'm looking everywhere but at Emerson, not wanting her to see the nerves on my face. Nail-biting is a tell-tale sign that I'm a hot mess inside, and Emerson will totally use that against me. So much for fooling the competition.

"It's gotta suck for you, right? Like, the nobody opening act usually goes *before* Beyoncé, not after. If they went after, no one would care. Everyone would leave."

I smile, and then Emerson's words actually hit me. What the eff? I keep the smile glued on my face, mostly out of shock. I have no idea how to respond. My initial "oh em gee, Emerson Bedford is actually talking to *me*" excitement quickly fades to "I can't believe this bitch is trying to psych me out." Yeah, so I haven't been on the elite scene for long, but I grew up in gyms that were all about encouraging your teammates, not pushing them off a cliff.

I consider this while gathering the rest of my things, which I toss into my duffel bag. "I'm gonna go grab a bottle of water," I say, speed-walking towards the cooler where Ruby's doing press handstands.

"Emerson talked to me yesterday because she saw my beam," I say, throwing my things down next to her.

"Yeah, and?" She finishes her set and drops down to her butt. "You're still crapping your pants about it?"

"She even brought up my start value, probably because it's higher than hers. She's totally afraid I'll beat her on beam and she's trying to mess with my head."

"Wait, what?"

I relay my Emerson encounter to Ruby's delight.

"This is your *third time here* and she's already terrified of you!"

"Why would she be afraid of me? There's no way I could ever beat her at anything. Except like, beam, I guess. Maybe."

"Okay, but even if that's true, being better than her on beam means you're better than her at *something*. That literally makes her homicidal. She's the best for a reason and it's not all about gymnastics. I've seen plenty of girls come through the ranks all talented with big skills, but Em's like a drug-sniffing dog with that stuff. She always finds them. And destroys them."

"Great, have a good meet, I'm just gonna get on the next plane home."

"No, because you're not gonna let her get to you. You're pissed off?"

"Um...yeah."

"Good. *Use it.* That's the problem with everyone else. When Emerson drags them down, they cower in fear. You need to be like...like a crazy ancient Greek warrior or some shit. Those guys just grabbed their weapons and went to town on each other without a second thought."

"Cool, I'll just trident her to death when she dismounts bars."

"Come on, *use your miiiiiiiiind*," Ruby yells, mocking our old bars coach who was convinced gymnastics is 99% mental, 1% physical. I beg to differ. "For real, I remember when you started at MGMA and everyone was like, 'well, she has zero talent, but she works *hard*.' You're a beast, and you have that weird Rain Man brain where you, like, zone out and become a rock star. You can have all the talent in the world – and you do, boo – but it doesn't matter if you're weak. You're not weak. You're gonna be awesome today and Emerson will be so jealous, her brain will leak out of her ears. Trust me."

"Okay, okay, okay. I'll stay pissed. I'll mentally destroy everyone here. I'll kick ass. I'll kick everyone's ass."

"Yaaaaas, bitch! That's my girl. Except don't kick my ass. I'm like 85 in gymnastics years."

I grin and give her a big hug. Ruby's pep talks are the best. I'm totally ready.

***

I am a competitor. When I first started training at a high level, my coach would fall over laughing at my form and style – or lack thereof – but she never doubted my work ethic or my ability to hit my routines.

"You're like an ox, Mal," Natasha would giggle. "Dependable and strong. A hot mess, but at least I never have to worry about falls."

Coaches would refer to my idols as graceful swans and nimble gazelles, so yeah, I was never exactly thrilled about my animal comparison.

"But think about it," Natasha would try to explain when I was 13. "Say you make a big team, for worlds or the Olympic Games. Even if you're not the headliner or the star, you're the reliable one anyone can count on. That's a big job. Not everyone can handle that pressure, but you can."

She had a point, but I didn't want to be known for my flexed feet or awkward dancing. I once overheard a coach say that my short muscular body and long arms made my uneven bars routine look like an ape swinging around on tree branches, especially compared to the long, lean, and elegant girls who swing naturally and beautifully with hyper-extended knees and perfectly pointed toes. Even when these girls are short on handstands or bend their elbows, judges don't take deductions because they cover their flaws so well with their beauty. Me? I would get hit with tenth after tenth because my clunky style made the mistakes all the easier to see.

I paid special attention to my problem areas going forward, attending ballet classes every morning before school and spending every ounce of free time working on my flexibility while drilling my coach's notes into my brain – "point your *feet*, not just your toes! Glue your legs together from toes to thighs in a layout! Hit every handstand on bars! Make flipping on a four-inch beam look as natural as walking down the street! Your movements should be quick but not jerky; it's all about being fluid!"

The harder I worked and the older I got, my skills grew cleaner and my routines got stronger. I mimicked the smooth movement of the gymnasts I admired, and while I knew I'd never have their natural ability, I became an expert at faking it.

My scores began to rise from good to great, and when it came down to me and Rebecca Miller for the level 10 title last year, I squeaked to the top of the podium by just a tenth of a point.

"It's that attention to detail," Natasha smiled, patting the gold medal around my neck.

Not one to upset the yin and yang in the world by handing out no compliments with no criticism to balance it out, she added, "Now if only there was a way to teach expression. You look like a serial killer on bath salts with that creepy fake smile pasted on your face. Do people from Washington not have emotions?"

Okay, so I'm no Emerson Bedford (who made people cry with her *Swan Lake* floor routine at worlds last year, by the way), and maybe my body line will never look naturally flawless, but my form is clean, my difficulty is solid, and Ruby's right – I have the strongest mental game in the country, a far cry from the little girl who couldn't do a somersault in front of gym moms at the Y.

I walk over to the floor and find an empty spot where I can get in one last stretch before I have to join the lineup. Moments later, Emerson takes a spot next to me, her eyes glued to her phone.

"Hey," I decide to be diplomatic. "Good luck!"

Emerson glances at me, smirks, and says, "I don't need luck. Save it for yourself."

My heart flutters for a second, but I've already made up my mind about my response.

"Your attempt at psychological warfare was adorable," I whisper. "But if my beam scared you so much that you felt the need to resort to middle school levels of terrorism, just wait until you see the rest of my routines. I hope you like second place."

My threats are mostly empty, I know. I'm not winning gold or beating Emerson in the all-around anytime soon. But the look on Emerson's face is more than worth the lie.

Vera saunters through the door just then, our cue to stand in line and at attention, but I can't help grinning at Emerson for one last blow.

"Good luck!"

Friday, April 15, 2016
112 Days Left

"You know the drill," Vera announces to the line of the 14 of us who compete at the senior level. "The first group of seven will start on vault and the second group will start on bars with touch warm-ups at 9. For vault, touch includes two practice vaults each, and for bars, you get 30 seconds. After everyone has competed, you'll trade places...vault group goes to bars, and vice versa. Then we'll move on to beam and floor for the third rotation, and again swap for the final. Head now to your first event. Touch starts in two minutes. All right?"

"Yes, ma'am, we are prepared and ready to win!" This is what we're supposed to shout in response to Vera's speeches before competitions, even though it seems ridiculous when we're just at the farm and not actually competing against other teams.

My first event is vault, and I'm third in the lineup. Natasha stays with me while our assistant coach, Polina, heads to bars with Ruby. Ruby can deal with things like coaching changes, but I'm pretty sure Natasha knows I'd lose my cool with even the slightest hair out of place.

"Still nervous?" Natasha asks.

"Well, yeah, but in a good way? Like, I'm pissed off, and that kind of cancels out the nerves."

"Mad? Why?"

"Just...nothing." The last thing I need right now is to rat Emerson out and have my coach tell Vera. "I'm 15. I'm mad at the world."

I sprint down the vault runway for my warm-up, a round-off back-handspring onto the table and then a layout with one and a half twists off. Vault used to be a nightmare for me, but it got easier once Natasha took me under her wing. My warm-up vault– a Yurchenko 1.5 – was once my competition vault, and now it's just practice. I used to struggle and now I barely have to think about it.

Panting, I jog back to Natasha, who smiles. "You looked clean."

I take a large sip of water. "Thanks. Now for the test."

For my second warm-up, I do my actual vault – the all-mighty Amanar.

The Amanar has an entire full twist on top of my warm-up vault, making it two and a half twists in the air before landing. One of the most difficult vaults in the world, it's something everyone wants, but only a few can actually hit. It took me a full two years to get it perfect, and this is my first time actually competing it, so it's a bit of a risk. But if you want to make the Olympic team, it's a necessity.

Hitting the Amanar all comes down to following laws of physics. I trust physics. I trust that the vault will go well as long as I do everything precisely right each time. Once I got the positioning down in the gym, I was able to hit the vault every single time in practice, so my goal is to just do everything the same as always. "Every variable is the same," I whisper to myself before running, picturing the vault in my mind. "You'll be fine."

And I am. The landing isn't my best; I guess I twisted a tiny bit too slowly, but even so, I still make it all the way around. The biggest problem is the step I take forward to steady myself, but even if something like that happens in competition, it's so slight, the deduction won't be too much. Saluting out of habit, I glance at Natasha, always waiting with a correction or two.

"Good girl. I won't talk about the step because I'm sure you know not to do it again. Notes...first, you piked your hips a little bit when you came off the table. Not bad, but your body was at maybe a 160-degree angle instead of a straight 180. Oh, and your pre-flight...when you did the back handspring onto the table, your feet came about three inches apart...one of those things judges might never notice, but try to be aware just in case. Glue your legs from thighs to toes."

"Anything else?" I'm still out of breath.

"No. You looked amazing. Do it exactly the same, but a little quicker, a little tighter, and a little stronger, and your landing will be perfect. You ready?"

"Yeah," I say, hopping in place to keep my muscles warm. "I'm ready."

***

We compete one at a time at the farm, alternating back and forth between vault and bars until everyone's done. I'm third in line in my group for the first rotation, and I move up a spot for each rotation that follows, making me second on bars, first on beam, and last on floor.

Kaitlin Abrams is first on vault. I never watch the other girls compete, preferring to lose myself in the world of my iPod, earbuds in and eyes closed. I know Kaitlin vaults a Yurchenko full, basically the easiest vault Vera allows her athletes to compete, and the rest of her routines are lacking in difficulty as well. She's not my competition at all.

As soon as she finishes, the first athlete up on bars starts, and then it's time for Emerson on vault. Okay, yeah, I don't usually watch the other gymnasts, but I can't help opening my eyes and peering sideways toward the runway as Emerson begins to run. She doesn't have my power, and comes up a tiny bit short on the landing, making the two and a half twists look more like two and a quarter. But she covers it up well, hoping the last bit around so she's facing front on the landing. She'll definitely get a good score.

I shove my iPod into my bag before jogging to the start of the vault
track as one of the Logan twins mounts the uneven bars. I close my
eyes, take a deep breath, and picture myself sticking the vault.

Natasha sidles up to me and whispers, "beeeee the vault," nearly giving
me a heart attack. No other coach would dare joke around at a moment
like this, but Natasha knows how intense I get before my first routine. I
need to loosen up, and a dumb joke always helped.

I smile but don't break concentration. I bounce in place for a few
seconds, stretch my toes, and do a final straightening of my leotard, a
deep ocean blue long-sleeved competition leo with lighter blue accents
along the sleeves and down my sides.

"You're officially wedgie-less," Natasha remarks just as Amaya Logan
lands her bars dismount on her knees. Ouch. Been there. "Just like
practice, okay?"

I take my place at the start of the track and wait for my cue, the green
flag. When it goes up, everything sets into motion. I take a large step
back with my left foot, putting my weight on it while pointing my right
foot, which I then gently place down before sprinting forward on the
left.

When I sprint down the narrow track, I reach around 17 miles per hour,
a superhuman feat. My run is so well-timed, I know it takes exactly 12
long strides down the blue carpeting to reach the vault table.

On the last step, I hop my left foot forward to join the right before
launching into my roundoff. I know how my hands need to be posi-
tioned as I cartwheel over, and muscle memory helps my feet hit the
springboard exactly where they need to be.

From there, I launch backwards, back arched and my arms outstretched
behind me, ready for the brief but violent contact with the padded table.

That backwards push with my hands, called a block, is what propels me into the air; the stronger the push, the higher I fly. If my hands touch even a centimeter higher or lower than my sweet spot, my block will be way off, which could result in a crash and possibly even a career-ending injury. I've seen it happen.

Once in the air, I jerk my arms inward, pulling them tightly against my torso to increase my torque, helping me quickly get the two and a half twists around while I'm simultaneously doing a back flip in the layout position, making sure my body is fully stretched – one long straight line from my shiny bun down to my perfectly pointed toes.

I'm in the air for less than two seconds, but if I do everything precisely right, I land facing away from the vault table, feet together, knees slightly bent to absorb the impact, controlling the landing so I don't have to take any steps or hops.

My feet smack the thick blue mat a nanosecond after I finish twisting. I reach my right arm forward tentatively in case I need to steady myself, but when I realize I'm fine, I flare both arms up. I hold the stick for a moment, and then turn to the right to salute to the judges.

My mind is racing. I stuck the vault. I didn't just hit it. I. Stuck. It.

Natasha is waiting for me off to the side, all smiles with both hands up for high fives.

"That was effing ridiculous," she says as I run towards her. "Yeah, sure, you could've gone for a bit more distance...but your body looked straight and your legs were glued. *Glued.* I have no idea how you did it, but you were phenomenal."

I finish my bottle of water, grinning from ear to ear.

"Just like practice."

***

The rest of my competition goes well, though it's not totally up to my impossible standards. I missed a connection on bars, but I nailed beam and hit floor – my worst event – about as well as I could.

After vault, I didn't watch a single routine, choosing to stay in my zone. With my eyes down and my earbuds in, my rivals fought to stay on or fell, struggled on landings or stuck them, and I was oblivious to it all.

Tugging on my white yoga pants, I glance around the gym to get a feel for the vibe. Ruby, who finished her day on beam, looks radiant. I smile, happy she's kicking butt at this camp. She needs it after her disastrous summer last year. *Then* I search for Emerson, whom I spot by the door to the locker room, hands on her hips, face completely stoic. Is it bad if I was hoping for a sobbing mess?

"Line up!" Vera calls, holding a clipboard with the day's results. I glance at Natasha quickly, nervously, but she shoos me onto the floor.

"Most of you did really well today," Vera starts once we're all in order. "You all need to do some work between now and this summer, especially on landings and on the little details. And that's okay. We don't want you to hit a peak here, or anywhere but the Olympics. The best performances of your *life* need to be in August."

Vera squints down at the list in front of her. "If you are called for the top five, step out of line and salute. I'll give score sheets and full results to your coaches after we finish. Fifth place, Irina Borovskaya."

Everyone claps while Irina steps forward. I bite my cheek. Irina was the silver medalist at nationals the year before and won bars at worlds. There's no way I scored higher.

"Fourth place, Amalia Blanchard."

Okay then.

I glance at Natasha, who looks totally unsurprised, giving me a thumbs up.

"Third place, Emerson Bedford. Second place, Maddy Zhang. First place, Ruby Spencer."

I can't believe it. I didn't beat Emerson, but one spot behind is huge. The whole point of verification is proving readiness for competition and showing that you can hit under pressure. If I can get fourth place here, I can definitely be in the top five at the Olympic team trials.

At the farm, Vera only gives medals to the first-place senior and junior all-arounders and to the winner of physical abilities testing, usually a tiny but muscular junior with the endurance to last through a rope climb, a handstand hold, the flexibility test, and endless reps of press stands and leg lifts. She places the medal over Ruby's head, and then grasps her shoulders while speaking directly at her, Ruby nodding and beaming in response.

After a brief announcement about tomorrow's practice – the last before we get to go home – we're dismissed. The second Vera finishes speaking, Ruby is already at my side screaming, "Congratulations!" while jumping up and down.

"Me, what about you?! First place?! That's amazing, Rubes."

"Yeah, the reporters who said I was 'finished' last summer can eat a dick."

"Nice visual," Natasha says, joining our little team. "And please, you'll be the subject of every single fluff piece before every competition this year. The sugary headlines are already making me nauseous, America's Sweetheart."

"As if she'd even give anyone an interview," I say, hugging Natasha.

"I knew you guys would be awesome. You seriously rocked it today. I'm gonna go wait to grab results and then I'll probably hang out in the viewing room to get some work done while watching the juniors. I'll meet you in the dorms after dinner?"

"Yeah, see ya," Ruby says. There are a million more tight hugs before our coach leaves, and then we run off to grab our things.

"Did you watch any of it?" I ask, slipping into my warm-up jacket.

"Some," Ruby replies. "But I couldn't watch you. I felt more nervous for you than I did for any of my own routines. But I *did* see Emerson eat mat on bars."

"She fell?!" Sweet. Karma.

"Yeah, on her Jaeger of all things. The rest of her routine was gorgeous, but she looked like she wanted to kill someone after she finished. Totally a fluke, but you could tell she was rattled."

"Wow." Naturally I'm thinking of my comments right before vault. I feel the *slightest* bit guilty, though honestly, not enough to truly care, sorry not sorry. Emerson still placed third, and probably would have won without that fall. So it sucks for her, but it's not like she crashed and burned.

"Whatever," Ruby shrugs. "She deserves a kick in the ass every now and then. Let's watch a movie."

We head into the locker rooms to shower and change into sweats before heading back to the dorms. I'm more physically and mentally exhausted than I can ever remember feeling, but as I turn around before stepping through the door, I get a glimpse at Vera from across the gym. She happens to look up right at that moment, catches my eyes, and smiles for a split second before returning to her laptop.

The exhaustion, the nerves, the shooting pain in my ankles from all of today's hard surface landings...all worth it.

***

"I can't believe vault was my best event." I'm poring over the results in the common room with Ruby and Natasha after dinner. "Vault has *never* been my best event."

"Ahhh, the beauty of the Amanar," Natasha says. "Your start value is a 6.3 and you're so clean, you'll probably get at least a 9.5 in execution every time you hit it. Automatic super high score. The only other event you come close to matching is beam, and there are way more deductions there, so you'd need to have the best routine of your life if you want it to match your vault score."

I look at the scores again, which at first glance are totally confusing. The majority of my career has been in the Junior Olympic system, which uses old-school perfect 10 scoring. Elite is a different animal with combined difficulty and execution scores, and I'm a little obsessed with analyzing everything.

"I still can't believe you got a 60 in the all-around," Natasha says. "I was hoping for 59, but thought even that might be a stretch. A 60 in your first senior elite competition...that's some prodigy nonsense."

"I could have done better," I huff. I'm a total type-A perfectionist, so I'm annoyed at losing difficulty on bars and beam due to missed connections, and I could've been cleaner on floor. Bars hurts the most, though. I should've had around a 6.1 start value, so getting knocked down to a 5.8 stings.

"You're fiiiiiiine," Ruby sighs, rubbing oatmeal lotion on her golden brown skin. "You heard Vera. 'Don't peak until the Games.' Today was all about the mental competition...can you handle it, are you tough enough, blah blah blah."

"Ruby's right," Natasha agrees. "We have two months until trials. That's more than enough time to make sure your difficulty's maxed out and to put the finishing touches on floor."

They've been doing this for years, so I know they're right. I trust them and change the subject.

"Ruby, I didn't see your scores!"

"Oh, yeah." Ruby gets up to search. I want to frame my results sheet, but Ruby has already crumpled hers up and forgotten about it.

She finds it under a magazine on the floor and hands it to me before plopping back onto the couch. She is way more into this *Grey's Anatomy* rerun than gym talk.

I see straight away that Ruby's difficulty is pretty balanced on all four, ranging from a 6.1 to a 6.4. Even bars, Ruby's weakest event, has tons of hard skills packed in. She isn't always the best at executing that difficulty, but with routines that complex she'd always pull in top scores if she just hit, period.

"We need to bring my floor difficulty up," I decide, jumping up from my seat. I'm in the mood to waltz into the gym to get to work right this second.

"Mal, even if we add a skill or two, it won't matter," Natasha tries to reel in my crazy. "If you fit into the Olympic team puzzle, beam and vault are where you'll add value, with bars as a back-up. The U.S. team has plenty of good floor workers. At best, you'd go up in qualifications, and

I wouldn't even bet on that. If your beam is the best in the country and your Amanar's consistent, your floor won't matter. Trust me."

I chew my lip and stare at the TV, watching but not paying attention. I can't get floor off my mind.

Natasha groans, grabbing both results sheets from my hands. "Enough of this. You'll only make yourself insane. I'm gonna go hang out with the other coaches. Gonna try to get them to go cow tipping with me. Spice things up. Bed by 10, okay? Travel day tomorrow."

"'Night, Tash." I curl my feet under my butt and bite my nails.

"Peace out," Ruby says, her eyes still glued to the medical drama unfolding on the screen.

Moments after Natasha leaves the room, Emerson slips in. It's only the three of us plus a couple of the youngest juniors, who can't be more than 12 and are freaking out – loudly – as if Emerson can't see or hear them.

I keep my face focused on the screen, no longer feeling as ballsy as I did during our last confrontation.

"Hey Ruby," Emerson says, squeezing between the two of us on the couch. "Hi Amalia." Her voice goes up a million octaves on my name.

Ruby gives her a brief, albeit fake, smile before turning back to the TV. I manage a weak "hey" in response.

"Good job today," Emerson turns to me as she talks. "I didn't think you'd get close to fourth."

"Thanks?" It's a clear insult masked as a compliment. I'd been planning on playing nice, but not after that comment. "Shouldn't you be doing better than third?"

Emerson stares at me for an awkward amount of time before opening her mouth again. "Look. You're really good. I don't want to bitch at each other every time we're in the same room. If we both make it to the Olympics, we have to be on the same team. We can't be juvenile little frenemies."

"Yeah, I get it. I didn't mean to be a bitch."

"I did," Emerson smirks. "But you took it like a pro. One time I told Sophia Harper her arms looked doughy before bars at nationals and she fell three times. It's hilarious how little it takes to make people lose their minds."

I don't even know how to respond. The whole conversation is bizarre to me.

"Whatever," she continues. "I'm competitive and I express that in obnoxious ways sometimes. But I made a bad first impression. I don't actively want anyone to hate me."

"I mean..." I start, and then try to gather my thoughts. "Like, you told me I was *nothing* before my first verification ever. You can't possibly feel *that* threatened by me?"

"Please. I am threatened by no one. I was testing you. Congrats, you passed! Fresh start?"

I shake my head, but know I have to do some adulting here and forgive her. "Fine. I don't want to have a problem with anyone, especially if we end up on the same team."

"Good." Emerson pauses. "I watched your routines, by the way. Your beam is seriously our best chance at gold on that event. Like, I seriously can't believe this was your first elite competition."

"Thanks. Actually, I did the Open last year, but I was terrible. I fell a million times and didn't qualify to nationals. I didn't watch anything today, really...but I did see your vault."

"Eh, not my best. And you missed my fall on bars."

I pretend Ruby hadn't already told me, and that I hadn't smiled in response. "Wow, that sucks..."

"My hands slipped on my Jaeger," she huffs. "I caught it, but couldn't hold it. I blame whoever went before me and I hope whoever it was seeks help for her hand sweat issues."

"I missed some connections on bars, if that's any consolation."

"I'm just pissed because if I didn't fall, I would have been first." Emerson glares in Ruby's direction, and then pulls out her results. "I mean, even Maddy beat me today. The laws of the universe are, like, set up to ensure that never happens. She's my friend or whatever but dear *Lord* she's a mess."

I peer over at her sheet of paper, mostly to get a glimpse at her difficulty scores. In the sake of friendly competition, I need to see how I compare.

She was right. That fall on bars cost a full point in execution, knocking her down to a 7.5; with a 60.2 total score, she would've finished higher than Ruby by at least a tenth if she didn't fall. And her difficulty is even more balanced than Ruby's...almost impossibly so at 6.3 or 6.4 on every single event. Every gymnast has a weakness but she could realistically get a 15 or better on any routine.

"Well, at least you don't have to prove yourself," I offer. "You're pretty much the only girl here who sealed the deal ages ago. Everyone knows you're going to Rio."

"Not if I start slipping now. I fell on my Jaeger today and, like, I'm a million percent sure Vera knew it was a fluke, but what if I stumble on floor next time, and like, sit my beam dismount the time after that? That's all it takes to call my credibility into question. Everyone will say I peaked at worlds last year and I'm done."

I can't believe it, but I actually feel bad for Emerson, who seriously looks upset at the prospect of falling apart only months before the competition she's been training for her whole life.

"You'll be fine. Literally everyone knows it was a fluke. One fall in your whole senior career won't be enough to keep you off the team."

"Thanks. You're really sweet. I feel bad for being a total c-word to you all weekend."

"Forgiven," I brush her off, looking away. It's almost embarrassing hearing her like this.

"Now that you guys have had your Lifetime moment, can you get a room?" Ruby says as the TV turns to a commercial. "Meredith just shoved her hands into a dude's chest and there's some kind of bomb in it and I really don't want you talking over whatever really emotional things Derek and/or Christina are going to say to her."

"Dude, this episode is, like, a decade old," Emerson scoffs.

"Sorry I haven't seen every episode of every TV show ever. I've been kinda busy?"

"Spoiler alert," Emerson snatches the remote. "They get the bomb out.

Meredith lives. The bomb guy explodes in the hallway."

Ruby grabs her blanket and gets up. "I hate you," she pouts, only half kidding, before turning to me. "I'm going to FaceTime my mom before bed."

"See you in a bit."

Emerson hands me the remote. "I'm actually going to get some stuff done before bed. Thanks for being cool."

"See ya." I watch her leave and then switch to a show about murder, though my brain refuses to let go of this bizarre day. Breaking 60 in the all-around, fighting with Emerson, becoming her...friend? Acquaintance? Teammate? Elite gymnastics is weird, but for the first time I've arrived at the farm, I'm starting to feel like I belong.

Saturday, April 16, 2016
111 Days Left

"Thank you, ladies," Vera says at the last lineup before we're sent home. Practice that morning was the easiest of the week, giving us a much-needed rest from full routines so we could focus on conditioning and working on individual skills.

"The next time I see you will be at the American Open, which is the last qualifier for nationals. All juniors and seniors must qualify, unless you were one of the six who competed at Worlds last year — Emerson, Maddy, Charlotte, Irina, Sophia, and the absent Kara Lennon. No more direct qualifications from your camp verification scores. However, because she had the highest all-around score in verification, Ruby is an automatic qualifier. Those of you already qualified to nationals are not required to attend the Open, though I suggest you make an appearance so you can get one last practice competition in before nationals and trials. Good work. Train hard."

"Thank you, Vera," we chorus, staying in line until we're dismissed.

Ruby and I trudge over to Natasha, who is checking her phone by the door. After quickly typing a text to her husband, she grabs Ruby and hugs her close.

"Automatic qualification!" she squeals. "I knew it would happen."

Ruby smiles modestly. "I still want to go to the Open, though. Maybe I won't do the all-around but I could definitely use the practice."

"Yeah, of course you'll go. You know Vera's 'suggestions' are actually law." Natasha tucks her phone into her purse and fiddles with the handle of her suitcase. "I'm gonna go say goodbye to my mom. She said she had something she needs to discuss. I'll meet you on the bus in a few."

Something to discuss? My awesomeness, I hope. Natasha heads to meet Vera in the office while Ruby starts toward the bathroom. "I'll be out in a minute. Wait for me!"

I check to make sure I have an eye on all of our things – backpacks, duffel bags, and vinyl drawstring carry-ons, all a deep blue with the Malkina Gold Medal Academy logo stamped on. As I'm about to begin lugging our things outside, I spot a guy standing in the doorway, leaning against the frame with his arms crossed, like a teen heartthrob being introduced in a cheesy 90s teen movie.

Mystery boy is obviously a gymnast – it's all in the shoulders – but the men's training camp doesn't start for another two days, so it's a little weird that he's already here. I'm lost in my own mind, hardcore staring at him, which I don't realize he notices until he makes his way over to me.

"Hey, stalker." He brushes his long sandy blond hair out of his eyes. "You're the new girl."

I take a second to gather my thoughts before responding. "Kinda new to the farm, yeah. But I've been a professional stalker for years. You're the first one to catch me."

"Amalia, right?" He ignores my lame attempt at a joke. "I'm Max."

"Yeah, Amalia. Blanchard. Nice to meet you."

Max laughs. "So formal. That's hot."

I immediately blush. There's no response in my head that doesn't sound ridiculous.

"Everyone says your beam is insane." Max is quick to pick things up again. "I can't wait to see it."

"Thanks...I haven't seen any of your routines yet." Stupid, idiotic, dumb, dumb, dumb.

"Yeah, you know, when they aired nationals last year you could kind of see me on floor in the background when that human dildo Sam York was on vault."

I laugh, realizing I know absolutely nothing about men's gymnastics and have no idea who this Sam guy is even though Max thinks I do. "I've never been on TV in my life, so...you win this one?"

"It's okay," Max says, putting his arm around me. "We'll run the show this summer. Every journalist will fight over us and NBC will show replays of our routines as if the other gymnasts competing don't exist."

I laugh again, but less at his joke and more because the physical intimacy of his arm touching my shoulders makes me feel giggly. Ugh. Our faces are so close, we're basically an inch away from kissing, so I turn away and catch a bemused Ruby watching from the water fountain.

"I think I have to go...sorry." I twist underneath his arm to escape. "We're supposed to be on the bus, like...five minutes ago."

"Yeah, yeah, planes to catch, coaches to bitch at you the whole way home..."

I roll my eyes knowingly, though I know Natasha will ignore her notes until practice on Monday, preferring to savor her wine and *America's Next Top Model* marathons on long flights.

"See you soon?" Max asks.

"Yeah. Uh, at nationals, I guess. It was nice to meet you."

"My pleasure, Lady Blanchard," Max responds in an exaggerated British accent, mocking my formality. "May your flight be safe and your ass-chewing be brief."

He walks over to one of the in-ground trampolines and starts jumping in place. Why? I have no idea. Mid-bounce he notices me staring for the second time in a matter of minutes. He grins, his blue eyes sparkling, before casually tossing a double front into the foam pit. I know almost nothing about him, but I'm hooked.

"Has Mal finally noticed the opposite sex?" Ruby smiles gleefully, making her way back to our bags. "Max and Amalia sitting in a tree..."

"Are you six? Shut up. He was just being nice to me. It's like a pity thing."

"Are you stupid? He thinks you're hot. And he wants dat boo-tay."

"You're high." I grab my duffel bag in one arm, my backpack and carry-on in the other, and lead the way out of the building.

"No, for real, he's a player," Ruby whispers, close behind. "He's like, fourth generation Russian but thinks he's Prince Andrei."

"I one hundred percent don't understand that reference."

"Hello? *War and Peace*."

"You've read *War and Peace*?"

"Um, do I look like I have time to read a book as long as Oksana Chusovitina's career? I watched the movie during my brief but inspirational Audrey Hepburn phase. There's a triangle between Audrey and two guys, and Prince Andrei is the hotter one. As hot as Russian dudes could get in 1812. I cried for a week after he died."

"Spoilers!"

"That book is a hundred and fifty years old. I think that passes the statute of limitations for spoilers."

"He *is* cute, though. Max, I mean." I exhale dreamily.

"Ew, no. He is gross. I've known him since I was three. We trained at the same starter gym before we moved on to bigger and better things. Besides, I'm not even kidding, he's a total slut. I'm like the only one on the national team he hasn't hooked up with, not for his lack of trying. Just trust me. He's pretty on the outside, but is all vapid, narcissistic frat boy in his soul."

I scowl, absent-mindedly playing with the straps on my carry-on as we board the bus.

"You're literally one of the top gymnastics prospects for the Olympic Games, inches away from a full athletic scholarship to Stanford, and you're pouting because I told you this boy is a creep? Priorities, Mal."

I'm the first to admit I'm a little immature when it comes to boys. I've never even really had a crush outside of *Grey's Anatomy*'s McDreamy, who is admittedly about 30 years too old for me and also not a real person. But like, who am I supposed to find attractive? The other 15-year-olds in my grade who laugh for hours at chair noises that sound like farts? The boys at my gym who smell worse than the foam pit and spend more time flexing in the mirror than actually training? Or Jack, my nerdy neighborhood best friend who is super smart but is basically dating Minecraft?

Max is the second teenage male I've ever spoken to who doesn't make me wonder if one entire half of the human species is devoid of intelligent life. And he's also super-duper-with-a-cherry-on-top cute. But Ruby is my life guru and if she says he's bad news, I listen.

Besides, every cheesy Lifetime movie about gymnastics is true. You literally can't train this hard with an Olympic goal in mind if you're distracted, and boys are a distraction. You make a million sacrifices if you want a chance at the Games, with every inch of your life planned by the professionals who can take you all the way. Eat lean protein, sleep eight hours a night, drink 70 ounces of water a day, get massages and see the chiro twice a week, don't go skiing or ice skating or anything else that leads to career-ending injuries, rest on weekends, no partying ever, and most of all, *forget about boys.*

No big deal. When I signed on to the elite level, I chose to follow all the rules. I make the sacrifices. I never cheat my conditioning, I don't eat pizza, and I live as pristinely as a 15th century nun. Someday the reward will be worth it, and I'm not going to jeopardize my future because a cute boy was nice to me for three minutes.

Ruby finds a pair of seats and pulls on her big headphones to settle in for the ride. The farm is in the middle of nowhere, just outside a little town called Shell Lake, Wisconsin. The trip to the Minneapolis-St. Paul International Airport takes two hours, mostly through the back roads of the dairy state before we get to civilization.

I watch Natasha climb aboard just as we're getting ready to roll. She looks annoyed, but that's pretty typical after a conversation with Vera. She and her mother are known for their little spats and disagreements, especially back when Vera was coaching Natasha. Natasha may seem all grown up on the outside, but deep down she's still very much a stubborn little girl who wants to challenge everything her strict, old-school, stereotypically Russian mother says. They're the mother-daughter embodiment of the Cold War, bickering back and forth for years with the anxious anticipation of eventual full-out nuclear attacks.

I reach for my calc textbook, and randomly realize as we're pulling out of the driveway that Emerson hasn't made it to the bus. Kinda relieved, to be honest...I wasn't looking forward to an awkward goodbye.

"Ruby." She's deeply invested in her music and doesn't answer. I wave my hand in front of her face, feeling more like an annoying little sister than a maybe future Olympic athlete. "Should we be worried that Emerson isn't here?"

"Chicago's not that far from here," Ruby explains. "She doesn't need to fly, and besides, she prefers the limo the gym rents for her and her team. Gotta keep her happy lest another gym steal their star!"

She goes back to her music and almost instantly falls asleep against the bus window. I crack my calc text, staring at pages upon pages of derivatives but nothing makes sense. That never happens. When I look down, my notebook is full of doodles instead of problem sets, and I see that I've written my initials paired with Max's inside a small heart, something I haven't done since the fifth grade when I had an imaginary boyfriend named Keanu.

I hate myself for behaving like the kind of girls I actively hate, the girls who give up everything they love and are good at because a boy gave them the time of day. Come on, brain. We were on the right track until about ten minutes ago. Is now really a good time to realize boys exist? I rip out the defiled sheet of paper, crumple it into my backpack, and slam my notebook.

Focus. That's what I need. I close my eyes and visualize. Me, on the Olympic stage, sticking my beam dismount in front of millions. American flags everywhere. A score of 16.0 flashing on the overhead LED screen. A gold medal around my neck. No boys in sight.

***

Four hours of practice, two hours on the bus, three hours before boarding the plane, a three-and-a-half-hour flight, and a half hour shuttle ride up through Seattle to my hometown of Lynnwood, Washington. I'm more than ready to crash.

I split up from Ruby and Natasha at the airport after Natasha reminds me to be at the gym at 6 a.m. on Monday. She and Ruby take the train into the city, Natasha to her Lower Queen Anne neighborhood and Ruby to the Bainbridge Island ferry.

Though she's 19 and technically an adult, Ruby is completely incapable of living on her own; 40 hours a week in the gym taught her how to do a double-twisting double layout, but she can't do laundry or remember to turn off the oven. She's super smart but has the common sense of a hamster, so a family with three young kids at MGMA hosts her in exchange for free tuition.

Many elites I know wind up in host family situations. There are only a handful of really good elite gyms, and while a few gymnasts move across the country with their parents to train with the best coaches, most moms and dads can't uproot their lives for their child's sport.

I lucked out. I grew up about 20 miles from MGMA, so when I left my YMCA for greener pastures, all I had to do was jump on the 535 bus. My parents try to make the drive when they can, and they pulled some strings so I could transfer to a school closer to the gym, but overall our sacrifices are small compared to the girls who end up moving thousands of miles away.

My shuttle ride home goes by quickly thanks to YouTube. Is it normal to watch roughly 20 videos in a row of small children falling off escalators? At least Max has all but vanished from my thoughts, thanks to my wonderfully fickle brain.

My mom and dad are waiting on the walkway with open arms when I get home, first for hugs, then for bag collection. My parents – Matthew, my dad, is a high school principal and Kate, my mom, is a legal secretary – were mostly supportive of my decision to take on the Olympic track. Their one demand was that I stay in public school and keep my grades up, though this has never been a problem. I take all AP and honors classes and had Stanford University offering a full ride after I won the level 10 title last year. That's way more impressive to my parents than Olympic gold.

"How did it go, Mal?" my dad asks as we walk into the house. "Did you make the Olympic team yet?"

"I came in fourth in verification, which is like...a mini-competition at the farm against the whole national team," I explain. "So yeah, it went well, but I still have to qualify to nationals."

"Didn't you win nationals last year?"

No one understands the intricacies of gymnastics less than my dad. No matter how many times I try to explain the levels, the scoring, the competitions, the rules, he just can't catch on, and his confusion only grew when I started elite.

"Dad, I won *Junior Olympic* nationals. That was for level 10. The nationals I'm trying to qualify into now are *elite* nationals. It's basically a level higher than level 10."

"I thought your coach was saying when you got your level 10 skills that you were at the highest level."

Oh God, it's lesson time again. I force a smile while unpacking my stuff.

"Level 10 is the highest in the J.O. program, which is the U.S. Gymnastics Association program all gymnasts begin competing in when they first start out. When you get to level 10, that's the highest you can compete. *Most* gymnasts who reach that level stay there until they either quit or compete in college, but about a hundred gymnasts in any given year decide to attempt qualifying to the international elite level, which is above the J.O. levels and is like a different program entirely. You have to be at the elite level to make the national team if you want to compete internationally."

"They should just call it level 11!"

"Dad, I have no idea how you can't figure this out. I think this is my 900th time explaining it? And yet you understand football."

"Football? That's easy. Straightforward. Your levels, the judges giving out a hundred different scores, multiple national championships...it makes no sense."

"It's confusing, but Mal's been doing gymnastics for 12 years!" My mom chimes in, laughing. "It shouldn't take you *this* long to pick up."

"I'll tell you what. If Mal makes the Olympic team, I'll sit down and read every single rule. I'll learn so much about it, they'll beg me to be a judge."

"Except judges for women's gymnastics are women," I remind him. "Are you willing to undergo some major life changes?"

My dad laughs and kisses the top of my head. "Go to bed."

"I'm gonna finish unpacking first, but I'll go to bed soon. Promise."

"Night, kiddo," my parents say at the same time before closing the door behind them.

I curl up on my fluffy cloud of a bed, fully prepared to catch up on homework while doing laundry, but the exhaustion from the week at the farm catches up to me all at once. As soon as my head hits the pillow, I'm out cold.

Monday, April 18, 2016
109 Days Left

"Whoever invented Monday 6 a.m. practices deserves a lifetime of pain," I pout, stretching my toes. Even with Sunday off to recuperate in front of 13 episodes of *Law and Order SVU* with my best and only non-gymnastics friend Jack, my body is sore and my mind sluggish.

"I blame Vera," Ruby yawns, zipping her gray cotton hoodie. "Vera and her sadistic Soviet torture methods."

I slam my locker and wait for Ruby. In a way, I don't mind coming in this early. We're the only two elites at MGMA and the gym feels calm even when we're working our butts off. In the afternoons, dozens of gymnasts of all ages and levels barge in with pent-up energy after sitting in school all day, making it way more difficult to concentrate.

Ruby finishes dressing and we head into the gargantuan warehouse of a gym. The locker room door opens up right next to the big blue square floor mat where we run the perimeter for five minutes before Natasha comes to lead us the rest of the way.

Today, Natasha's already there.

She's a statue in the middle of the floor, arms folded in front of her. There's a smile on her face, but it seems forced, her eyes narrow darts. She's pissed about something.

"What did we do now?" I whisper as make our way over.

"There's no way this is about us." There's a weird tone to Ruby's voice. She reads Natasha way better than I do.

"Ladies," Natasha says, uncrossing her arms and clasping her hands together. "Line up."

We never line up in the mornings. Another clue telling me a drama tornado will soon be swirling before my eyes.

"We have a visitor today," Natasha chirps, her voice cartoonish and shrill. "Three, actually. They flew in yesterday and are in my office doing paperwork. They'll be out in a minute."

I don't want to ask questions. Thankfully Ruby doesn't have my self-restraint. "Who?" she blurts.

"My mom."

"Vera?" I instantly tense up. I picture Vera watching us in our natural habitat and feel sick at the mere thought of the pressure that comes with being under her critical eye. If this is her way of testing potential Olympians, it's super rude.

"Vera's only here for the day. We also have a new gymnast and coach joining our team."

Ruby scoffs audibly while my brain shifts into full-on freak-out mode. I can't tell if this is better or worse than Vera watching us like a hawk. Natasha said gymnast *and* coach, so okay, logic brain to the rescue, it's not like we'll have to share our coach's attention. But for real, it'll definitely change the vibe in the gym. With the Olympics not far away – a hundred and nine days, who's counting? – we can't just start doing things differently. My thumbnail finds my mouth out of habit and I begin to gnaw.

"Well, who is it?" Ruby finally blurts after an interminable silence.

A big sigh from Natasha, who closes her eyes and grits her teeth. "Emerson Bedford."

I realize I've been holding my breath for like an hour. I let it all out in one long overdramatic exhale while Ruby laughs in a "you've got to be kidding me" kind of way.

"I'm sorry. My mom...*Vera*...spoke to me after camp ended and said we're the only elite gym equipped to take them in. There was some sort of squabble...I don't know the details but Emerson felt like the owners of her gym were turning her into a cash cow and tried to get her to sign some contract requiring her to turn over a portion of her earnings. It's been ongoing, but Vera doesn't want this ruining her focus, and only just made the decision over the last week, so..." Natasha trails off.

"This is bullshit," Ruby yells. "We've had our whole team dynamic going for over a year now. If Emerson comes in, it will change everything. We're supposed to completely rearrange our lives, like, three months before Rio?"

"I know. It sucks. But it's Vera's decision. We have no choice. Any other national team club coach in my position would have to listen. I don't get special favors just because she's my mom. Besides, it won't be so bad. She and her coach will just be using our space, not joining the gym. Nothing has to change."

Ruby huffs, hands flying to her hips as she stomps her foot. One of her more deserved tantrums. She's had enough trouble in her career...if this throws her off course again, there won't be many more chances. If any.

I try to make myself believe that it won't be so bad. So what, we maybe do warm-ups together like at the farm, but there are four events. Emerson and her coach can train on one side of the gym while we stick to the other side. Easy.

Except not really. One of our biggest rivals in the gym with us every day, watching us train and learning every weakness? I'd rather have our biggest international rivals spying on us than someone who could mess with my head before I even make the team.

Vera pushes through the office door, giving a cursory nod to me and Ruby before smiling stiffly at her daughter. Emerson and her coach, Sergei Vanyushkin, follow, Emerson looking confident but avoiding our eyes.

"Thanks so much for squeezing us in on short notice," she says when she reaches Natasha, like she's making a last-minute spa appointment and not barging in on one of the best gyms in the country during the most stressful time in our lives.

"Happy to have you," Natasha lies, though her face betrays no emotion. "We'll do a full welcome later, but we're already off schedule. Let's start with the warm-up, and then my plan for the morning was half-sets on bars, beam, and floor before moving onto some leap drills before break. I know you and Sergei probably have your own routine, but feel free to join us. If not, we'll work out a way to share the equipment."

"I'd like to train with you guys for today...if you don't mind." Emerson finally looks over at us, her rivals, and flashes a picture-perfect Patrick Bateman *American Psycho* smile.

"Fine. Ladies, get started on your jog. I'm going to have a word with Vera."

I give my back a big stretch before beginning to run. A bit of a conspiracy theorist, I immediately think there's more to Emerson moving halfway across the country than money battles with her gym owners. Vera's up to something.

As if reading my mind, the national team coach smiles mysteriously at me like she's Napoleon plotting the invasion of Russia. Fantastic.

***

"Snap your shoulders up, jump *taller*, Amalia...don't lean forward. You're leaning forward. Pull *up*...like you're a marionette and someone is pulling a string on your head."

Assistant coach Polina is running this morning's leap drills on the floor with the three of us each stationed at a folded panel mat, Emerson already stealing the spotlight in dead center.

Ahhh, leap drills. We basically just work the individual leaps we do on beam and floor...boring but necessary. Today's focus is switch leaps with a half twist, which we each have somewhere in our beam or floor routines. The goal is to make them as perfect as possible, with a quick twist, pointed feet, straight legs, and great height. We start each leap on the floor but land them on the mat about eight inches higher than the starting off point to really enforce the whole air time aspect.

I try another one with Polina's corrections in mind, making sure to pull up on everything. I get so much height this time around, I could've added another two inches at least to the mat and still landed well.

"Better height, but Amalia, you are really struggling to do everything correctly all at the same time. A minute ago, your legs were perfectly straight, but you were low and leaning forward. So you worked hard on pulling up and got great amplitude, but your knees were bent. Stop focusing on the last correction I give you. You need to do it *all at once*." Exasperated, she adds something she knows will motivate me more than any correction: "Watch Emerson."

Emerson's switch half is perfect, from the second her front leg kicks out to the perfect 180 degree split high up in the air as she changes legs and turns her body to the opposite direction. Her toes are pointed, chest high, shoulders back, and she even lands it completely balanced with a smile on her face. She probably could have finished on one foot and still looked better than me.

"*That* is a switch half," Polina squeals, clasping her hands together. She is clearly thrilled about getting the chance at running drills with someone she doesn't have talk through each skill a thousand times. "Emerson, you look like a ballerina."

"So join the Pacific Northwest Ballet," Ruby mutters.

Emerson laughs. "If I join the ballet, I won't get to beat you in Rio. I'll wait until after I get my gold, thanks."

I sigh and try my millionth switch half of the day, but I'm so frustrated, I miss my footing and land on the edge of the mat, my ankles bending awkwardly as I slip to the floor and land on my butt.

"Shit, Mal!" Natasha runs over as I stand up gingerly. "Is everything okay?"

"Yeah." No. *Ow*. Goddamn. But it's nothing. "Nothing tore, nothing broke. They're just getting a little weak this far into practice...I probably didn't wrap tight enough."

"Polina will give you an ice wrap before school. Let's end a few minutes early today, ladies...we're all a little over it. Your skills looked good, leaps are getting better...just think of it this way. Leaps are *so easy* compared to the big acro skills in your routines, and yet they're often the most heavily deducted. If you can keep them clean, you'll be able to focus on everything else."

She clears her throat. "The animosity in this gym is gold medal-worthy, by the way. Yes, Emerson's leaps are worthy of the Bolshoi, but Ruby could teach everyone in here a thing or two about powerful tumbling, and Amalia has a head for competition like no one I've ever met. You might not love everything about this new situation, but consider it an opportunity to learn from one another. What a concept."

Ruby stands on her mat, hands on her hips, face almost a challenge to Natasha, but she backs down at Natasha's famous "I take a lot of crap from you, but I've had it up to here" look.

"Emerson, after you change, meet me and Sergei in my office...we can order brunch and make everything official. Amalia, see Polina for an ice wrap before you leave. Ruby, don't do anything that will end with jail time."

The three of us walk back into the locker room without saying a word, though our silence doesn't last long. As soon as the door closes, Ruby – already half out of her leo – is more than willing to start a conversation.

"Why here?" she asks, hands back on her hips. "There are, like, a billion gyms in this country."

"I didn't make the decision, so get over yourself." Emerson pulls on her shorts and I almost feel bad for her; she doesn't even have a locker yet and is already under fire. "Vera told me my gymnastics looked rough compared to last camp, and thought getting me out of Chicago would help. I mean, *you* were able to beat me at verification. Obviously I'm in a dire situation."

Ruby is practically foaming at the mouth. "The truth is that no gym wants to work with the teenage girl version of Satan, so Vera forced her daughter to take you."

"Whatever. Natasha knows I'm basically guaranteed at least one gold medal in Rio. It'll look good for this gym's reputation after you failed to come through in 2012."

The silence is so deadly you can hear an Achilles snap. For a full minute, Ruby burns fire from her eyes into Emerson's smug little face. *Awkward*. When I can't take it anymore, I physically step between the two.

"Excuse me, but I have to get ready for school."

I begin to spin the knob to open my lock, but then whip around.

"Emerson, seriously, it's weird as hell having you here three months before the Olympics. But I believe you. It's not your fault." I turn to Ruby. "What Vera says goes, and if she thinks Emerson belongs in this gym, there's a reason. Natasha said we should use this as a way to learn from each other, so I mean, really, it doesn't take a 180 IQ to figure out that's exactly Vera's plan. She wants to make us better gymnasts. There's no way in hell she'd risk Olympic medals for some twisted little game."

Usually I'm not one to make a scene, but my speech is pretty kickass, so I don't stop there.

"If petty drama is more important to you than making the Olympic eff-ing team, you need serious help. You're both a few routines away from boarding the plane to Brazil and you don't even care, while there are thousands of girls in this country who would *kill* to be you even for a second." Yeah. *Me.*

I storm into the shower stalls, leaving the other two stunned. I'm actually kinda stunned as well; I've never gone against Ruby before and I've never stuck up for girls like Emerson. I'm almost proud? I grin a little before turning the nozzle and unwinding my bun. I desperately want to make the Olympic team, and I know my own standing depends more on how I perform and less on Emerson's presence invading my gym. If anything, having her there would push me to be better, just like it did at the farm.

When I'm happy with the water temperature, I step in, my ankles already feeling better as I stretch them under the hot pulsating stream. I revel in this brief but amazing alone time between the four-hour morning practice and my half day at school before returning to MGMA for afternoon practice, which I hope won't be as draining as the first.

I still have absolutely everything to prove. It's not going to happen if I let my frustration show in my skills like I did today. I need to train like the best so I can compete with the best, and Emerson is the best. It is going to take every ounce of patience I have to get through each day without strangling her, but if the end result is me in a Team USA leotard, it's worth the torture.

Monday, April 25, 2016
102 Days Left

A week after Emerson's first day, the tension at MGMA has weakened, if not fully dissolved. Emerson is still hard to read, but while she comes off as confident and unbreakable in the gym, her life outside is a mystery and I can already see the cracks in the surface when she talks about anything but gymnastics.

"She's a serial gym hopper," Natasha had gossiped between sips of her much-deserved margarita at our team lunch over the weekend. "She hasn't stayed at the same gym longer than a year."

"It's shocking that she's been successful at all, let alone become the world all-around champion two years in a row," Polina added. "The longest she's been at any gym was when she spent the year at Wallace's leading up to 2014 worlds. The second she got gold, she was out, done."

According to her bio on Wikipedia, Emerson trained on her own at the busy elite factory Windy City in her hometown of Chicago for a few months after that, until Vera practically forced Sergei to take her. He moved up there and the whole situation seemed under control until Vera yanked her out last week after camp.

"She's still claiming it's because Windy City was trying to get their hands on her endorsement money, but I'm pretty sure Vera just wants to bust my ass," Natasha groaned.

I'm the first to show up today, and am already out of the locker room and beginning to stretch as Ruby and Emerson arrive almost simultaneously, both grumpy thanks to the 6 a.m. call time. When they finally join me for our jog, neither makes an attempt to offend the other. For the first time since Emerson showed up, the atmosphere feels almost normal.

Natasha and Sergei come out of the office together. They actually make a kickass team, and he's already given me a ton of tips for floor, my weakest event. Natasha asks us to line up, which we rarely do before practice, but the American Open is in just over three weeks. It's crunch time.

"As we all know, this is a qualifier for nationals," she says, glancing at her clipboard with the day's schedule. "Amalia, you need to qualify. Don't freak out, you'll definitely get the required score – a 54.00 or above in the all-around. Your goal isn't just to qualify, because that would be like giving a MENSA member the goal of learning the alphabet. Instead...your goal is to win. No pressure."

I nod seriously, half confident, half ready to jump out the window. A year ago, I didn't make it past the Open. Why earn your qualifying score when you can fall six times on four events?! It's probably more difficult to do what I did than to actually make it to nationals. With all of the praise I get for being a killer competitor under pressure, last year I completely floundered doing elite-level routines for the first time. It's not easy to forget.

"Emerson and Ruby...you will *not* be doing the all-around. Unlike Amalia, you've both qualified already...Ruby from winning verification and Emerson from her participation on the worlds team last year. Instead, you'll use the Open to get one more practice competition in before nationals. Ruby will compete bars and beam, and Emerson will compete vault and floor."

"Um, but bars and beam are my best events?" Emerson glances over at Sergei, her eyes begging him to tell Natasha she's wrong, but he smiles and stares ahead, pretending to be oblivious to her pleas. "Shouldn't we show our strengths?"

"Good question, Emerson, and as a reminder, you don't speak during lineup, okay?" Emerson actually blushes slightly, but then rolls her eyes to make sure we all know we are but mere peasants beneath her feet and do not deserve her respect. "No, you shouldn't show your strengths because Vera knows them already. If we're using this as a *practice* competition, shouldn't we practice our weaknesses?"

Ruby nods, smirking, although a second earlier I bet she was about to make the same complaint. Emerson just beat her to it.

"Sergei and I decided on a joint practice today, to make it a little more competitive. We're looking for consistency, and want to see multiple full routine hits in a row. If you're gonna be flawless at the Open, you're gonna need a ton of numbers under your belt. Let's start at the beginning and go through each event with hard landings, competition surface. First routine is like a warm-up, a freebie, no mistakes count...and then we'll look for mistakes in your second. If you take a step on a landing, if your form is a mess, and of course, if you fall, we do it again until we get the execution level we want to see on the podium. Got it?"

"Yes, Natasha."

"Good. Move to vault and chalk up."

We go through the first three events in competition order – vault, bars, and beam – with almost no mistakes, making it through with only two or three routines apiece.

Then comes floor. We're all a little tired, and here come the blunders, like machine gun bullets into Natasha's heart. There's no way we can do our full floor routines more than a couple of times each, so we focus just on tumbling. As if that's really any easier.

"Emerson, you need to compensate for your lack of power going into your triple full," Sergei yells, shaking his head. "If you can't get a nice high set into the layout, you're going to have to twist even faster than you already are, which I don't think is physically possible. You're landing either a quarter twist or sometimes even a half twist before you're supposed to, and you need to make sure you get it all the way around, okay? If anything, you want to twist *more* than three times...I'd rather see you overdo it than fall short. Then the judges can't devalue the skill. They can only deduct. Try it on the track."

The track is a long trampoline down the length of the gym with a mat at one end and a foam pit at the other. Emerson starts at the end with the pit, gets a good run into her round-off and back handspring, but loses power somewhere in the middle of it all and stumbles onto the mat. She definitely would've crashed it had she done it on floor instead of a bouncy trampoline.

"I don't know how she lands this in competition," Ruby whispers. We're watching from the floor where we stretch out our shoulders with re-sistance bands. I'm done after bouncing out of pretty much every pass because I lack control, but Ruby has yet to come under the chopping block.

"It's all adrenaline," Natasha says, her eyes still on Emerson. "And wanting the win. Like when a tiny woman can lift a car if it means sav-ing her baby. Adrenaline is good, but it's dangerous to rely on it and nothing else, especially at the Olympics. You need to have the building blocks down too."

Emerson is deep in conversation with Sergei, gulping to catch her breath between nods as she accepts his notes.

"Ruby, last up!" Polina calls. "I want to see all four of your passes on the floor. We've seen you stick all day, so take it easy on the landings if you need to."

Despite her exhaustion, Ruby manages her incredibly difficult tumbling with ease – a double-twisting double tuck, a full-twisting double layout, a triple full, and a full-twisting double tuck. Every pass is stuck, seemingly without even trying; she just explodes off the floor. For her, adrenaline during a competition might give her too much power, but even then she knows how to handle it.

"Very nice." Polina jogs over to give her a high five. "Strong but controlled. Compete like that, okay?"

Sergei also gives her a high five and a hug. "Emerson, these are the landings I want to see you hitting, okay?"

Emerson nods and smiles, but I catch another eye roll, as if a queen can learn anything from her servants.

"Great work today, guys," Natasha calls out. "Let's line up real quick before we break."

I wrap my resistance band into a coil, throw it in the bin, and tug my sweats on over my chalky legs before joining the group on the floor for Natasha's instructions.

"You all looked consistent and strong today. Don't pat yourselves on the back too hard; that's what I expect from you every day. Today just looked extra good. Threatening you with extra routines works."

Ruby throws her head back and laughs. "Spot on!"

Natasha smiles. "Okay, so every training session, every warm-up, every competition, pretend the alternative to hitting is having to do ten extra routines. Actually, at the Open, new rule. Anyone who falls gets to come back to the gym straight from the airport and practice sets until you're perfect. Deal?"

"Deal."

"But yeah, that aside, it was a good day. Nice attention to detail, and

good job taking corrections and actually using them to fix your skills."
Natasha turns to Sergei, who clears his throat.

"Since you were so on top of things, we have a surprise for you. On
Wednesday, one hundred days before the Games, NBC will begin their
official 'Road to Rio Countdown' in Times Square. There will be interviews, athlete demos, freebies for fans, all that good stuff...and Vera
wants you three there to represent the U.S. Gymnastics Association."

I look at Ruby and squeal. She grabs my hand and squeezes, a big smile
on her face. Emerson remains cool, shaking out her ponytail and running her fingers through her long blonde hair.

"We're going to New York?!" I screech.

"Yes, we'll take the red-eye tomorrow night after practice," Natasha explains, scrolling through an itinerary on her iPhone. "Get extra rest tonight and prepare to sleep on the plane. We'll land around 6 a.m. on
Wednesday morning and have to go right to the athlete tent. We'll
probably have to be there until, oh...noon? Probably. But we don't fly
back until the evening, so you'll have a few hours to see the city."

I literally don't believe it. Also, is it weird that I'm more excited about
the day off from practice than about the trip itself? Either way, I'm over
the moon.

"Why us?" Ruby asks.

"Vera wanted girls who can legitimately contend for the Olympic team
so if...*when* you make the team, people will remember you."

I'm starting to get the feeling this was supposed to be a trip for Ruby
and Emerson and I'm just going along as a third wheel since it'd be
awkward to leave me behind. But no complaints. I'm going to New
York.

"Don't think of this as a freebie day off," Natasha warns. "We'll do a Sunday afternoon practice to make up for it. If you want to *keep* getting this attention you have to actually make it to Rio?"

She dismisses us, and I basically skip back to the locker room. I want to text my parents with the news. Crap, actually, they'll be pissed about missing school. It's a battle just getting them to accept me only going for half days while training elite, but this is an opportunity of a lifetime. How could they say no?

"I don't know why you're crapping your pants," Emerson scoffs. "It's only New York."

"I've never been."

"Actually, neither have I," Ruby adds. "Sorry some of us aren't cyborgs and actually have feelings and emotions and get excited about things. How are you not even a little happy about the break in routine?"

"I've known for like, a month," Emerson says. "Vera was waiting until camp to see who else she'd send. Ruby, obvious choice after you won verification, and Amalia...you have a good story. Audiences will eat up the underdog angle."

"Well, I'm excited," Ruby announces. "Mal and I are gonna have a blast."

"Good for you," Emerson retorts. "You guys have fun staring up at tall buildings, omigod, so cool, while I sign autographs and listen to my agent bullshit sponsors into giving me more money."

I ignore her humblebrags and sing along to Taylor Swift on the loud-speaker as I get ready for school. There aren't many exciting things happening in my life, and competition trips aside, I don't get out of Seattle much. New York is going to be awesome.

***

"Dad, I *have* to go, you don't get it!" I'm bordering on whine territory, quickly regressing from tenth grade to preschool. "When the national team coach gives you an assignment you can't just say no!"

"Mal, you had to miss an entire week of school this month for what, to go camping? We said you could train at this level if you keep school your priority and it doesn't seem like you're sticking to your end of the bargain," my dad says, opening his laptop.

"It was a *national team training camp*, we didn't *go camping*." I swear, my dad is impossible. "This isn't a stupid club bonding trip where we talk about our feelings and pee in the woods. We train to become Olympians. It's like a legit job."

"But this New York trip is unrelated to training." He's glancing through his agenda for the next day, trying not to look at me. "It's late. I need to be at school early tomorrow for what could be a life-changing meeting. Not everything revolves around you. My answer is no. You can do Olympic publicity when you're an Olympian."

My dad clicks his laptop shut, stands up, and heads to his bedroom. I'm not trying to be a brat, but tears brim in my eyes and I want to slam stuff.

In a last-minute effort, I grab my iPhone and tap my way through my recent calls, knowing Natasha will be close to the top.

"Hey, superstar!" Natasha yawns. "It's 10 pm! Didn't I say get *extra* sleep tonight? What's up?"

"Um, I know, I'm sorry, I was getting ready for bed when my dad got home." Why am I nervous? "He said I can't go to New York. He said I already missed my absolute maximum days of school this month when I went to the farm, and he said he doesn't think going on TV is an appropriate use of my time..."

"Oh, for Christ's sake." Natasha sounds more awake now. "Put your dad on the phone."

"He...he said he's going to bed, end of discussion basically."

"*Get him.*"

I've only heard that tone once before, when Ruby threatened to quit after nationals the year before. I run to my parents' room and knock quietly.

"Don't think you're going to get a different answer when my Ambien kicks in!" he jokes.

"Dad, you're the least funny human being alive, and also, my coach is on the phone. My cell. She wants to talk to you, like, now."

My dad doesn't respond but I hear him shuffling to the door. When he opens it, I'm holding my phone out in front of me with a nervous smile. Dad looks less than thrilled.

"Go to your room." He grabs the phone and I bite my lip to keep from smiling. "Yes, Natasha?"

I skid down the hall, a huge smile forming on my face. There's no possible way my dad can say no after talking to my coach. On the parental hierarchy, Natasha usually finds a way to outrank my actual mother and father.

I grab my empty duffel and throw in a pair of jeans, a few tops, sweatpants, socks, underwear, an extra training leo, and my travel toiletries. I make sure to leave extra space for the national team apparel I'll get from Natasha tomorrow – the Team USA leo and warm-ups Emerson and Ruby already have. When my dad comes in a few minutes later, I'm double-checking my backpack to make sure my gear's all there, even though I haven't removed anything after practice just a few hours earlier.

He stares at me from the doorway for a few moments before tossing my phone on my bed and sighing dramatically. "You're going to New York."

"*Yaaaaaaaaaaaas!*" I jump up and hug him.

"Quiet, your mom's already asleep," he laughs, then kisses the top of my head. "That coach of yours has a lot of faith in you."

"What did she say?" I'm insanely curious. I know Natasha can be persuasive, but my dad is a pretty hard sell.

"She said I have no idea how talented you are, that putting you in the public eye now will give you fans and support once Olympic Trials roll around, and saying no to this opportunity would be like saying no to Harvard after they throw a full-ride scholarship at you," he says, pausing to give me a look. "You're kind of a big deal, huh?"

I blush. "Dad, I'm a nobody. But the U.S. team is pretty rough on beam and Natasha thinks mine is so good, they won't be able to turn me down. She said I'm the missing piece of the puzzle and that I can probably even win a medal on beam in event finals."

"She said her mom hasn't seen a combination of raw talent and hard work like yours in years. She wants Natasha to do everything in her power to get you to the top."

"Wait, *Vera* said that?!" My heartbeat quickens.

"Yeah? I guess?" My dad looks delirious. "I'm sleeping on my feet, kiddo. I wasn't joking about the Ambien. Goodnight...mom and I will try to stop by the gym tomorrow before you leave for the airport, okay?"

I nod and give him a quick hug before turning off the light and jumping under the covers. For the hundredth time this month I'm having a Vera-induced freak-out. I try to breathe slowly and deeply to quiet my brain, which is on overdrive, not letting me finish one thought before starting another.

Before I can even talk myself into the idea of Vera's attention being good for me, I'm already thinking about how much it could add to the enormous pressure I'm already under. Training and competing with Vera keeping tabs on my every move would be like a serial killer going after his prey in the FBI's backyard – there's nowhere to hide.

I bite my nails, moving methodically from finger to finger as my brain flies. Eventually, my body begins to chill out once the extreme fatigue finally catches up to me. My eyes flutter as I drift into a light sleep, but my brain continues to battle itself well into the night.

***

I breathe in sharply as the plane takes off, biting my bottom lip and gripping the arm rest. I used to love flying. The first time I went on a plane was for a competition when I was nine, and my eyes were glued to the window for the entire trip. I loved the feeling of leaving the ground, and I felt safer thirty thousand feet in the air than I did anywhere on earth.

Now I turn into a jittery mess when I walk into an airport. It's not really the flying that scares me – it's the anticipation that something could go wrong on the way up or down. Two years ago I saw some Discovery Channel show about how most plane crashes occur within the first three minutes of taking off, and now I can't think of anything else.

There's zero logical thought going into this, but the second the plane leaves the earth I slowly count to 180 – the amount of seconds in three minutes – while tapping along with my finger against the armrest, eyes closed and breathing slowly. Like with any of my competition rituals, once I finish, I feel totally fine. I know it has absolutely zero effect on my fate, but the repetitive motion soothes me.

Normally I sit with Ruby on gym-related flights, with Natasha and Polina together in the row behind us. Ruby is used to my crazy brain and doesn't even notice my bizarre habits anymore, but today I'm sandwiched between Ruby at the window and Emerson on the aisle. I can feel Emerson's eyes burning holes into me as I tap quietly away.

"*What* are you doing?" Emerson finally asks, wrinkling her nose out of both curiosity and amusement.

"Shut up," Ruby replies without removing her sleep mask. "Leave her alone." She wants to take advantage of every second of sleep on our overnight flight.

"I wasn't talking to you," Emerson huffs. She crosses her legs, takes a sip of her chamomile tea, and opens her copy of *Glamour*, scanning the table of contents before turning back to me. "Really, what are you doing? It's weird as hell."

I reach 180 a few moments later, exhale slowly, and open my eyes. "You're gonna think I sound nuts, but if I don't count up to three minutes, the plane will crash and we'll all die a fiery death in Puget Sound."

Emerson narrows her eyes but then relaxes her voice. "No, I get it," she finally responds. "It's like when we compete. If you don't smack your hands together exactly twice after you chalk up or if you don't tap your toes on the carpet three times before running on vault...it's like, it doesn't actually do anything, but it puts your mind at ease."

"Yes," I breathe, shocked that Emerson also needs to play games with her head. Ruby isn't like that at all. She can empty her mind and just compete without needing to trick herself into thinking that everything would be fine if she followed a silly ritual. "It feels ridiculous but like, I've never fallen on vault or died in a plane crash, so why stop now?"

"Totally. I mean, I've never done it for anything outside of gymnastics, but it's the same thing."

I nod, not knowing what else to say. I still feel awkward speaking to the girl who only a few weeks ago was no more than someone I idolized in magazines and on TV.

"I'd better go to sleep," Emerson yawns, putting her magazine in the seat pocket. She pushes her seat to recline, and groans when it stops after just an inch. "Not being in first class sucks."

"Goodnight." I push my own seat back and shut my eyes.

After a few moments, Emerson is lightly snoring. I've always been too jumpy to sleep on planes, but know I have to force myself to somehow get a couple of hours in. I pull my arms inside my sweatshirt and hug my body tightly before counting down slowly from a hundred. Eventually, somewhere over Montana, the hum of the engine begins to lull me into a deep and dreamless slumber.

Wednesday, April 27, 2016
100 Days Left

"Where are the gymnasts?"

A production assistant on her fourth cup of coffee buzzes around the Road to Rio staging tent with the day's itinerary on her iPad.

I've never been this overwhelmed in my life. After landing at JFK, we were whisked away in a black SUV that flew into Manhattan, careening through the busy narrow streets. Our driver dropped us off just before 7 a.m. at a hotel in Times Square, where two makeup artists and a hair stylist were awaiting our arrival. Less than an hour later, Ruby, Emerson, and I were out the door in our Team USA gear, ready to go.

An intern walked us the two blocks from the hotel to the staging area, a large white tent like the one my cousin James had at his high school graduation party. Except this one takes up about ten billion times as much space.

The actual stage is smack in the middle of Times Square on 43rd and Broadway, a slightly elevated square platform carpeted a bright blue. American flags and patriotic balloons decorate the street, where dozens of U.S. Olympic Team tents are spread out over Broadway, boasting Team USA swag and athlete signings for the fans.

"You're going on *The Today Show* at 8:41 a.m.," the assistant reads off of her device. "They'll interview you in a group but will ask questions directly to each of you, one at a time, so you don't jump over each other."

"Don't speak until we're spoken to?" Ruby grins.

"Exactly. The opening ceremony and speeches will start at 10, followed by a tribute honoring some gold medalists who competed at the 1956 Olympic Games, and finally, athlete demos go on 11. I have you ladies going on at 11:20. Sound good?"

We nod. As if they'd change anything if we responded in the contrary.

The production assistant turns to Natasha. "You'll be signing autographs in the 47th Street tent at noon with...Emerson Bedford, right?"

"Correct."

"And we have a set of uneven bars and a balance beam in the tent. Whoever is doing tumbling will go up first on the floor, and then we'll bring the equipment out. Who's doing what?"

"Ruby is doing floor, then Emerson on bars, and we'll end with Amalia on beam."

"Perfect." She runs over to another group in a huff.

"Hurry up and wait," Emerson sighs, examining her newly-manicured nails. "Welcome to live television."

"You nervous, Mal?" Ruby asks. The demo would be no sweat — we were showing nowhere near our actual routine difficulty — but Ruby knows I have a tendency to lose it during interviews. When GymnaSTICK, a social media site for gymnasts and fans, interviewed me after my level 10 title win, I didn't know to look at the interviewer and instead stared straight into the camera, my eyes wide and my face bright red. My answers made me sound like a baby uttering her first word. Seriously, when the interviewer congratulated me on a strong performance, I responded, "you too."

"A little nervous. Natasha coached me a bit this year. I have answers ready to go on autopilot even if my brain stops working."

"Interviews are nothing," Emerson shrugs. "You have more talent in one skin cell than any reporter has in her entire body. They should be afraid of you, not the other way around. Act like you're untouchable, a legend, and you'll be fine."

I grin as a thank you for her advice, but don't see how it's so easy for her. I go to bite a nail, stopping only when I realize I'm about to destroy the American flag manicure I got between school and practice a day earlier.

"Just remember, everything you do from now on is work," Natasha instructs. "You need to be professional in your interview, you need to hit your skills in the demo, you need to make people love you so people tune in for nationals and Olympic Trials because they want to see you make this team."

Natasha runs through a half hour of last-minute interview advice, most of which Emerson ignores, and then finally another production assistant enters the staging tent looking for us.

"We're putting you guys in places now. There will be a live shot before a commercial break where you wave to the cameras and smile, and then we'll go in with the live interview after the commercial break. Ready?"

"Yes," Natasha replies for us. "Have fun!" She leans in for a quick group hug.

The assistant leads us out of the tent and to a small shaded area in front of a countdown clock next to the demo stage. I look out at Times Square and the hundreds of people crowding around the roped-in area, cheering in their "Go USA" t-shirts. I gulp, and then notice a girl no older than six in a knockoff mini version of a Team USA workout leo holding a sign that reads "Amazing Amalia."

"How does that girl even know who I am?"

"How does who know what?" Ruby asks.

"There's a girl with a sign. It has my name on it."

"They handed them out to everyone." Emerson points out the rest of the crowd, where I spy more "Amazing Amalia" placards in addition to some "Rooting for Ruby" and "Extraordinary Emerson," all red or blue with white lettering. Cheesy, but my nerves immediately flip over to excitement.

I peer back over at the little girl with my sign, waiting for her to look at me. When I catch her glance it's pretty clear she has no idea who I am. I smile and wave, and she turns to her mom, probably alerting her to potential stranger danger because I definitely look like a creep.

But then she turns back to me, holding a silver sharpie. I'm sure this goes against the "official plan," but I take three seconds to run over, sign the poster, give her a high five, and run back to my group. Interview, schminterview. Let's do this.

***

"With me now at the Road to Rio Celebration in Times Square are three of the best gymnasts in the entire country," a young field reporter named Danielle Cruz announces cheerfully into the camera while Ruby, Emerson, and I smile brightly at her side.

"They come from all over the United States, but their families made big sacrifices so these talented young ladies can train with the best coaches on earth, Sergei Vanyushkin and Natasha Malkina. Sergei won the Olympic gold all-around medal for the United States in 2008 when he was just 18, and Natasha was the first American gymnast to win an individual gold medal at a fully-attended Olympic Games. With their help, Emerson Bedford, Ruby Spencer, and Amalia Blanchard also have a shot at gold medal glory."

Danielle turns to Emerson, standing immediately to her right.

"Emerson is already a golden girl," she continues. "She's never lost a competition, and that includes back-to-back world championship all-around gold medals. Emerson, how did it feel bringing those medals home for your country?"

Emerson pastes on a smile to answer this question for the millionth time. "It was truly an honor to represent the United States," she says, managing to sound humble. "I trained my whole life for the opportunity to compete at worlds, and it didn't hit me right away when I actually won. Even when you train hard, anything can happen on the competition floor. I thought I did my best in the moment, so I was thrilled to see my hard work really paid off."

"Just a few weeks ago, you stopped training at Windy City Gymnastics and moved with your coach to Natasha Malkina's gym. What was behind that decision?"

"Windy City is a great gym with a lot of great athletes, but I felt like I needed a change. I've worked with Natasha a few times at the Olympic Training Center, and we really connected. Her gym has better elite facilities, which is what I need going into the Olympic Games, so my coach and I thought it was for the best."

"You already have two all-around gold medals. When you were considering a gym change, did you wonder if changing that part of the recipe could mean messing with success?"

"I won each medal with a different coach and gym," Emerson replies sweetly, before adding in the kick she knows would be the gymnastics news of the week. "Gyms, coaches, they're the variables. I'm the constant. You can change any variable you want, but at the end of the day, success comes down to me."

Ruby is fighting hard to keep from rolling her eyes, which I totally notice. Now I have to try not to laugh.

Danielle looks almost taken aback, but smiles. "Well! There we have it. I'm afraid to ask how you think you'll do this summer? I think I already know the response..."

Emerson laughs coyly, expertly twirling a stray piece of blonde hair around her fingers. "How do I think I'll do? I think I need to start shopping for a third display case. Preferably one that doesn't clash with gold."

The crowd cheers and Danielle fake laughs as she turns to Ruby. She already knows the first question by heart. It's the same question every reporter has asked for four years.

"Ruby, when you were fifteen, you were so close to making the 2012 Olympic team, and then you got injured. How did it feel knowing you'd gotten that far and then had to watch it slip through your fingers?"

"You know, it still feels surreal," she answers, managing to sound genuine but wanting to scream. "When I fell in practice, when I went to the hospital, when my doctor told me I wouldn't go to London...none of it felt real. It finally hit me when the team was announced and I didn't see my name on it. I was devastated and thought I was done with the sport forever. It was like I worked my entire life for nothing."

"When you came back to gymnastics last summer, you had a pretty rough outing. The press was brutal, calling you 'washed up' and 'tragic.' Did that make you want to give up?"

Another question she'd answered in every interview for almost a year. "When I read what the press wrote, for a split second I believed them and almost retired a second time. But I got over that real fast." She flashes a smile. "I love proving people wrong, so I used what they said to get me going harder and stronger. You know those cheesy motivational posters? I blew up a quote from one of those articles and that became my poster."

"Now you're back on top and your teammate is your biggest competition. What's it like having Emerson in the gym?"

"She's a pain in the ass," Ruby answers. I laugh out loud while Emerson continues to force a smile. "I mean, you heard her talk about herself. I've known her for a really long time. She's a perfectionist, she's obnoxiously competitive over every last detail, and she always has to be the best. Sometimes I want to slap her, but mostly, I just try to one-up her. That's how you get better...and nothing pisses her off more."

"A little friendly competition never hurt anyone!" Danielle says gleefully into the camera, after which Ruby quickly blurts out, "It's not *that* friendly."

Everyone in the crowd laughs. Danielle ignores the comment, grimacing underneath her grin. "Finally, Amalia, you're the baby of the team. What is it like training with superstars?"

I brighten my eyes and smile before answering. "Are you kidding me? It's amazing!" I gush, my voice sounding more bubbly and upbeat than normal. "This is really nerdy, but up until last year, I had pictures of Emerson on my wall! It's like a dream come true to get to train with her. Ruby, we've been training together for a long time, and I was in the gym when she got injured. It's an inspiration seeing her work every day after what she's been through. She's my best friend and the person I want to be when I grow up."

"You've only been training at this level for two years, you didn't qualify to nationals last summer, and you have no international experience. Do you think the Olympics are a possibility for you?

I swallow while carefully forming an answer. I am the all-American girl-next-door underdog and have to sound grateful for the opportunity, but confident enough in myself to prove I belong.

"I credit who I am as a gymnast to my coach, Natasha," I start. "Before I began elite gymnastics, I was still training at my highest physical capacity because she didn't want to limit me, even though back then my biggest goal was getting a college scholarship. Natasha treated me like I was on the same level as Ruby, which made my transition into elite training pretty seamless because I already had the strength, the endurance, the mental toughness...she used that foundation to help me reach the highest level of U.S. competition in a short time, and now she's gonna coach me all the way to the Olympic Games."

The crowd roars as I smile shyly.

"Thank you very much, ladies, and good luck this summer!" Danielle says before turning to face the camera for a close-up. "Tune in tonight to see highlights from today's Road to Rio Celebration, including demo performances from sports like fencing, volleyball, archery, taekwondo, and of course, gymnastics."

We freeze in place, smiling as the camera pans out to get a view of Times Square behind us, and then finally exhale when the director gives us the cue.

"Nice meeting you, ladies," Danielle says, sounding a bit colder than her on-air personality. Before we can answer, she is rushed away by a small entourage.

I spot yet another assistant speed-walking toward our group. Like the reporter, we're about to be whisked away to our next stop on the itinerary, back to the hotel to train our routines quickly in the conference center.

Ruby nudges me, directing my gaze to Emerson, who is taking selfies in front of the staging area. Selfies she'll send out to her hundred thousand followers through Twitter and Instagram with a caption like "Can't believe I'm only #100days from making my dreams come true!"

I laugh, but I want selfies of my own. I drag Ruby over and we take a bunch of snaps, first just the two of us but then surprisingly, Emerson joins us and for a second it feels like we're all best friends.

Until the assistant, mid-panic attack, spots us. "I'm going to have a heart attack and I'm only 27!" is his frustrated shriek. "You're throwing us off-schedule! Hurry up!"

"It was their idea!" Emerson. Of course.

***

"At least you're not boring," Polina quips, closing the door to the conference center doubling as a practice gym. "No stock answers here!"

"I don't even remember a word I said," I mumble, out of breath from the mad dash back to the hotel. "I was so nervous."

"You were actually great. Articulate. You looked at ease. The crowd loved you, and you came off confident but down-to-earth," Natasha remarks. "It's the other two who need to start begging for Vera's forgiveness. Emerson doesn't need a coach? Ruby wants to stab Emerson? There goes our whole 'we're all great friends in addition to teammates!' vibe."

I jog around the perimeter of the room to start warming up and don't notice until the middle of my second lap that both Ruby and Emerson are slumped in the corner of the blue floor mat, snacking on granola bars and bananas.

"Dude, we have, like, two hours," Ruby laughs. "This is literally our only free time until after the Olympics."

I change my route and run over to my teammates, grabbing a banana on the way as Natasha checks her watch. "You can start warming up at 10," she says. "Thirty minutes for general stretch, ten minutes of basics on your demo events, ten minutes of full routines...just hit three demo routines each and we'll head back down."

"I don't even know what I'm doing for my demo," Emerson whispers, moving into an over-split as naturally as most normal humans breathe.

Of course, Natasha overhears. "Sergei went over it with you before you left," she scolds. "Glide kip mount, toe-on to handstand, or a toe-on half if you're feeling up to it, pike circle around, jump to the high bar, giant full, layout flyaway dismount. No releases. No transitions. Easy and clean."

"I've done demos with releases before," Emerson tests the waters.

"No. Don't even try me. Absolutely not. The last thing we need is you falling at a demo to get the press talking about the gym change being a bad decision, you not being mentally ready, you peaking at worlds...just no."

"Not even, like, my shaposh? I have literally never fallen on a shaposh in my life. Sergei would let me do the shaposh."

"Sergei isn't here, so you answer to me. I don't want your hands leaving the bars except for your kindergarten-level transition." Natasha gives Polina a look of exasperation. She usually keeps her cool with Ruby's attitude, but Emerson is a whole new level of hell. When Natasha reaches her limits, one glance at Polina puts the strict former ballerina in charge.

"If you do anything outside of the routine Sergei gave you, even in training, you're on mommy and me duty for the next month," Polina threatens.

"If you *ever* make me go near a toddler, I'll have Vera on the phone so fast...I'm sure she'd love to hear that the best gymnast in the country is thinking of early retirement."

"Please," Natasha laughs. "You're good, Emerson, but everyone's replaceable."

"She got that from *Dance Moms*," Ruby whispers to me, and I stifle a laugh. I can tell Emerson and Natasha are still testing things out, but I can't imagine ever talking to an adult – especially my *coach* – the way Emerson does. My feelings for my coaches have always been a bizarre mix of tension, fear, respect, admiration, and trust with only a tiny bit of friendly rebellion thrown in once I hit 14. I always get so close to my coaches, and feel like I can tell them things I can't even tell my parents. With Natasha especially, there's a good balance of business in the gym and friendship outside of it.

Coaches are the big decision-makers in a gymnast's career, but there's always teamwork in the best relationships, especially as a gymnast gets older. But Emerson sees herself as an equal, or even like the coach is only there as her personal assistant, managing the schedule and moving mats but not actually an authority figure.

Emerson is independent and doesn't seem to need or want anyone, a self-made champion who always fends for herself. At nationals two years ago, she didn't hit her super difficult double arabian beam dismount even once in training. Her coach at the time said she should go back to a double pike, her dismount from the year before, even though it wasn't worth as much in difficulty points. Emerson refused.

She stumbled out of it in the first day of competition, but still wouldn't relent. When she finally landed it on the second day, it was flawless and has been ever since.

"If I did what he said, if I downgraded, I wouldn't have won my first title at worlds," she'd told me one morning before practice. "It came down to practically hundredths of a point between me and the girl who got silver. If I changed my dismount to play it safe, I wouldn't have won, period. Coaches don't always know what's best."

And because Natasha isn't even really her coach, Emerson trusts her even less.

"I'll try not to do anything crazy in the demo," Emerson finally concedes, though she always had to have the last word. "But you can never know what might happen *in the moment.*"

***

After a seamless training session in the makeshift gym, another faceless, nameless production assistant collects us and herds us back to the white tent. We're beginning to lose steam from crappy airplane sleep, and I can only pay a tiny bit of attention to a fencing demo on the monitor while trying to keep my muscles warm.

Finally, right on schedule, someone shoves us over to the main stage and we're introduced to the crowd.

"Give a big welcome to three of the 2016 Olympic gymnasts, Ruby Spencer, Emerson Bedford, and Amalia Blanchard!"

I gulp, nerves hitting me the second I hear my name. Plus, I'm feeling the superstitious side of me flare up when the announcer calls me a member of the Olympic team. I don't really believe in jinxing things, but with something this big I also don't want to take any chances.

We march out in front of the crowd, walking with straight backs and chins up. I picture us as the Von Trapp children marching out in front of their whistling father before they learned how to sing and for a second it makes me smile.

When we reach the middle of the floor, the announcer asks us to introduce ourselves, something I wasn't prepared for. Compete death-defying skills under intense pressure to win gold with millions of people around the world watching at the Olympic Games? No big deal. Say my name in front of a couple hundred people only barely watching? Terror.

"I'm Ruby Spencer, I'm 19, I'm from Clear Lake, Iowa, I train in Seattle, and I'll be showing off some tumbling from my floor routine. Anything else?"

"No, you're good," the announcer smiles.

"My name is Emerson Bedford, I'm 18, I'm from Chicago, Illinois, and I just moved to Seattle to train at the best gym in the country." She adds a sweet smile for good measure. "Today, I'll be performing on the uneven bars."

I wait a couple of seconds to make sure Emerson's done talking before I start speaking. "Um, I'm Amalia Rose Blanchard, I'm 15, and I was born and raised in Seattle, where I train...oh, and I'm doing a beam routine."

Ruby gives me a grin that says, "See? Talking is easy."

Emerson and I step off to the side while Ruby gets ready for floor. She does a couple of round-off back handsprings before nodding to the sound engineer, who gets her music ready. Not Ruby's real floor music, but something the crowd here could clap along to while she did tumbling she learned when she was eight.

Though Ruby has one of the most difficult floor routines in the world, her performance today includes nothing more than a back tuck, a front tuck, and a layout. She tosses in some leaps and turns to go with her last-minute choreography, but it doesn't matter what a sad, thrown-together routine it is. The crowd loves it.

She waves to everyone before jogging off, laughing when she sees me politely clapping. "You like that? Where's my gold medal?"

Emerson snorts, tapping her foot impatiently while she waits for the crew to anchor the uneven bars to the floor. When she gets the green light, she marches out, waving, and begins performing the routine she was told to perform.

But instead of dismounting after her full pirouette on the high bar, she takes a couple of extra swings, building her momentum around the bar before throwing her signature skill, the one she had named after her in the official Code of Points at worlds the year before. The Bedford is a tricky skill, combining a piked stalder with a release move called a Tkachev, during which she lets go of the bar, soars over backwards to the other side, and catches it again as gravity brings her down. She does the Tkachev with her body piked, a bit more difficult than the typical straddle position, making it a pretty big risk.

She catches it with no problems, however. Those watching gasp as she lets go of the bar, thinking it's a mistake, but then they cheer wildly when she wraps her hands safely back around again. I watch her smile to herself as she dismounts with the planned layout flyaway, and she walks off the stage without even acknowledging the crowd.

"I'd watch my ass if I were you," Ruby warns, arms crossed.

"Natasha isn't my coach. She can't do anything to me." Emerson smirks. "I'm not teaching babies how to roll down triangle mats and she knows it. Besides, I did Natasha a favor...the crowd was bored to tears with the demo routine. I got them interested."

I nibble the corner of my thumbnail, watching the seamless transition as one set of stagehands drags the bars away while another pushes the beam out. I figure Emerson is right, but can't believe she actually did it...especially since it was such a dangerous skill; she didn't warm it up earlier, and she didn't have someone spotting her. Girls have broken their legs and necks on Tkachevs before. Stupid.

My own routine is simple...a couple of easy leaps and turns, front and back walkovers, a back tuck if I felt like it (which I did), and a layout dismount. Easy. But nothing thrilling. I move through it with no problems, receiving a polite smattering of applause from the crowd. A smile, a wave, and I'm off. Anticlimactic.

We march back out to take a press photo in front of the Team USA banner, and then are dismissed back to Natasha, who has a pasted-on smile. She doesn't say a word about Emerson's routine, which I know from experience is worse than getting yelled at.

But I'm pretty sure Emerson's right. Natasha's not her coach. There's nothing she can do.

Wednesday, April 27, 2016
100 Days Left

"Why are you even here?" Ruby asks Max as she barrels into his hotel room-slash-apartment. "You're like, the worst guy on the team."

"I know, right? I'm pretty sure that's the point. The good ones keep training while the suckers get sent to do the dirty work," he snorts. "Opposite from the women's team strategy, *obviously*. Hey Amalia."

He remembered my name?! I smile, and think about how awkward my face is while I'm doing it. It's definitely too cheesy, like an elementary school photo. I take it down a notch and respond smoothly. "Hey."

While Natasha and Emerson spend an hour signing autographs in aggressive hostility after what Emerson pulled on bars, Ruby and I have free reign in New York City. The thing is, we're so exhausted, after ten minutes of walking around Times Square, we're ready to crash. Neither of us knows anyone in New York, but then Ruby remembers Max's parents have an executive suite at the Palace.

It's a super fancy hotel, and while his parents are off traveling the world for work (his dad) and shopping (his mom), Max is the king of their little urban castle. I didn't want to come, I swear, but we don't know the city and have nothing else to do.

"Nice digs," Ruby says, throwing her backpack on an armchair. "You mind if I shower? I'm covered in makeup and sweat."

"Go for it. I'll order room service. Salmon and veggies?"

"Always."

"I'll make it three." Ruby gives him a double thumbs up before sprinting to the bathroom.

Max dials the restaurant, winking at me like a real-life Prince Charming. I sit on the couch, feeling more like an ugly stepsister than Cinderella. Come on, Mal. It took you five minutes to develop a crush on this guy and an entire afternoon to get over it. Let's not go through that again.

He hangs up and gives me a quick smile. His eyes seriously look like they're twinkling.

"Have fun today?" he asks, moving into the kitchen.

"Um, yeah, kind of. I'd rather be training?" I immediately blush. I sound like a freak. "I mean, like, I just hate interviews so much," I add, rolling my eyes as if I do interviews on the regular.

"You'd rather be training, I'd rather be living," Max laughs. "I'm probably gonna blow off this crap later, honestly. What a waste of time."

I don't know how to respond. The only thing that comes to my mind is "but you'll get in so much trouble," though I keep from blurting it out. Instead, I force a horribly fake laugh and glance out the window, waiting for him to say something else. After the longest ten seconds of my life, he does.

"So, New York, huh? First time?" He pops open a bottle of champagne and pours two glasses. "Bubbly to celebrate?"

"Sure." I grab the glass and sip as though I've done it a billion times, though in real life not a single drop of alcohol has ever touched my tongue. At first taste, I think, "this is terrible," and try not to make a face. I'm so nervous about the drink, this hotel room, everything, I forget he asked me a question.

"This is your first time in New York?" he asks again.

"Oh, yeah. First time." For some reason I blush at this as well, and re-member an episode of *Grey's Anatomy* where some girl had surgery to stop blushing. I need that. Stat. "Um...I mean, it's not like I get to see anything when I'm here but like...we were in Times Square? I've only seen it on TV before. It was really cool."

"Times Square is the worst place in this city, and probably even the world, bro. If you loved it there, wait until I show you the real New York."

Ouch. Nerdy tourist 1, cool Amalia 0. "I mean, I didn't *love* it. I just thought it was cool to see it up close, like, after watching New Year's Eve stuff every year, the ball dropping, I don't know."

"Nah, I get it. I was just being a dick." He lounges back on the couch, sinking into the plush cushions. "I know your time is probably tight but after you win every gold medal in Rio, I'll show you around."

Again with my face and the blushing. He can probably see heat lines radiating off of me like a cartoon. "I'm...I don't think I'll win any golds. I don't even know if I'll make the team."

"You will. Maddy was whining about you after the last camp. That means you scare the crap out of her."

"Really?" I try not to smile. "That's a surprise."

"Well, yeah, like, you're better than her on beam. You're a natural and she works her ass off and is nowhere near as good as you. That kills her."

"Unfair. I'm nowhere near a natural," I argue playfully. "I also worked my ass off. I'm just good at making it look simple. So is Maddy, like, your girlfriend?"

"Yeah, 'girlfriend,'" Max laughs. "She wishes, bro. We hooked up once last summer after she bombed nationals and now she thinks we're married. She's obsessed with me."

Ew. I don't even like Maddy, but I feel duty-bound under some code of girl honor to defend her. "Obsessed with you?" I roll my eyes. "Maybe she just likes you, *bro*?" I feel bolder than usual and thank my few sips of champagne, its bubbles scrubbing off my outer layer of tension and anxiety, making me assertive and feisty. I sound like Ruby.

"She's annoying. All of the elite girls are. You care more about what Vera thinks of you than what guys..." He stops, but the hideousness of what was about to come out from his mouth is already in the air.

I don't know whether to laugh or riot. "Than what *guys* think of us? You really think we care about what you think?"

"I didn't mean it like that. I mean like, at worlds, you guys win gold medals and then you go and lock yourselves in your hotel room until it's time to fly home, and you just go right back to training even though you have two months before you have to be at the farm again. You don't celebrate anything. Everything's all work all the time. There's more to life than gymnastics."

"Says someone with no chance at actually making the Olympic team."

"You don't have to be a bitch, okay? Jesus. I'm not saying go out and party or get drunk every night, but there's this thing called balance. Don't you remember *The Shining*?"

I haven't even heard of *The Shining*. "No?"

"Jack Nicholson typing away day after day? 'All work and no play makes

Jack a dull boy?' He went nuts and tried to murder his family with an axe and then froze to death. Just saying."

"None of us are going to murder our families just because we train hard. And I know I'm just another 'crazy elite' girl who doesn't care about fun, but if the upside to hard work means getting to go to the Olympics, I *think* it's a pretty fair payoff."

"It doesn't have to be one or the other, though!" He looks exasperated and I'm just smirking. "All I'm saying is that it's annoying to hang out with girls who talk about nothing but rips and leg workouts and beam upgrades. You can be a good gymnast and have a personality. Maybe then I'd give frigid little Maddy the time of day."

"Okay, I get that your whole 'thing' is being an asshole, but newsflash, not everyone has parents who make a billion dollars a year and can therefore throw money at the best coaches in the world for their son who only wants to waste everyone's time. My daddy isn't going to buy my way onto an Olympic team, and neither is Maddy's or any of the other girls'. None of our spots are a given. We *need* to put every molecule of energy into our training plans. If we don't, we don't make the team because the girl who *is* focusing 24/7 will make it instead. It's cool that you don't have to care about these things, but I do, and Maddy does, so you can call us frigid or bitches or whatever demeaning adjectives you pick up from your He-Man Woman Hater's club meetings, but at the end of the day, no one has to apologize to you for working hard."

Max stares at me with a stunned grin as Ruby steps out of the bathroom in clean clothes, towel on her head. "What's the matter with you?" she asks Max. "Mal charming your pants off?"

He picks up our champagne glasses, mine still half-full, and dumps them into the sink. "Oh yeah," he responds, avoiding her stare. "She's a barrel of laughs. Enjoy your food, ladies. Should be here soon. I have to get ready for a date."

"What a douche," Ruby says after he closes himself into the bedroom. "What did you guys talk about?"

There's a knock on the door before I can answer. Lunch. Perfect timing, universe.

***

The rest of New York is a blur. A cab ride back to Times Square, a black SUV to the airport, and before I know it, I'm back in Lynnwood, exhausted but too worked up to sleep.

I still can't believe how pissed off I got at Max. The more I think about what I screamed into his stupid beautiful face, the angrier I get at what a selfish dick he is, and at myself for finding him remotely attractive.

As I crawl into bed, my phone suddenly dings with a text notification. Jack. We grew up together, born only two months apart, and now he's like the only friend I have outside of gymnastics. He's one of the smartest people I know, nerdy cute in a John Green anti-hero kind of way, but completely oblivious to the fact that this is something girls are now into. He hates sports, preferring to spend time on the laptop he built from scratch, writing code and playing video games. He also possesses the ability to think reasonably and logically about things instead of letting his brain explode into an emotional fireball the way I do, so we're a hundred percent different in every possible way, and yet somehow, we're a good fit. Yin yang and all that.

"Lights on? Back from NY? Famous yet?" I smile and swipe to reply, but before I do I glance outside and see him making faces from behind the small rectangular window that looks into his basement, where he spends every waking hour. I motion for him to come over, up onto the roof of the porch overhang and then in through my window so we don't disturb my parents.

"Am I annoying?" I blurt when he gets inside. Might as well get to the point.

"What? Hi, by the way."

"Hi. Do you think I'm annoying? Like if you wanna hang out but I have to train or whatever, is it annoying? Would you be mad if I chose training over partying with you?"

"Um." Jack pauses for a second, pushing his too-long brown hair aside. He won't lie to me, but he always phrases his responses in the most diplomatic way possible so they don't sound so bad. "I mean...well, first of all, we don't 'party.' And no offense, but when you can't hang out, I survive. There are other things in my life."

I sigh, and relay the Max debacle to him, starting from our first meeting at the farm and taking him on a joyride through my vapid verbal assault at the Palace. I leave out the part about me being totally in love with him for the better part of an afternoon because really, who needs to know?

"What a dick," Jack says once I'm done.

"I know, right? I can't even articulate why I'm mad about what he said, but I don't think I've ever been this angry."

"Well, he's belittling your sport, so there's that. Oh, and there's also the fact that he's taking feminism back to the 1950s by expecting women to throw out everything they love and work hard for when a man shows interest."

"All I could think of was like, elites only have a couple of years in the sport before they're done, and you have to work your ass of just to get to that level. But making it to the Olympics is like...you go even beyond that. You give every little part of yourself to your sport and it still might not happen. Or it does happen, but one thing goes wrong and it's over."

"Like Ruby?"

"*Yes*, exactly. One microscopic miscalculation while tumbling and everything ends in an instant."

No wonder I'm so mad. Ruby. I still remember the sound of her Achilles rupturing over the beat of her floor music back in 2012. I was there for it all; the recovery, the depression, hitting her lowest low, and moving back home to Iowa. That's why she trained for her entire life? And then she said screw it, and decided to come back knowing she'd have to go through it all over again because that little bug was still inside her. There's something that pushes you from deep down that tells you no matter what the outcome, the worst thing you can do is not try, and that's why we do it. Because we have to. That's who we are. The goal is the Olympics, but the pushing yourself to do what 99% of humans can't is why we keep at it even knowing how impossible it might be.

"It's just offensive that some guy thinks he's more important than something we kill ourselves trying to achieve."

"He sounds like he has no direction in his life, and he's jealous of those who do," Jack shrugs. "Don't even give him the satisfaction of knowing he got to you."

"Too late for that," I grin. "Whatever. Thanks Jacks. I'm around gym nonsense all the time...I get so trapped in that bubble I forget how normal people think. I was so embarrassed after I freaked out...it felt like I was overreacting."

"Coming from an outsider, your anger is well-placed. Seriously, if I could do anything even half as well as you do gymnastics, I wouldn't spend a second thinking about anything but how to make myself the best. If anyone gave me crap about it, they wouldn't be worth having in my life."

I'm about to emphatically agree, thrilled that someone understands where I'm coming from, but before I can speak, my dad does a slow clap from the arch of my bedroom door.

"Hi Mr. Blanchard," Jack says cheerfully.

"Hi Jack. It's after midnight, Jack. Go home, Jack."

Jack grins sheepishly and disappears through the window. I watch him run across the lawn and slip through his own window, and then say goodnight to my dad before climbing into bed. Even after Jack's visit, I can't stop thinking about Max and my justified outburst, and I spend a good amount of time replaying it in my head as I try to fall asleep.

The good thing is that if I wasn't over my little crush before, I'm pretty sure this seals the deal. If nothing else, my priorities are back on track. And I won't lose sight of them again. I am *so* done with boys.

Monday, May 9, 2016
88 Days Left

Practice, school, practice, sleep. Practice, school, practice, sleep. Lather, rinse, repeat. The past two weeks have been like living the movie *Groundhog Day*.

"You have *two days* until we leave for the Open," Natasha drills into us at today's morning practice, as if we haven't been thinking about this season our entire lives. "We're officially in crunch time. For the next three practices, we're going into competition mode. Three vaults, three bar sets, six beams, one full floor routine. I need you to attack the equipment and work to stick dismounts. But don't push too hard...I don't want any messed up feet, ankles, or knees until after the Olympics this time, okay?"

I sneak a glance at Ruby, who actually smiles at this. It's been four years, so she's definitely had "closure" or whatever but I never got there. I still want to cry for her.

"Because we want to save your lower extremities from untimely collapse, we'll work problem tumbling passes and dismounts into the pit until we're happy with how they look in the air, and then try one or two on a hard surface," Sergei adds before giving the floor back to Natasha.

"Amalia, you're doing the all-around, so start on vault...you'll be with Polina today. Ruby, you're starting on bars with me. Emerson, I believe Sergei will start you on floor."

Our mouths say okay, but all three of us are starting to mentally check out. We've all been putting in way more effort than usual, going on team jogs before practice in the mornings, doing no-impact pool conditioning at night, and even trying hot yoga on the weekends at Emerson's suggestion.

"That's exactly what you need to relax, clear your mind, and get centered," Emerson had said after I almost burned down the uneven bars out of frustration one afternoon. Every day it's something new on bars, and at this point I'm just hoping things will all fall into place when they need to.

It's been nonstop routine repetition at MGMA. Multiple full routines each session, hard landings, pressure sets...but the second any of us shows signs of burnout, we're immediately pulled and sent away to regroup.

"Training routines when you're mentally at your limit leads to injury more than anything," Sergei had lectured. He won the Olympic all-around gold when he was 19, two quads ago in 2008, and after his victory immediately went to the press with a story of the extreme pressure he was under at the hands of the men's program. He almost walked away from the sport several times, so while he may be a no-nonsense drill sergeant as a coach, he also totally understands what it's like to reach your breaking point.

Though Emerson wasn't fully on board.

"If you can't train under pressure, how do you expect to win medals?" she scoffed, noting that Sergei's own story ended in a win. "This isn't some spiritual retreat where we all hold hands and sing 'Kumbaya' after discussing our feelings."

They're both right in a way, though I'm with the coaches on this one. In the gym, the more frustrated I get with a routine, the more likely I am to go into complete disaster mode. I have a better handle on things in competition, but training is a different story, so I'm grateful for the mental vacations.

We are eating, sleeping, and breathing gymnastics. When I'm at school, I'm going over routines and corrections in my head instead of doing any work, and when I'm home all my parents talk about is the gym.

My one reprieve has been Jack, who comes over at night to literally Netflix and chill, no double entendre necessary. He asks me how training was each day, I say "fine," and that's it. It's the perfect symbiotic relationship, with Jack the host and me the parasite, grateful to have someone who doesn't care at all about gymnastics, though I honestly don't know what he's getting out of our friendship. I'm asleep 20 minutes into whatever movie he chooses, and have pretty much never asked him about how his computery things are going. I'm the worst.

I jump in place to wake myself up a bit before jogging over to the vault table. By the time I start my sprint down the track, I feel my body respond, my muscles finally waking up and ready to get to work. But I doubt they're ready to get me through a vault warm-up and three stuck Amanars.

After getting started with just a layout and then a layout 1.5, I prep for my first 2.5 of the day. And it's not bad, considering how exhausted I am. Not stuck, but that's basically on purpose to give my knees and ankles a break. I can tell Polina's fine with it. She sees me absorb the impact the way I would if I was working hard to stick; I'm just hopping out a little at the end.

It still baffles me that I can do this vault at all, to be honest. I was only competing the 1.5 a year ago, and the added difficulty alone tacks on a full point to my score. Tenths can make or break you in this sport. I've seen girls miss out on qualifying spots by hundredths and even thousandths before, so a full point is a gift from the heavens. Not that it comes for free...I don't think I've worked on anything harder than the Amanar, though once I got it down to a science, it ended up looking better than any of my easier vaults have ever looked. Bouncy landings aside, today is no exception.

I wish I could say the same for bars.

For some reason, people have it in their heads that I'm a decent bar worker but what I'm actually good at is faking it. I work hard on my technique and I usually stay on, so normal people think I look pretty, but when you get up close with the careful eye of a judge, it's still kind of a mess. I mean, I've worked a ton on it so I no longer look like a monkey swinging on vines, but it's pretty clear I'm uncomfortable up there and if I'm not careful, I attract millions of minor form deductions like a magnet.

Today, the issue is my van Leeuwen. It's not an easy skill, I guess...from a handstand on the low bar, I have to pike down with my toes on the bar as I swing around back to a handstand position and then at the last second, I let go, using the momentum of the swing to propel me back to catch the high bar. To complicate things further, I do a half twist to face the high bar before I catch. *Voilà*, the van Leeuwen, named for a Dutch gymnast over a decade ago.

I'm miscalculating the distance between the two bars. How?! I catch this skill all the time. When I release the low bar on the first few tries it's clear my swing wasn't strong enough. My fingers graze the bottom of the high bar, I can't quite wrap them around, and I slam my knees on the mat below.

"You need more oomph, Amalia." Thanks, Polina.

I start throwing myself hard around the bar, only now my frustration is making me lose my focus and I overdo it a bit, my hands now slightly too high to catch the bar; instead, my wrists bounce against it and I drop to my feet. Better than my knees, but still...not good.

"Control. Focus. Breathe. Take a second to regroup, and then try again."

I can't regroup. My brain is enraged and no amount of breathing will help me chill. It's a skill I've been able to hit a thousand times before; I'm mad because it doesn't make sense that I suddenly have no idea how to catch it. Where's the logic?

After re-chalking and taking a sip of Gatorade, I let Polina know I'm better. Facing the low bar, I decide to work just this one skill rather than starting from the beginning of my routine. I mount the low bar with a glide kip, cast up into a handstand, and in the nanosecond I hold the position, I tell myself to hit.

My feet come down on the bar as I pike swing around, and I know a split second after I let go that my hands come off too soon. See what frustration does to you? I forget everything I'm supposed to do in the skill, my legs come apart, my knees bend, and I only get the half twist about a quarter of the way around. When my hands approach the high bar my body is still basically facing sideways and I'm only able to grasp the chalky fiberglass with one hand.

I can't hold onto it at all. My body crashes to the mat in a heap, and I think about how I don't even have control over my fall. When you're a kid, pretty much the very first thing you learn in gymnastics is how to fall – how to brace yourself, how to roll out of it, how to not get hurt. In case you were wondering, dropping eight feet onto your ass is a great way to get hurt.

"You okay?" Polina asks, jogging over to me.

Thankfully, yes. It won't be much more than a bruise. My legs weren't at weird angles when I dropped, which is good. I once watched a team-mate break her leg after falling leg-first, her own body weight crushing the bone.

"I'm good." I stand up; nothing hurts. "Fine."

"You're done with bars," she says. "Actually, with all routines. Take the rest of the morning off to cool down and condition before school."

Fine with me. I thank her and put on my warm-ups before heading over to the treadmill, always a good way to work through aggression. My one saving grace is that Ruby and Emerson were too busy with their own work to notice my meltdown.

Natasha didn't miss it, though. I watch her nod as Polina gives her an update about my failure. She catches my stare when Polina's done and gives me a thumbs up, her way of asking how I'm doing. I give her a thumbs up back as my answer and she mimes wiping sweat from her brow.

I am physically fine. It's the truth. I just can't let my mental game crack like this again.

***

Our afternoon practice is the last we'll have with the other kids in the gym, so our coaches decide to have us do a mini competition in front of everyone – the lower-level J.O. girls, the boys, and the rec kids, who train for fun and don't compete – at the end of the afternoon.

With a full day of school between me and this morning's bars errors, my mind is no longer in meltdown zone. I hit my van Leeuwen in all three routines in the first half of afternoon practice along with all of my other skills on bars as well. They're not all perfect, but I'd rather have a few messy skills than crash and burn due to mental errors.

"Thank you all for your undivided attention!" Natasha yells over the noise of the hundred girls and thirty boys in the gym today. Though they have their own training to focus on, we like to pull them away every now and then as we prep for big competitions, not because we're really vain and demand attention, but because the cheering helps us get a feel for an actual arena.

The J.O. girls have all met Emerson, but we're usually kept pretty separate from the rec kids and this is their first time really seeing her up close and in person. At least half are hyperventilating. The boys, mostly young teenagers hoping to reach level 10 so they can earn college scholarships, are equally enthralled, but more because she's hot and less because they admire what she's done in the sport.

"Today our elites are excited to share their routines with you before they go off to compete at the American Open, the first stop on the road to Rio!" The younger girls scream in applause, but the older girls and guys don't look thrilled about being forced to leave their own training. "I hope you will all cheer really loudly for the girls before, during, and after their routines so they can be super pumped up for this weekend. Have fun!"

More applause. My heart flutters. I don't know why I'm suddenly nervous about doing my routines in front of a bunch of kids who work out at my gym every day, but even though I know this is just a rehearsal, the overall meaning is something bigger.

We start on vault with no problems. Considering neither Emerson nor I are naturals here, we're both so solid, so perfectly prepared, we could probably stop training this event and still go out and stick in Rio. Don't tell Natasha I said that. For real, bless the Amanar for being worth a crap load in difficulty points and for happening so quickly; there's very little chance to screw it up if you've had good training and get a good enough block.

Bars, meh. No major mistakes for me, thankfully, though it could always be better. But Ruby looked *fantastic*. Even though she's not an aesthetically "pretty" gymnast on the event – like me, she's noticeably muscular, whereas the conventionally "pretty" bar workers tend to be long and lean – she's super clean, and has a natural swing. People will still call her bars work gross because she doesn't fit the stereotypical look, but the fact is that she hits her skills better than basically every "pretty" bar worker I've ever seen.

By the time we get to beam and floor, the younger rec kids – some of whom are only four or five – are over it and I can tell they'd rather be doing their own flipping and flying. Some are actually doing splits and handstands and cartwheels while their teenage coaches play on their iPhones. Total anarchy.

Even in the mild atmosphere, our routines are fine. Before Ruby does her floor routine she tries to get the kids riled up, which works but only for a few seconds and then they're back to their distractions.

My tumbling on floor is a little low-energy, but there's nothing really bad about it. I just tend to lose endurance a bit when doing a full routine. The passes on their own are solid, but by the time I finish a full 90 second routine complete with choreography and dance elements in addition to the four big tumbles, I'm too winded and my muscles want to go on strike, so I am barely able to get everything around. In a competition setting, the added adrenaline should help, but even if it doesn't, I'm not in *such* a bad place that I need to be concerned.

We line up at the end of the mock meet, which takes all of 20 minutes, and everyone goes wild with applause again before running back to their own activities. Natasha gives notes to me and Ruby while Emerson and Sergei do their thing, and then there's just an hour left, split into polishing problem skills, one more set of competition routines, and a cool down before we can leave.

My floor needs the most work, but with so many strong floor workers in the country we tend to not care about it as much as we do my other events, where I have more of a chance at making an impact on this team. Besides, two floor routines within the span of a half hour would probably kill me, so bars it is.

I make it through a first time with no problems, impatiently listen to notes and corrections, apply them to whatever skill gets picked on, and do it again, following this pattern for a half hour until every skill has been critiqued and fixed. Just make it through, I remind myself. Survive this. This is nothing.

"Good work," Polina says with a pat on my back when we're finally done. "Just do vault and beam, and then throw your tumbling into the pit. No need to kill yourself."

Fine with me. It's the easiest end of practice ever, and after landing my final tumbling pass – a double tuck – into the foam pit, I close my eyes and breathe for a second because I don't have enough fight in me to pull myself back out. Only one more day of torture, and then it's meet time.

Tuesday, May 10, 2016
87 days left

I honestly don't believe what's happening.

After a productive morning practice and my last day at school for the week, I stepped out into the rainy spring day expecting Polina in her trusty little Honda Civic.

Instead, I get Emerson in a brand new BMW 6-series convertible, Ruby strapped into the passenger seat looking like she's been kidnapped. "Surprise!"

The "surprise" in lieu of Tuesday afternoon practice is something Emerson cooked up, called "Treat the Elite." One of her old coaches started doing it when she first made elite as a junior, and she kept the tradition going because it always led to good results.

First we go for mani-pedis, so our nails look cute for competition. Because that's apparently important? We're getting the works – salt scrubs and massages – and it's amazing.

But then we get to the gym. When we walk into the front office, a grimacing Polina is waiting with blindfolds, which she ties over our eyes. She leads us to the locker room, tells us to put on our Team USA warm-ups, and after a few minutes we hear the John Williams NBC Olympic score blasting through the speakers.

"What the hell?" Ruby mutters. Emerson giggles.

One of the little rec girls takes our blindfolds and escorts us out, where – I kid you not – there are three thrones made out of mats in the middle of the floor, surrounded by the gymnasts as well as some of the MGMA parents.

Ruby raises her eyebrows and wrinkles her nose, her face working hard at betraying no emotions, which right now for both of us is a mix of "are you kidding me?" and "yep, seems about right." Of *course* Emerson would include public worship as part of her tradition. I catch Ruby look bewilderedly at Sergei, who responds with the most aggressive eye roll I've ever seen.

When we sit down, Natasha sees our faces and breaks into a smile. She walks towards us and claps her hands together, signaling an upcoming speech.

"Well." She exhales and I giggle. "Thank you, everyone, for taking time out of your workouts to wish our 2016 American Open competitors luck. I believe a few of you have some gifts for the girls here, so I won't keep you. Thanks again for supporting these Olympic journeys and to the parents who set all of...*this* up."

Jillian Bergman, a superstar level 10 Natasha is keeping under wraps until she's a bit older before unleashing her in the elite world, bounces over to us with a gift bag. The bubbly 11-year-old mini-Emerson pulls out crowns – like, the kind bachelorettes wear in Vegas with fluffy pink feathers hanging from the sides – and places one on each of our heads. Ruby can't contain her laughter anymore and is now capturing the madness on her iPhone.

Don't worry, there's more. Custom sashes that read "Miss Olympics 2016." We are bachelorettes winning a beauty pageant. Natasha has tears rolling down her cheeks from laughing so hard and Sergei has an apologetic "I swear this wasn't my idea" look on his face.

"Ruby, Amalia, and Emerson," Jillian begins, reading from a piece of lined paper. "You guys are an inspiration to everyone in this gym every single day. You are focused, determined, and strong. Even when you fall, you are brave enough to get back up and do it again. Ruby, you showed us that you don't have to give up on your dreams even if you think you miss your chance. Amalia, you showed us that if you work hard, you can achieve the impossible. Emerson, even though you're new to our gym, you are amazing and talented and beautiful and my favorite gymnast ever, I swear, I love you!"

The crowd laughs at Jillian's outburst. Ruby and Natasha share a look, most likely about Emerson's reaction which I don't see but can imagine it's one of faux humility. If she had her way, she'd make Jillian bow at her feet and probably, like, wash them too. And Jillian would love it. She should've volunteered for that job at our nail place.

After Jillian sits down, Sasha Watson — another top level 10 who's a year older than me and clearly embarrassed — brings over small gift bags for each of us.

"The level 9 and 10 training group pooled our money together to give you good luck gifts before you go," she mumbles, her face turning red. "We hope you kick butt in San Diego."

Short and sweet. We open the little bags to find Alex & Ani bracelets. We each have two beaded bracelets — one red, one blue — and one gold bracelet with a USA 2016 logo charm dangling from the metal. I immediately put mine on and hold out my wrist in front of me, thanking Sasha, who smiles and mouths "kill me" before walking away. I giggle.

"Get used to that gold!" A parent yells out and everyone cheers. Oh, hey, it's my parent. My mom and dad are standing in the back of the gym by the office door, and wave when they see I've spotted them. I don't think they've ever come to the gym during practice. I hope they think this is how we spend our time on a daily basis, me sitting on a throne receiving gifts and worship.

Natasha comes back up, ready to break up what she no doubt considers a silly distraction. "We want to let our teams get back to practice, so elite ladies, if you'll grab your things and follow me to the parking lot, we have another surprise waiting."

My parents come with us, and it's not until we're walking out that I notice Ruby's family — her parents and three brothers — are all here too. She runs up to them and gives them all big hugs, and the six Spencers all talk at once, yelling over one another as we make our way out the door.

There's a limo waiting for us in the drop-off zone. I've never been in a limo, and run towards it. Ruby's not as impressed — back in 2012, she always had sponsors doing cool things like this for her, and she's so happy about seeing her family, she doesn't notice (or care) about something as trivial as an extra-long car.

We all pile in — me, my parents, Ruby and her family, Natasha, Sergei, Polina, and Emerson. It's only then that I notice Emerson is the only one of us not engulfed in her family's attention. She's on her phone, quietly texting or tweeting or something while my mom sarcastically comments on how classy the neon ceiling lighting is.

"We're going to some place called Mistral Kitchen?" Natasha says, checking her phone. "Emerson picked it out. It's in Belltown, supposed to be delish. I trust you."

"I made sure it was gymnast diet-friendly, but don't worry, non-gymnasts, the normal people food is also good," Emerson quips.

"I'll never forget your birthday last year, Amalia," my dad begins. "Our whole extended family is around the table eating cake and she's sitting there with a popsicle. I'm surprised no one called children's services."

Everyone breaks into laughter. "To be fair, it was a Firecracker popsicle, and those are amazing," I add.

The whole ride into the city is loud and cheerful, but Emerson only smiles occasionally, pretending to react to what's going on but not really paying attention. On a whim, I take out my phone and scroll through Twitter, casually shielding my screen so no one peeks and sees me stalking my teammate. Because that's what I'm doing.

Aha, there's one posted with a photo of the limo just as we were leaving the gym.

Emerson Bedford @EmersonBedford – 31m
Limo ride to Belltown for dinner at Mistral! Celebrating with the whole fam here. :) Best way to kick off the #USGAOpen2016!

Um. I give her a glance. She's staring at the window, watching raindrops drip down. I used to pretend they were in a race when I was a kid.

Does she think Ruby and I won't see what she wrote? I mean, yeah, Ruby probably wouldn't notice, she barely reads her own messages let alone what others are blabbing about, but still. It's weird.

My mood drops from over-the-moon excited to kinda bummed when I realize I don't know this girl at all. There's obviously a reason her parents aren't here, and probably an even bigger reason why she's pretending they are. Now to just figure out what it is.

***

Dinner is amazing, even if I can't eat the good stuff.

"Don't worry," my mom says, enjoying her whiskey apple turnover with brown butter ice cream. Ugh. "In three months the Olympics will be over and you guys can eat whatever you want."

"Yeah, and then when you step out in public for the first time, the press will call you obese because you weigh 110 pounds instead of 96!" Ruby retorts cheerfully, sipping her water. Funny because it's true. Ruby stopped training for a few months after her injury and when she made an appearance at the Women in Sports banquet in 2013, people were brutal even though she was still in better shape than 99% of those with opinions.

Emerson is perfectly charming throughout the meal, really playing it up to my star-struck parents. I blame myself. I'm the one who forced them to watch her every routine and TV appearance during my obsessive days. At the restaurant, there's no hint of the sad girl from the limo. Girlfriend is amazing at faking it.

The limo takes everyone around the city after we leave, doing drop-offs at or near homes and apartment buildings. Since my family doesn't actually live in the city, we get the car to ourselves as it brings us back up to the suburbs, my parents finally able to examine every button and amenity without looking like the Beverly Hillbillies in front of the more sophisticated guests in our party.

When we get home, my mom makes tea and we all collapse onto the living room sofas.

"So, are you ready for this thing?" my dad asks.

Am I ready? Physically, mentally, yes. I've never been more ready. The easy answer is yes, which is how I respond. No need to bring up the fact that I am emotionally a nervous wreck. I'm pretty good at dealing with my neuroses and anxieties at this point, and I know when it's time to compete I'll be fine. The last thing I want is my armchair psychologist dad analyzing me.

"We wish we could be there," my mom says, frowning. "Flights are so expensive, but the Spencers are going...it's sad that you won't have us."

"Nah, it's just the qualifier." I brush her off, though whenever she brings up money related to my gymnastics career, I can't stop myself from feeling guilty. "You'll see me in Boston. That's when it counts."

"It'll be even cooler watching you on TV," my dad adds. "You know, there's probably going to be some little girl out there watching you the way you used to watch Emerson."

I think about this 600 times a day and my mind is continuously blown by how crazy it is. Last year when I did the qualifier, I wasn't very good. Because I was so super consistent as a level 10, Natasha and I both thought I'd stay mentally strong even when we upped my difficulty for elite. We were very, very, very wrong.

I was lucky to make it as far as the Open a year ago, but when I got there and fell six times on three events – the only thing I didn't screw up was my relatively easy vault – we knew elite just wasn't in the cards yet. My newer and bigger skills were too much too soon, and I totally let my nerves take over. So the fact that I'm now at the point where I'm one of the gymnasts the cameras will follow is ridiculous.

We lounge on the couch for a little while longer, something we don't often do because by the time I usually get home from the gym, I have dinner to eat and homework to do, and my parents are usually so zonked from their own busy days, there just isn't much time for family hangouts. We watch that night's DVR'd episode of *Jeopardy*, yelling out the answers the way we used to do, until the tea – chamomile – makes me sleepy and I say goodnight.

"Have a good flight," dad says. "Call my office when you get to San Diego."

"I will. Love you." I give him a big hug and he kisses my cheek. My mom's taking the morning off to drive me to the airport for my 7:30 a.m. flight. My alarm is set for 4:30, so I should be able to get about seven hours in if I fall asleep immediately.

"When you get back, let's set up a time to chat," my dad says as I trudge up the stairs. "I have a, uh...I have a surprise for you."

Surprise? My mind goes right to car shopping. I do turn 16 in November...a car would be a pretty sweet early birthday slash congrats on making it to nationals gift. And it makes sense, too...my parents would finally be off the hook for gym and airport trips.

I grin to myself during my entire shower, throw on a cozy XXL cotton t-shirt, and climb in between the freshly washed sheets, wet hair and all. I click my small bedside fan on, more for the white noise than air circulation, and picture myself on the high bar when I close my eyes. I imagine myself swing giants, around the bar and back up into a handstand on top of the bar, over and over, counting swings instead of sheep.

Eventually, it works – I feel myself slowly fading instead of listening to my mind race about every little worry I'll have over the next few days. Before long, I'm totally zonked.

Wednesday, May 11, 2016 -
86 days left

The Pacific Ocean is inviting as we loom overhead, getting closer and closer to earth. I've been pretty chill the whole way, but now seeing the city and beaches below, knowing I'm minutes away from disembarking in the city that is home to the Viejas Arena, the place where I'll hopefully – okay, definitely – get one step closer to my Olympic dream? It's too much.

Everything has me on sensory overload. The landing, the airport, the car ride to our hotel, checking in – it's too much, my mind is swimming with overstimulation, so I retreat into my head, trying to focus on breathing. It's not until we get to our room – which is beautiful and overlooks the ocean – that I'm able to function like a human again.

"You okay, Mal? Ready for the meet?" Ruby asks. We're rooming together. Everyone else has their own rooms, including Emerson, who got a suite. Like, the craziest suite I've ever seen. Her bathtub is a whirlpool and when you lay down in it, water reflects off the ceiling and walls, making it look like there's a waterfall rushing around you. What is the point? I have no idea, especially when the ocean is inches outside the door. But I love it.

"I'm good! I'm amazing!" The California sun is energizing as hell. I want to go for a run on the beach, do yoga every morning, eat avocados until I turn green, teach surfing to kids, wear sundresses every second of every day...why isn't everywhere like Southern California?

"I think I'm gonna nap before practice," Ruby yawns, flopping onto the big bed with its thick down comforter.

We don't have to be at the arena until 3, so we have a little time to unwind. I want to be outside, so I grab my math book – cool, right? – and a towel, making up my mind to get my homework done on the beach. If you have to do math, you might as well do it while ogling surfers.

Pacific Beach is literally steps away from our hotel, Tower23. It's a small beach, not many tourists, mostly locals with surfboards. I easily find a spot close to the water, set my phone alarm for an hour from now, and engross myself in the world of calculus. Rio is up in the air, but finals are happening, and soon. Like, whether I fail massively at nationals or sweep the titles, I still have to go straight home and take exams.

I sprawl out on my stomach and dig my feet in the sand behind me. The waves crashing are great for concentration and I'm actually making it through a good chunk of these problem sets. Until...

"Hey."

Emerson.

"Hi!" I slam my book shut. In the math versus Emerson battle, Emerson wins, though it's a close contest.

She has a big blanket and spreads it out on the sand next to the ratty *High School Musical* beach towel I've had since second grade.

"You ready?" she asks.

"Yeah. Why does everyone keep asking me this?"

"Well, you bombed it last year. Doesn't it make you nervous? History repeating itself?"

"If this is a psych-out attempt it's pretty lame. Last year I was 10% the athlete I am now and it was my first time competing elite. History only repeats itself if people don't change." Note to self, become a motivational speaker after this whole Olympics thing.

"Good one."

"Are *you* ready?" Classic turning of the tables.

"Why wouldn't I be?"

"You're doing your two worst events."

"This is just practice for me. Nothing at stake. Besides, my two worst events are better than most of these girls' two *best* events."

She's right. I'd kill for her floor, which sometimes actually ends up being one of her highest-scoring routines because her execution is so perfect.

Because I'm feeling bold, I bring up dinner. "I saw your tweet last night."

"What tweet? If it sounded sub-tweety, I swear it wasn't about you."

"No, the one where you said your parents were here."

"Oh." She brushes sand off of her blanket as though she's brushing off the question. "Yeah, it's easier for sponsors and fans to just assume everything is normal in my life."

"You're a back-to-back world champion. You took Zayn Malik to prom. Why would people assume things are normal?"

She pauses, trying to figure out how to phrase what she's going to say. "Normal isn't the word. Perfect. People want perfection. They think because I'm good at gymnastics and win every title I must have everything together, perfect grades, perfect family, perfect life. It's easier to let the myth be the truth."

"But it's not the truth."

"No, Sherlock Holmes. It doesn't have to be. People just have to *think* it is. Like when you're nervous at a meet but you can't let it show so you stand perfectly still, arms by your sides, staring straight ahead and not moving a muscle so no one's the wiser."

Yep, that's me exactly. Emerson knows every last detail about those she considers her competition.

Moments pass as we just watch the waves roll in and out. Finally, I have to ask.

"So what is the truth?"

Emerson sighs. "It's complicated." Just then a gaggle of junior elite hopefuls in swimsuits catch sight of Emerson, whisper excitedly to debate approaching her, and ultimately decide to run over. Emerson flashes a megawatt smile as she gets up to take photos and chat with the girls and their coach.

I take this as my cue to leave. I shake out my towel, walk back up to the hotel, and climb the stairs to my floor. My hotel room door swings open as I turn the corner, but Ruby doesn't come out. It's Sergei.

What the eff. I slip back into the stairwell undetected and peer through the window just in time to see Ruby pop out to give him a hug, her arms wrapped around his neck and his around her waist. Definitely not a "thanks for the pep talk" hug. More like an "I want to have your babies" hug.

I wait for Sergei to go back to his room and count to a hundred before I return to the hallway so there's no reason for Ruby to suspect I know anything.

Emerson's family drama, Ruby's inappropriate relationship, ain't nobody got time for that. We have practice in an hour.

Before I swipe the key to get back in the room, I pinky promise myself that I won't obsess over anyone's personal lives. Drama-free is the life for me, and I have other things to worry about. Like making it to nationals on Saturday. I push open the door, smile brightly, and exclaim, "the beach was *amazing*!" Emerson's not the only one who can fake it.

***

The Viejas Arena is massive.

We come in through the athlete entrance, weave through the confusing backstage area that I'll never figure out even with the signage, and walk out onto the floor. Normally San Diego State University's basketball games happen here, and I've heard it also hosts the occasional concert. I stare out at the rows and rows of seats going what feels like miles up into the rafters. It's crazy that in three days, these seats will be filled with butts. 12,400 butts if it sells out.

As a level 10 gymnast my meets were usually in hotel conference centers or gyms, a few rows of folding chairs or collapsible bleachers set up for the parents. This is...pretty different. Even last year's Open was in a comparatively small peewee hockey arena. People only really care about gymnastics during the Olympic year.

The other major difference is the podium. Most meets are done with the equipment right on the floor, but the big U.S. meets get these raised podiums that are basically a bunch of table-like structures on top of steel frames. They're like little stages, with each apparatus on its own perch.

This is how the International Gymnastics Federation does things at worlds and the Olympics, so Vera makes sure everything down to the layout of the equipment in the arena is exactly as it will be on the international level.

I competed on the podium last year and didn't feel much of a difference…the equipment was maybe a little bouncier, but overall it's not a huge adjustment. Still, before all of the big meets, we get to train on the podiums for a couple of days in advance just to get a feel for everything.

I'm still gazing up at the seats when Emerson grabs my wrist and pulls me to the floor podium where we'll start getting warm. "Get over it," she hisses. So yeah, she's probably mad about me prying into her personal life. Fantastic.

We're the first ones here. Emerson chooses a select spot on the floor where we begin stretching casually before the formal warm-up with the rest of the competitors. Girls slowly file in, many as excited as I was to see the gargantuan space, but some – like the always-charming Maddy Zhang – are more like Emerson with their "been there, done that" attitudes.

"Is this gonna be super awk for you?" Ruby asks Emerson, nodding toward the group from her last gym, Windy City, walking in.

Emerson, who's in a middle split, gives them a glance and then turns back to us, stretching down into the floor until her back is flat and her face touches. "Nope."

"Look at Maddy," Ruby sniggers. "She's totes the new queen bee and she is *loving* it."

"Enough idiocy," Natasha retorts. She'll brief us as we stretch. Sergei the manwhore is at her side.

"As usual, this is a structured training. Team warm-up and general stretch will last a half hour, then each rotation group moves to their first event...that's bars for you guys. It's a half hour on each event, and we take turns with the other girls in our rotation."

She continues with our training goals for the day.

"On bars and beam, you'll want to get at least four turns each. We'll start out working a couple of skills, then you'll do the first half of your routine, then the second, then the whole thing twice. If there's time – and there definitely will be – we'll work any problem skills. For vault, I want to see three Yurchenko layouts, then a 1.5, then the Amanar, twice. For floor, you'll work your tumbling separately first and then each of you will get a chance to perform with the music. For today, just do a dance through. Sergei, anything to add?"

"Yeah, keep your turn in the rotation order in mind. You need to be quick – in place to start the second the girl before she finishes – but don't just stand around waiting to go. Chalk up in your down time at bars, and when you're on deck, stand in your position to mount so you're ready as soon as the last girl gets off. During beam, work your acro on the side, and during floor, work dance elements. Vault...there's not much you can do without the table, so just stay warm and on your toes."

Warm-ups officially begin with a quick jog around the floor exercise mat, and we make our way through the national team workout before going through some leaps and light tumbling...tucks, handsprings, nothing killer. We eventually begin to disperse around the gym to finish things up using the different apparatuses, like bars for pull-ups, the beam for press handstands, and the vault table for plyometrics.

The real fun starts when it's time to get into our rotation groups. 31 girls are competing this weekend. We're split into four groups, three with eight girls and one with seven.

In my group, it's me, Emerson, and Ruby, obviously, some girls named Elise Connor and Madison Kerr (neither was invited to national team camp and I don't know them at all), and then the twins, Amaya and Nalani Logan, both 17. The Logan twins got lots of international assignments as juniors but didn't really improve enough to make a splash when they joined the senior ranks. But if I have a chance at a team spot, anyone does.

The seven of us crowd around the chalk bowl to begin prepping our hands for our start on bars. This will be our rotation group all weekend, and I'm smack in the middle of the lineup, between Nalani and Ruby.

A few people chat at the chalk bowl. Emerson isn't one of them, preferring to stay in her own world. She's not competing on bars this weekend but needs to put in the training hours so she doesn't regress.

I find out Elise and Madison train together and it's their first year attempting elite. When Emerson goes up, they both stare in awe, completely forgetting about their own preparation.

"Oh man," Madison breathes. "I remember watching her bars the first time she went to nationals and being like, oh my *God* I want to be her."

"I used to have her posters on my wall," I confess. "Like, very, very recently."

"Doesn't it feel insane to actually be here with her?"

Everything feels insane. "Yes," I smile, aggressively rubbing chalk over my hands, occasionally giving them a spray from the water bottle. Gotta get the consistency of this nasty paste juuuuust right.

When Nalani mounts the uneven bars I move in front of the low bar, preparing for my own mount. I thought I'd be nervous, but as I stand there I realize as intense as this is, it doesn't feel any different than a regular practice. Even being on a podium in front of thousands of seats, I'm just going to work the bars the way I always do. I have zero reason to freak out.

Nalani hops off after a few giants on the high bar and it's my turn. I glide kip on, cast into a handstand, work a few toe-on handstands, jump to the high bar, swing through a few giants, and go in for a layout fly-away dismount, all basic, no problemo, skills I've been doing for a thousand years.

"Your toe point was fantastic," Natasha says as I head back to the chalk bowl. She puts her arm around my shoulder and speaks quietly, as if we're guarding a national secret. "Work it like that in your routine and the judges will eat it up."

"Thanks. I'll keep it in mind." I loosen my grips and then tighten them again out of habit. "Anything else?"

"Your handstands were a little short...nothing drastic, only a tenth off here and there, but still costly. You're not doing much on this event...other girls have start values close to 7.0 and you're only at 5.9 or 6.0 so you really need to maximize every possible tenth in execution."

I nod. Nothing new there. I feel like I'm just hanging out in the gym, like if I walk through the arena doors right this second, my locker will be right outside.

"When you go up next time, start your routine like normal, go up to the Gienger, and then drop off."

I nod again, and turn back to the chalk bowl for a touch up just in time to see Ruby bust out a Tkachev pretty much right off the bat.

"Show off," Emerson grunts. Again, it's just like home.

***

"You ladies were excellent," Natasha says in the van back to the hotel. "Very productive day."

"Compete like this on Saturday and you'll sweep every event," Sergei chimes in. "Really, I think we could definitely end up with the top scores across the board. Amalia, you're gunning for that all-around title...there are probably three girls who can beat you and their training was nowhere as tidy."

I grit my teeth, not letting his praise take away from the fact that he is a disgusting animal. "Thanks."

"And Ruby, damn, you look kickass even on your weak event. For real, those bars are getting to the point where they're pretty on par with everything else. That's unbelievable...you're a true all-around talent."

My eyes are going, going, gone, rolling all the way into my skull. I think I see my brain.

Okay, so here's my beef. Ruby has worked her ass off to get to where she is now. The last thing she needs is a distraction, and yet here one is, in the form of a 26-year-old former Olympic champion-turned-*Dancing with the Stars* disco ball winner. He's hot and everything – like in a ridiculous way – but is hooking up with a hot older man worth missing the Olympics *again*?

Watch, and like, he's totally not even really interested in her. Why would he be? His girlfriend in Chicago – oh right, he has a girlfriend – is a model. He's a carbon copy of Max. All men are the worst. He probably isn't even a real coach...I bet Emerson hired him just to take Ruby down.

Okay, okay, I'm a conspiracy theorist. But for real, I seriously question Ruby's life decisions right about now. We have less than three months left. You've gone this long without a guy in your life...why start now, right when everything is finally happening for you?

I haven't been paying attention to the conversation in the van at all, but snap back in when I hear Natasha mention media day. Crap. Tomorrow.

"I can't decide if I want you to go all-out in front of the press or hold back and keep them guessing," she ponders, tapping her iPad in between typing out notes. "It would be awesome to just walk right out, do full routines, stick Amanars, the whole nine yards, because can you imagine the write-up? But then the pressure we'd be under on competition day will be insane. Expectations would be way too high."

"I'm all for giving people the absolute lowest impression possible," Ruby shrugs. "I'd even be up to falling on purpose multiple times throughout the day so I can blow everyone's minds on Saturday."

"Yeah," Natasha thinks for a second. "I tend to agree that seems like the best way to go. Minus the falling. We can train the bigger skills in the practice gym in the afternoon, and then just do basics for the media. A few skills but no full routines."

"You really want to risk not getting in enough full routines on the podium just to keep the press at bay?" Emerson sounds like she's ready to battle this one.

"We still have the afternoon practice, and then Friday morning. It's not like you're not getting enough training time."

"Well, I'm doing full routines. People's expectations of me are already high."

Ruby snorts. "Em, we get it, you do what you want when you want. There's no need for a humblebrag. Chill."

"So it's settled then," Emerson retorts. "You two can look like you don't know what you're doing and I'll look prepared. Good strategy."

I'm actually on Team Emerson here, but don't say it out loud. It's not missing the extra full routine practice that bugs me, but the chance to get my name out there. If the press at media day can see me doing big skills, I'll get attention going into the meet...pressure, sure, but I can handle pressure.

Without some pre-meet attention, I'll be the one on the broadcast they'll refer to as MGMA's third wheel, sitting in Ruby and Emerson's shadows. They'll air a clip of me stumbling on floor or something, and they'll be like, "we don't know much about Amalia Blanchard, but we do know she isn't ready for this level of competition."

"Oh, and don't forget, one-on-one interviews happen right after training," Natasha remembers to add. "You'll have a few minutes to cool down after training, but not enough time to change. Just put your warm-ups on so you look more professional, less sweaty and gross."

We pull in front of the hotel and decide to grab dinner at the restaurant on the ground floor. After we eat, we go our separate ways, leaving Ruby and I alone for the first time all day. I want to ask her about Sergei but I don't want her to think I'm prying or being a dick.

"You want first shower?" she asks, rifling through her gym bag. "Crap, I think I left my pre-wrap at the arena."

"Yeah, thanks." Under the hot water I think about what I'd say if I bring it up, and I almost work myself up into actually doing it, but when I head back into the bedroom Ruby's already passed out. It'll have to wait.

Thursday, May 12, 2016
85 days left

"What is it like training with two of the best gymnasts in the world?"

I bite the inside of my cheek. This is the fifth reporter to ask this question in the past ten minutes. They also ask how I thought my training went today, and then they leave to talk to someone more interesting. Fun.

They all want sound bites like, "Ruby and Emerson are *such* an inspiration and make me want to be a better gymnast," which is exactly what I say. I'm incredibly bored and would rather be doing ten pressure sets on beam in front of Vera.

Emerson and Ruby both have at least five reporters crowded around them. We're in something called the mixed zone, each of us in a chair with our names on placards over our heads. It's basically a three-ring circus of journalists shoving iPhones in our faces so we can talk into their voice recorder apps, though there's also the occasional old-school reporter armed with nothing but a notebook and pen.

I've had more one-on-one stuff, usually reporters who want to talk to my teammates but can't get close enough, so they hang with me until they can sneak on in. In between interviews, I play Trivia Crack.

Finally, a younger woman with a digital camera walks up. "Is it okay if I film you?" she asks.

"Uh, sure."

She smiles. "Great. I'm Anna Young." She fiddles with the buttons, a red light flashes, and she points the camera at me. "I'm with the *Seattle Times* and we're going to be following you and your teammates this summer, putting together a little video documentary as part of our online coverage. How was your trip out here?"

"Great. You?"

"Not bad, thanks. So you're coming out here a relative unknown but really have a chance at winning the all-around tomorrow. Can you tell me where you are mentally?"

"Um...honestly fine. I don't think it's really hit me yet. We'll see how it feels when I walk out on the competition floor Saturday night and see the people, the judges...but right now I feel like it's just practice."

"That's good. Do you consider anyone here your competition for the title?"

"I mean, I'm really not even thinking about the all-around title...I'm more concerned about just getting a good enough all-around score to qualify to nationals. Obviously I want to win, but beam is my thing and my biggest goal is to win that title. There are so many top girls here doing the all-around, I think there are like ten who could win it if everyone hits. Maddy Zhang and Irina Borovskaya could definitely do it...and then probably Zara Morgan? She looked really good at training camp. Oh, and Bailey Dawson and Charlotte Kessler, and probably the Logan twins too."

"You said your goal is to win beam. Who is your competition there?"

"Oh man, so many...Irina, definitely. She's probably number one. Maddy and Irina again, Sophia Harper, maybe Olivia Nguyen, and then Ruby...I'd also say Emerson but she's not competing beam this weekend, lucky for me!"

"How badly do you want a spot on this year's Olympic team?"

"Are you kidding? It's something I've dreamed about since I was four. Pipe dream, I mean...I didn't think it was even a possibility until a year ago, and even then it was still really far-fetched. Now that it's something I can actually achieve? I don't think there's anything I could ever possibly want this badly."

"Be honest, no sugar-coating. Do you think you can do it?"

"Honestly? The odds of it happening are definitely low, and I am a pretty realistic person. I know my place on the team, I know what I'm good at, and I know that it might not be something the team needs. I think if I show that I'm the most consistent person on beam in this country and can also hit good scores on my other events, it can happen. But there are other girls who have good beam routines and they're stronger than me on other events. I have as much of a chance as any of them, so it'll come down to how we all do and then obviously what Vera needs the most."

"Is there anyone you think is a lock for the team?"

"My own teammates, Ruby and Emerson. They're the best all-arounders in the country. That aside, it's anyone's game."

"Aside from your teammates, you said Maddy, Irina, and Sophia are your biggest competition for beam, right? You seem like you have a great analytical mind. Can you compare your shot with theirs?"

"Well...they all went to worlds and have major international experience. That's a big edge over me. Sophia only trains two events, so that could be bad for her. Vera always says she likes when girls can do the all-around because even if they never go up on like, floor or whatever, they can still be backup in case someone gets hurt. Irina...she does the all-around and she won gold on bars at Worlds last year, so like, why wouldn't you take her? She's probably the one who worries me the most. At camp I beat her in the all-around by two tenths, but she looks incredible on bars and I don't have a second event that's as good as her bars. Like, my vault gets a high score because I do the Amanar, but like, vault is basically everyone's best event so it's not like they really need it. Maddy's similar...she won vault last year, beat me in the all-around at camp...it's hard to ignore her."

"Great. That's all excellent. Thanks so much, Amalia, and best of luck this weekend."

"Thanks!"

I breathe a sigh of relief. That was way easier than I thought. I probably look ridiculous on camera...I never know where to look. But I think – hope – I sounded smart.

Natasha gives me a thumbs up from the other side of the press zone. A few people have interviewed her, too, but more casually.

A few minutes pass before a bored-looking journalist in a Padres hat approaches me. "How did your training go, Amelia?" he asks. I sigh. This one doesn't even get my name right. Such a letdown after that last interview, which was actually fun. I grit my teeth, take a deep breath, and throw out a stock answer, all the while watching the clock and counting down the minutes I can get back to what actually matters.

***

"Get back up and do it until you can get it right."

I brush my hair out of my eyes. In the midst of my *six* falls on bars in this morning's training session, my bun has completely unwound itself and my bangs are everywhere.

It's my freaking van Leeuwen again. When I propel up from the low bar to catch the high, my hands are either not close enough or they extend over and I bang my wrists instead. The more I miss, the more frustrated I get, and the more frustrated I get, the harder it is to focus. At this point I'm basically hurling myself into the bar without even trying to catch because I know I won't.

"Just move on to the next skill," Polina yells from the floor next to the podium. I guess she didn't hear Natasha tell me to do it again. Or she feels bad and wants to save me the embarrassment and pain.

"No, you need to get back on. I need you to catch it at least once before we leave here. It's the last practice and if your last memory of this skill is the inability to do it, you up the risk of not being able to do it in competition."

"It's just a bad day," Polina says. "She's been catching it all week. She should move on and then do it in the warm-ups before the meet tomorrow. If we push her, it'll get her more frustrated and the rest of her day will be a mess."

Natasha glares at me. The two rarely disagree but when they do, they're always able to back up their reasoning...though it's Natasha who usually ends up getting her way.

"I can do it," I say, pushing myself up off the ground. I mount the low bar, do a couple of toe-ons to get in the swing of things – literally – and then pretend I'm doing the Maloney instead. I've been catching the Maloney all day, and it's the same exact skill, minus the half twist.

When I'm ready, I release and reach up to catch the bar, and then do the twist at the last possible instant. I feel my grips wrap around the bar and I'm definitely a little too close when I catch, which makes me kind of dead hang for a second and I have to muscle the kip cast. But I caught it, which is what Natasha wanted, and then continue the routine with no problems and stick my double front like a final "eff you" to the apparatus that is killing my soul.

"See?" Natasha grins. "That was fugly as hell but you'll go into the meet tomorrow with the memory of catching. Clear your brain of the falls."

I nod, and painfully walk back to the chalk bowl. I can see my knees bruising practically before my eyes from all of those eight-foot drops.

"You're thinking too much," Emerson hisses. "Just go on autopilot. You're like, going over the physics of the skill in your head when it's your muscle memory you need to rely on."

"As if clearing your head is an easy fix," I snap back. "I'm not the Dalai Lama."

I still have one more turn on this event, our last of the day. We start on bars tomorrow, so I'll be happy to just get it out of the way. Otherwise I had no problems this afternoon, though we did decide to downgrade my floor a little bit so I don't freak out about connecting elements, which is always a pain in the ass on a podium, which gives the floor springs a little extra bounce.

My last turn ends up being fine. I use the same cheat on my van Leeuwen, twisting super late and catching close but catching being the key word. Ruby also struggled on bars today, not so much with falling on skills, but she did look messier than usual, so at least I'm not alone.

When all is said and done, we walk tensely to the chairs where our stuff is parked. "I'm almost happy," Natasha starts. "Obviously, not everything went our way today, but as they say in the theater, a bad dress rehearsal means a good opening night. Use the car ride to the hotel to think about training and what you need to do tomorrow. Visualize your routines, and then just breathe. Close your eyes. Relax."

The three of us are in various states of disarray, exhausted from training, as we trudge to the van. Emerson claims the back seat for herself, probably so she can text or scroll Instagram instead of listening to

Natasha.

When I sit down, I lean my head against the window and close my eyes. I try to focus on my van Leeuwen, and remember catching it at the farm during verification, where it looked great. The problem now is the force I'm using when I release the low bar...my hand position is usually accurate, but I'm either giving too much or too little when I let go.

Sometimes you can blame the bars...if the set you're on is tighter or looser than you're used to, which can wreak havoc on your routine, but the bars at the arena are the same brand we use in our gym and feel equally bouncy. Besides, everything else is working out, including the Maloney.

The problem is that I fear the twist, I realize. The Maloney is straight up and back, but with the twist on the van Leeuwen I'm going up, I'm going backwards, and then I'm turning my body around, all while trying to keep my legs tight and my toes pointed. For a skill that takes a second, it's too much happening at once. The twist should be easy, but because it's freaking me out, it's suddenly the most difficult task in the world.

I'm giving myself less of a push back so I rebound more slowly in the air between the bars giving me a tiny bit more time to twist, but then I'm not actually making it far enough...and when I get frustrated and give myself more of a push so I *do* make it, I over-compensate and give too much, everything happens too fast, and I miss the mark completely.

"Why can't I just find a balance?!" I whine.

Ruby laughs. "What?"

Cool, now I'm saying things out loud instead of thinking them. Just one stop further on the crazy train that is my head.

"Nothing." I blush. "Van Leeuwen drama."

Ruby nods and wraps her arm around my shoulder. "Mini huddle," she whispers, glancing at Natasha, who's listening to her iPod. "Seriously, do a different transition. You've competed the stalder shaposh plenty of times...you'll lose a tenth in difficulty, but that's a hell of a lot better than falling and losing a full point. Try a few in warm-ups tomorrow and if they feel better than the van Leeuwen feels, change it up."

"But Natasha..."

"Natasha is pushing you to do the harder skill because she wants your difficulty higher so she can make you a great bars gymnast because she believes in you and is thinking long-term," she interrupts. "You're not a great bars gymnast, and you might never be one. Not with that swing."

I laugh. Funny because it's true.

"For real, you're not going to be in a bars final anytime soon, so why push it harder than you have to? You need a short-term solution. Do what you can to get a respectable score and focus on what really matters, which is killing it on beam."

Ruby is absolutely right. "If Natasha is pissed, I'm fully blaming you."

"Cool," she shrugs. "She'll find something else to be pissed at soon enough. Even if she's mad, it'll only be until you go off and destroy everyone on beam, and then she'll forget this ever happened, and you guys can have a serious chat on the flight home about changes to your routine for the long haul."

We arrive at the hotel, where Ruby, Emerson, and I are scheduled to have massages and some light physical therapy just to make sure our bodies stay in working order.

The rest of the day is free, and Natasha wants us to relax as much as possible so we're rested for the meet. I'm thinking beach time is just what I need to gather my thoughts about today's bars session. A massage, a hot shower, the beach, a nice salmon dinner in the name of pre-meet tradition, and nine hours of sleep, glorious sleep.

It's the perfect way to chill before tomorrow, one of many days this summer that will determine my gymnastics future. Deep breaths. No big deal.

Saturday, May 14, 2016
83 days left

The crowd starts filing in an hour before the meet is set to begin, which is awesome. It gives me time to get used to having people screaming and cheering...or worse, gasping collectively when something goes wrong. The funniest is when we vault timers on giant mats to our backs on purpose to save our legs. I'm pretty sure people think we're falling and our bones are smashed to bits.

So far, so good. On bars, I warm up both the van Leeuwen and the stalder shaposh, also known as a Chow. It's super similar to the van Leeuwen aside from the very beginning, where I straddle my legs while swinging around the bar in lieu of piking with my legs together and toes on the bar. It has the same feel in flight and like the Maloney, you catch the high bar without doing a half twist, which is obviously what matters.

"Changing your routine on me?" Natasha asks, amused.

"My low back hurts a little," I lied. "The straddle feels better than the pike."

She thankfully brushes it off, too distracted to realize that if the pike in the skill made my back hurt, I'd also have pain on the Maloney, which also comes from a pike position. That was a freebie.

Following warm-ups, every gymnast meets in in the tunnel that leads to the floor. In five minutes, we'll march right back in, where we'll be announced to the crowds, stand at attention for the national anthem, and then run to our first events for a final touch warm-up before the meet begins.

We hang out in our rotation groups, in competition order, which thankfully means Ruby is right behind me. She grabs my shoulders and shakes them a little to rile me up. "Ready?!"

"So ready." I turn to face her and she's jumping up and down to stay warm. "I'm doing the Chow, by the way."

"*Good*. Trust me, it'll be a billion times better. It looked great in practice."

"Thanks." I stretch my shoulders and back until I hear the walk-on music beginning and then I join Ruby in bouncing, which loosens me up and gets me energized and excited all at once. I feel a vibration in the drawstring bag I have slung over my back, and though I usually ignore my phone from warm-ups until the end of the meet, I don't want to miss a good luck text from my parents.

"Good luck, Mal!!!!" Except it's not from my parents. It's from Jack, who has also included about 600 emojis – smiley faces, random animals, the shooting star. I smile, but turn my phone off completely without responding before tucking it back into the little pocket. No distractions now.

When we march out onto the floor, the main lights are off, neon lights are flashing, fog is shooting out of machines by the entrances, and big spotlights dance across the floor podium. I hear the vault competitors listed one after another, and then the announcer begins with my group as we climb the podium stairs.

"Beginning on the uneven bars, please welcome Amaya Logan from Waimea Sports Center, Emerson Bedford from Vanyushkin Gymnastics, Nalani Logan from Waimea Sports Center, Amalia Blanchard from Malkina Gold Medal Academy, Ruby Spencer from Malkina Gold Medal Academy, Madison Kerr from Great Plains Gymnastics Club, and Elise Connor from Great Plains Gymnastics Club!"

When our name is called, we take a step forward and salute to the

crowd, first facing those in front of us and then turning to those behind
us before stepping back in line. Emerson gets the most applause, Ruby
gets a good amount, but not a ton, and the rest of us get polite smatter-
ings.

After each of the four rotations is introduced, we stand and face the big
flag over the beam, hands over our hearts, while the Christina Aguilera-
wannabe national anthem singer riffs her way through a too-long rendi-
tion of the song.

And with that small ceremony, we're off. Our rotation leader guides us
to bars, as if we can't make it across the arena on our own, and we all
frantically wrap our forearms, dig for our grips, buckle them over our
wrists, and dash to the chalk bowl for the touch warm-up. We each have
30 seconds to quickly run through a few skills, so I work my transitions
and releases before hopping off the apparatus and leaving the podium.

Emerson is sitting in a split next to the folding chairs where we're supposed to sit when someone else is competing. I almost say good luck,
but for some reason, don't. Instead, I grab my iPod, scroll down to "Eye
of the Tiger," close my eyes, and picture myself nailing this routine.
Everything else in the arena disappears, and I know I'm gonna kick ass.

***

"Up next on uneven bars, Amalia Blanchard from Malkina Gold Medal
Academy."

I'm at the chalk bowl giving my grips one last dusting, waiting for the
bars judges to put up Nalani's score. I wasn't watching, but I'm guessing
she fell...she looked absolutely suicidal when she left the podium.

I walk over to take my place to mount, my mind automatically blocking
out the distractions of the arena – the screaming crowd, someone's
floor music blaring over the speakers, and the flashy scoreboards

around the perimeter of the place. I glue my eyes to the green flag; when it goes up, the judges are ready and I'm allowed to start my routine. My competition at the 2016 American Open officially begins.

Big, deep breath, and I jump into my glide kip mount. Maloney to pak, no problem, I can do this in my sleep. But now for the test. I kip cast out of the pak, and then stalder through my next swing, gritting my teeth before letting go. I rebound up to the high bar, squeezing my legs together as hard as I possibly can, pointing the crap out of my toes, hands outstretched over my head and ready to catch.

Bam, right in the sweet spot. My skill anxiety subsides and I am focused and fluid for the rest of the routine: toe full to Gienger, giant half to front giant to Markelov, toe-on to handstand, and then finally the giant half to front giant right into my dismount, a double front tuck.

I take a tiny step forward to steady myself, feel my body absorb into the mat, and then hop my feet together before saluting to the judges, a big smile on my face.

I made it through. That's all I wanted. I didn't have a single major error, and I was even able to concentrate on my form after I hit my transition. Competing here was mentally no different from competing in front of the few dozen parents who showed up at my J.O. meets. It's actually super easy to forget about the crowd, the television cameras...

Actually, it's when you get *off* the podium that you notice the cameras, because the dudes lugging them around shove them into your face to get your reaction, as if me grinning from ear to ear makes for great TV. If you're leading the competition, they never leave you alone. I almost want to lose just for that reason.

"Sneaky routine change," Natasha says, giving me a side hug after I hop off the podium. We walk back to our seats, cameras following us. "If you felt you couldn't compete the van Leeuwen, you could have told me."

"It was a last-minute decision," I lie. "I got scared and didn't want to miss it."

"Well, at least you were smart enough to train your 'last-minute decision' before you did it, liar. But great job, really, you were crisp and clean, just some leg separation here and there, and the handstand on the toe full wasn't really precise. Overall, good work, and we'll talk about taking your van Leeuwen out for real when we get back to the gym."

Good. I take a sip of water and nod. Ruby is on the podium, chalking and waiting for before she gets her own green light. I don't want to look at my score until it's all over, and Natasha promises that she won't say anything when she sees it.

"Come on, Rube!" I yell right as she's about to mount. Her routine has some crazy elements, but the one that's going to freak everyone out is this combination she's been training all year – a Ray half to a straddle-back half. The Ray is a release move starting from a toe-on before launching into a Tkachev, up and back over the bar before catching on the other side. Finally, right before you expect her to catch, she twists and *then* grabs the bar. Insane.

As if that's not enough, she immediately transitions right down to the low bar, releasing her hands pretty much the second she catches the Ray half. She flips her body upside down to face the low bar, and then goes for another half twist before blindly catching. Just ridiculous. No one else in the world does either of these skills on their own let alone connected, and I know the crowd is going to explode when they see her do it.

Normally I don't watch routines, but this is my best friend, and she's doing something so unbelievably fierce, I know I can't miss it.

She starts out well, catching her Church release skill without a single problem, and the crowd applauds politely. Then comes the combination out of nowhere...she catches the Ray half, releases, does the straddle-back half, and expertly grasps the low bar, causing the crowd to actually *gasp*, totally shocked.

The arena erupts into thunderous applause, but it doesn't faze Ruby, who continues nailing big skill after big skill before sticking her dismount, a double layout with a full twist. Again, monster applause, and it's 100% deserved.

"*Yes!*" Ruby screams after her salute, fist pumping before jumping off the podium and running into Natasha's arms for a hug. Natasha is beaming. She has no notes, no corrections, which is super rare. I hold up my hands for a double high five from Ruby, who looks like she just won a billion dollars in the lottery. I'm bananas proud of her.

The celebration doesn't last long; only Elise and Madison are left to compete before we have to head over to beam, and we need to use this time to mark our routines. I take a bite of the banana I keep in a Ziploc bag for a little energy boost, and find some space off to the side where I can throw my leaps and practice my acro series.

I don't want to see my bars score, but I'm dying to see Ruby's, and I know it flashes when I hear the crowd go berserk. I make myself finish my routine choreo, not wanting to break my focus, and then glance up.

15.4, and on her "worst" event. Holy crap. She is going to *dominate* this summer.

***

On beam, I know my routine is nearly perfect but I don't get excited until I feel my feet plant firmly on the mat. My chest is angled a tiny bit down, which will be a deduction, but it's one of the hardest dismounts in the world and I stuck it, so I'll let that slide even if the judges won't.

More hugs from Team MGMA before the focus shifts back to Ruby. I get nervous for her here, and glance down at my nails when she's about to land her more difficult skills, but she looks great. There are pretty, fluid beam workers, and then there are the girls who are super aggressive and attack the beam like it just tried to steal their wallet. Somehow, Ruby is both.

The arena goes wild again when she lands her dismount, and multiple cameramen track her as she leaves the podium to high five everyone in our rotation group.

Emerson is the only one not celebrating. She sits in a middle split, listening to music and fiddling with her phone, trying to ignore Ruby's rekindled fame. It's gotta suck for her; Ruby's two "weak" events are actually pretty awesome, especially in their public debuts. Emerson is basically old news now. Sure, she has her world titles, but her floor – while gorgeous and difficult – isn't the type of routine that gets people on their feet, and vault goes by so quickly, most people miss it, especially with four events happening all at once.

With three more beam routines to go in this rotation, I need to keep my muscles warm so my flexibility looks good on floor. My tumbling may never be anything amazing, but as long as my leaps don't get deducted, I'm happy.

"Good job," Emerson says, not looking up as I slide into a split.

I point my toes, flex, and point them again, harder the second time. "Thanks."

"Nervous about floor?"

"No? I haven't really been nervous all day."

"Well, good luck."

"Thanks, you too."

Great convo. Still in a split, I bend my back knee so that my toes are pointing up and lean back as far as I can until my toes graze my forehead. The switch ring in its true form...looks good on paper but throw it in the middle of a fast-paced routine, and most girls don't get halfway to the correct position. Always good to give my muscles a reminder of how it's supposed to look beforehand.

Finally, Amaya finishes things up for our group on beam. She looks okay from what I can see – no falls at least – but has downgraded some skills since I last saw her do this event. Not good.

When the rotation officially ends, we march over to floor, salute to the judges, and begin our touch warm-up. We each chuck one pass at a time, and when we're not tumbling, we're working leaps and choreography off to the side.

My passes are fine, except I think with the added adrenaline from the competition, I'm getting a little bit more bounce than usual and stumble back a few steps on each.

"Get it out of your system now!" Natasha yells-slash-threatens before we're forced off the podium moments later.

The competition order shifts up with each rotation, so I was fourth on bars, third on beam, and now second here. Not enough time to work myself into a full-blown panic attack over my mistakes in the warm-up, thankfully. I linger off to the side, jumping up and down to shake off the jitters and keep my mind off of everything.

When it's my turn I give myself one last bounce to jostle the nerves out, smile to the judges as I salute, and then slip into my opening pose. The music begins and I'm easily able to forget how rattled I was moments earlier.

Once upon a time, I was so bad at performing on floor – not tumbling, necessarily, but expressing myself and engaging with the crowd, what's referred to as "artistry" in the gym world – my coach had to choreograph emotions for me. No joke. I felt like a sociopath. But with a few years of practice, I've been able to "feeeeeel the music!" – as Polina would scream at me – a bit better. I'm still not a natural performer but at least I don't look like I have no soul behind my eyes.

First up, double arabian, and I take a step forward instead of sticking. Not terrible but not great, either. I nail my triple full in the second pass, and then finish up with a double pike and a double tuck, both of which are fine, no big mistakes. But they're also not stuck – I stepped back twice on both. For such easy passes, they should be stuck every time.

When I come off, Natasha gives me a big hug and hands me a cold bottle of water as we walk off to the side for her notes.

"I'm sure you already know your landings were sloppy," she starts. "Except the triple. That was gold. I'll give it to you this time because it's your first time competing this routine on a podium in front of a crowd, but you have to learn to tame it, okay?"

I nod, still out of breath.

"Good job connecting with the crowd, though. There was one moment in your choreo where you heard applause and actually gave a genuine smile with a little head nod, and that was a little detail that comes across so huge…especially to the judges. Your dance elements were mostly on point, good extension on leaps, but I saw some little deductions there. We'll work on it. Your landings weren't *terrible* but you know that's what sticks out in their minds, so it kind of negates the good stuff you did. But overall, I'm happy."

Phew. "Thanks." She rubs my back a bit and then leaves me to recover.

Only vault left, and it's basically impossible for me to mess this up on a grand scale. At least I'm going to come out of this day alive, and with a pretty decent all-around score, if I had to guess.

Ruby, done for the day, comes over to congratulate me and we watch the rest of the rotation together from our seats on the sidelines. On floor, Emerson looks good but not her best. Nothing really bad, but it's not a standout routine, either. When you're not doing all four events it can be super difficult to stay in the zone all meet, so with her hour of doing nothing, it's no wonder she's not on her game.

Emerson is the last to go. Ruby, who doesn't like to see her own scores in a competition but loves checking out everyone else, glances up.

"Have you seen the standings yet?" she asks casually as we pick up our bags and get ready to walk on to the final rotation.

"No. Why? Don't tell me."

She smiles and stands behind me in our little line. "I won't." But her smile says it all. I never do this. There's so much else to focus on, but my most difficult work is behind me at this point and I seriously can't help myself. My eyes dart up to the big screen hanging from the center of the arena and see the list of the top eight ranked going into the final rotation.

43.5. I'm in the lead by one tenth. I try to play it cool, but I can't force my smile away and march over to vault looking like the happiest ventriloquist dummy in the whole world.

***

"This is it," Natasha whispers, hands on my shoulders after the quick touch warm-up before vault. "It's been a great day so far, so keep that momentum going and finish it up strong. You've done this vault a million times, you know what you need to do. Consider it practice. You got this."

I close my eyes and inhale, hold my breath for a second, and then exhale deeply. The little bell dings, signaling the end of warm-ups and the start of competition. I climb back onto the podium, wait for the signal, smile, salute, and get into position.

My sprint is on point. I hit the table with the power I need, and then twist as fast as I possibly can, my form immaculate. I can feel the landing approaching, and I realize right as my feet hit the mat that I came in with a little too much power and twisted a little too hard.

My body wants to keep rotating beyond the 2.5 twists but I'm no longer in the air, so that's obviously a problem. I manage to stop myself before I over-rotate too much, but I land facing slightly to my right, and have to cross my left foot over the right to steady myself. And then my right foot steps out to the side and over the line. One-tenth penalty. Damn.

Salute, smile, and exit the podium. All on autopilot.

Natasha comes in for a hug but it's a "good job" hug, not "you just killed it at your first major elite competition" hug. Had I nailed this vault, she would have run up and whisked me off the ground the way she did at level 10 nationals last year.

"What happened?" she asks.

"Nothing...adrenaline?" I respond, out of breath.

"It's okay, it was fine. It was a very strong vault, control aside. Landings are clearly your biggest problem when you get excited, and we need to harness that, okay? As soon as we get home, that's what we need to work on."

I feel a lump come into my throat. I know I had a great meet and I can't let minor mistakes ruin it, but the feeling of not having a *perfect* meet because I got a little too excited pisses me off. I'm not really upset about the couple of steps, but I am a little bummed about having it go so well, making everyone rally for me, and then not following through.

My smile stays glued to my face as I hug and/or high five the rest of the girls in my rotation. I finally sit back, drain my water bottle, and wait for the score to flash.

15.4.

The crowd cheers, and I grin, though I'm not thrilled. 15.4 is terrific in this crazy bizarre scoring system we have now. Anything above a 15 on most events would make you one of the best in the world, but on vault a 15.4 is below average if you're doing an Amanar. Vault is where gymnasts tend to get the least amount of deductions, because it goes by so quickly and there's so little to it...how badly can you possibly screw it up? Even girls with falls can manage an execution in the 8.0 range.

With a 6.3 start value and a penalty off for the step out, it means my execution is a 9.2. It's good, but the best in the world on this vault are getting 9.6 or 9.7 execution. Those few tenths are everything, especially when I look up at the rankings after Maddy Zhang finishes floor.

She must've had an incredible routine, finishing with a 15.6 to end her meet with a 59.0. I'm right behind her with a 58.9. One tenth separates us, which means had I hit my vault, I definitely would have won.

Winning isn't *everything* to me, I guess, but the thing is that I know I won't beat Ruby or Emerson when they do the all-around at the next couple of meets. This was basically my one shot to get that all-around gold, and I blew it, which stings. Sure, I blasted past the nationals qualifying score by over five points, so that's something to celebrate? I guess. I bite my nails watching the last few routines, hoping no one breaches my score, and after Irina Borovskaya finishes things off on floor, it's settled. First place, Maddy Zhang with a 59.0, second place, drum roll, *me* with a 58.9, and third place, Charlotte Kessler with a 58.7.

In the next few spots I spot Zara Morgan in fourth, and then 2015 worlds alternate Bailey Dawson in fifth, and world bars medalist Irina Borovskaya in sixth. Zara, a shy gymnast about my age, was elite last year, but only a junior, so it's kind of cool that she and I are the two newbies beating last year's golden girls. Well, silver girls. They only got the silver team medal at worlds. Yes, *only* silver. I feel your pain, ladies.

"Congratulations!" Ruby comes running up for a big hug. Emerson, who got a 15.9 on *her* Amanar, trails behind her and also hugs me. "You were amazing."

"Thanks guys, though I have to admit I feel like I blew it."

"Please, it's so close at the top right now the rankings don't even matter. You're all equally fantastic, so don't let the color of your medal determine how you think you did," Ruby advises.

"Yeah, you guys in the top three were within three tenths of each other," Emerson adds, somewhat surprisingly not rubbing it in. "If this competition happened again tomorrow, your spots could be completely swapped around."

"Thanks. Deep down I get it, but I'm probably going to be bummed for a tiny bit. Silver is the worst."

"You are allowed to wallow for the rest of today, and then tomorrow it's back to fighting," Ruby says, grabbing my shoulders and staring me in the eyes, mildly creepy but it works when she has to talk her teammates off of cliffs. "Use it as motivation for being better next time."

"One time I got silver and my mom custom made a t-shirt that said

'Only Second Best.' That was motivation enough for me," Emerson adds with a friendly pat on the back.

The medalists are waved over to the floor podium for the ceremony, and Natasha is already right in front with her camera, beating all of the reporters for the best spot. The 16 or so bars of music they have playing for us repeats over and over while we listen to short speeches from various people connected to the meet and I can see Natasha impatiently stomping her feet to the rhythm, which makes me smile.

Finally, the medals come out, awarded by Vera, who shakes our hands and then places them over our heads. Her skin is papery thin but her grip is like an arm wrestler's. I would love to see her forearm muscles.

I lean in for a brief hug. Vera then grabs my face in both hands and whispers, "You surprised me. You are a great competitor." I pull back, stunned, and she smiles, adding, "It's only up the hill from here" before moving on to her next victim.

Suddenly silver doesn't seem so bad.

Monday, May 16, 2016
81 days left

"And then there were 22," Natasha beams.

That's how many of us qualified to nationals. Of the 31 at the American Open, nine didn't reach the qualifying score of 54. You think I was being dramatic about tenths? One girl, Leah Manning, qualified by the skin of her teeth with a 54.1 and is probably on her knees thanking Nadia for remembering to keep her toes pointed or not wobbling more than she did. Then there's poor Danielle McIntyre with a 53.9, missing out by a tenth and most likely cursing Satan for that tiny step on a dismount or not hitting a handstand quite right on bars.

Having Sunday off after traveling and the stress of training and competing felt like a blessing from the gods. It's not like I can kick back and eat chocolate cake for every meal, but my parents got me a little fruit bouquet and I'm not gonna pretend I didn't eat pretty much everything in it while watching an entire season of *30 Rock*, Jack working away on his laptop at my side.

But now, back to square one. Training in the gym resumes as if nothing is different, the American Open feels like it didn't even happen, and we have bigger goals to attack.

"This week is all about the three C's," Natasha goes on. "Consistency, control, and...competitivity. Is that a word? Competitiveness? *Being competitive*. I know we just competed five seconds ago, but nationals are three weeks away. Only twelve will continue on in the hopes of becoming America's next top...gymnast to compete at Olympic Trials."

Oh my God, this is the weirdest pre-practice speech we've ever had. I'm guessing Natasha had several long hours of nothing but margaritas and Tyra Banks on her day off.

"The cutoff is twelve athletes? I thought it was a score cutoff." Ruby butts in.

"Yes, twelve total, unless Vera changes her mind but I doubt any of you will have a hard time making it. If you hit, that is, which is why we're going to work these routines to death so you're hitting them every single time without wobbling or falling."

Sergei steps in with a list. "I have the results from the Open, and based on how other girls are doing, you ladies would probably make the cutoff if it was six. But it's close. If I had to guess, I'd say the lowest all-around score we'll see making it in is probably around 57. At this rate you'd each need to fall twice to score that low, so we're not worried, but at the same time we want you in the top half of the top twelve. Just to be safe."

I feel a little more confident knowing this, and I know I can make top six even with Ruby and Emerson in the all-around. But it's gonna be close. I'll definitely be borderline in that group.

"Okay, Emerson, go with your coach, Ruby...just go through routines with Polina, and Polina, do something like...have her start over if she makes a mistake or something, you know what to do. Amalia, you're my special project."

Natasha smiles and I grimace. This is going to be a killer workout.

"So, we know your problem," she starts. "Adrenaline. You have too much of it in competition, and that's hard to prepare for. Even if I bring in the rec kids to watch you, it's not the same as doing this live in front of a huge crowd on national TV. I don't want to tell you to under-rotate your tumbling in practice with the hopes of your adrenaline carrying you through in competition because it's dumb to rely on adrenaline alone. What if you're not feeling it? You're screwed."

I have no idea where this is going. I yawn without thinking. I miss my bed. And my fruit bouquet.

"Basically, we're going to prepare for the worst. We're going to over-rotate everything so your body can get used to how that feels and we're going to train your body to find the landing even if you do come in with a bit too much power. Make sense?"

"So I'm just going to be doing my passes but with too much power?"

"Yes. We'll use the tumble track into the pit at first so you don't wreck your legs on landings...your body and muscle memory will still get the sense of how it feels to be over-rotated so you'll be able to recognize it mid-pass. Then we'll try a few on the floor, doing it how it's supposed to be done and then giving yourself a bit too much power so you pick up on the difference. You might not be able to stick an over-rotated pass, but we'll at least get them to the point where you won't stumble them back either. Controlled lunge is the name of the game."

I actually like this idea. A lot. The last thing I want to do at nationals is stumble back so far I sit the pass and count a fall.

"What about the Amanar?" I ask. "Should I practice over-rotating that as well?"

She thinks for a moment. "I feel like that was more of a fluke. Like you knew you were about to win the meet and so you tried to go out with a bang. I'm not as worried. You're usually solid there and I don't want to mess with a good thing."

She totally knows I looked at the scores before doing vault, and I hadn't thought of it before but now it makes perfect sense. Looking at the rankings between rotations, seeing myself in first place, wanting the win – that's a hundred percent why I went in too hard.

"So, no more counting our chickens before they hatch," she adds knowingly, a small smile on her lips. "And besides, your score on vault was still decent. Your floor score in comparison is pretty abysmal. If we clean up your landings there it's going to add close to a point."

I run over to the tumble track and bounce a little before getting into place. We try a double back first because it's the easiest for me, and I don't even have to really give it any extra power; the trampoline does it for me, and I feel myself rotating past the point where I'm supposed to land. If I were going onto a mat instead of in the pit, I'd be on my back right now begging for ice.

We repeat this drill a few times, until I have a decent awareness of my over-rotated body position in the air. Then we move to the floor. "Push harder than you normally would, and then slow your rotation on the second flip," Natasha yells from the other side of the springy square. "Make sense?"

"Yep." Deep breath, then I go. I give myself way too much of a punch off the floor out of the back handspring, can tell in the air that it's too much, and then try to curb it, but I curb too much and end up with my chest down and a step forward, which is probably worse deduction-wise than taking the steps back. If you under-rotate a pass, it shows the judges you don't have enough power to do the skill, which also adds killer deductions.

"Good job," Natasha says. "We'll find that happy medium."

"My thing is like...this is easy because I'm *planning* to give myself too much rotation so I know before I go that I'm going to stop myself. I don't think mid-competition it's going to be easy to realize in the split second I'm in the air that I'm rotated too far back."

"Right, but based on how you did this weekend, the adrenaline is probably going to carry you over so you'll still be able to plan for it. We'll have to take it as the day comes. If you're warming up with too much power we'll have some idea what to expect in competition and we can go from there."

It's a decent plan, but still not fine-tuned enough for my need to have everything planned and ready to go exactly as it needs to be done in the meet. I almost feel like she has no idea what to do with me and is just grasping at straws until she can figure it out.

I try the pass again, give too much, pull back, and land it straight up. Not stuck, but I'm not over- or under-rotated. I just take a little steadying step back into a lunge, which used to be an acceptable way to land your passes. I yearn for those good old days.

"Better!" is my feedback. "Again!" is my command. I groan internally, but accept my fate, because no matter how much this kills my ankles and exhausts my muscles, nothing will destroy me as much as finishing behind Maddy again.

***

"For homework tonight, copy down all key terms for the section — the *section*, not just the last chapter — and be prepared for team vocabulary Jeopardy tomorrow. If you don't do the work, you're only letting your team down! Trust me, you won't want to lose this reward."

Ugh, I don't have time for this. There are over a hundred terms in this section about World War I *and* I have a math test tomorrow. Oh, and I'm trying to make the Olympic team, which I'd say is a little more important than history class Jeopardy. The first day back at school after a competition is always a pain in the ass, but with being Natasha's "special project" at this morning's practice, I am pretty over everything.

I slam my book perhaps a little too hard when the bell rings, and one of my inbred d-bag classmates decides now is his opportunity to shoot me when I'm down.

"Hey Shoulders," he says. Cool. Observational humor. On point. *Saturday Night Live* is going to be calling for you any day now. I mean, sure, my shoulders are larger than average due to the fact that I use their muscles to hurl my body around a million hours a week? I can probably bench press your whole family and you wish you had even a tenth of the muscle that I do.

Except I say none of this out loud. Instead, my face explodes into a hot pink mess as I try to gather my belongings without dropping anything or falling over. Because whenever I'm confronted, I somehow turn into Mr. Magoo.

I duck under his arm, which is poised aggressively against the door frame. He laughs at this, and for some reason, some girls who literally didn't even see what happened laugh along with him. I loathe girls.

"Don't run away from me," he says with a half grin and a swagger only rock stars and prepubescent high school boys who think they're more important than they'll ever be have. "I need to ask you to junior prom."

Well, consider me blindsided. The girls begin whispering angrily, their day clearly ruined by watching my bad fortune turn to "good," if you can call this good.

"Why do you want to go to the prom with me?" I ask, truly curious.

"I heard you telling Emma Kaufmann that you weren't going. I was planning on going with my buddies, didn't want any girl drama, but I felt bad that no one asked you."

"That's very romantic," I grunt, shifting the weight of my backpack to one of my ginormous attention-grabbing nickname-inducing man shoulders and turning on one foot to walk away from this weird situation.

"Wait," he yells. "It's not like you have anything better to do Saturday night. This is like, the best offer you're gonna get."

I turn back and smile insanely, to the point where I think I legitimately terrify him. "*Bro*, sorry, but I'm gonna have to turn you down," I start. "I do have plans this weekend, actually. On Saturday I will be in the gym for seven hours sweating and bleeding and crying and making my shoulders even bigger than they are right now, if you can imagine that. And every second of agony and misery will be a billion percent more preferable than spending two hours at a lame high school dance with you."

Point for the nerd. Those who were still following our little spectacle look stunned but also angry, as if they're mad that I dare rise beyond my place in the universe to give back what I'm just supposed to take. I kinda wish my life was a 90s movie so they would take my side and slow clap.

I hear the jock moron whose name I honestly don't even know yell out "bitch!" as I turn my back to head down the hallway and out the door. Without turning I yell, "you're mistaken, I'm not your mom," right back, just as I see my own mom waiting to pick me up for the gym, something she tries to do at least once a week because otherwise I'd basically never see her.

"That seemed unpleasant."

"It's high school, Mom. It's supposed to be unpleasant."

"Why did he call you a bitch?"

"Because I wouldn't go to prom with him." I spot my dad in the driver's seat as we approach the car. Two parents on the same day?! At least he didn't witness my outburst. Something tells me as a school principal, he wouldn't be super pleased. "Hi, pops."

"He asked you to prom!? And you turned him down!?" My mom is seriously thrilled for me. Like, more thrilled that a guy deigned to speak to me than she's ever been about any of my major gymnastics accomplishments.

"Mom, he's literally garbage. You'd *want* me to say yes to a guy who calls me a bitch because things didn't go his way?! Also, I have gym all day Saturday. As if I'd have any time to make myself look presentable to other human beings afterwards. Besides, I'd rather be in an ice bath and in bed at 8 pm. *That's my choice,*" I joke.

"But *prom*, Amalia. I know, I know, I know. It doesn't compare to the Olympics. Nothing does. But you know that's not a given. Don't you think you'll have even the slightest regret about missing these normal high school milestones because you're training all the time?"

This conversation happens at least once a month. My mom is convinced that when I'm 30 I'll look back on my life and be really upset that I missed out on crucial high school memories like washing cars in a bikini whilst sucking a lollipop in a Walmart parking lot or giving birth at a school dance and trying to hide my baby in a trash can.

"It's not like I'm sitting at home doing nothing. I'll have *other* milestones and memories, and just because they're different than *normal* high school memories doesn't mean they don't count."

"You're so smart and grown-up," my dad sighs. He's mostly been mentally elsewhere for this conversation.

"I trust you to make your own decisions here, but just don't want you to feel like you have to give up every single quote-unquote *normal* activity just because of training," my mom continues. "One night away won't kill you."

"But I'd *rather* be in the gym, that's the thing. I know plenty of girls who choose dances over training every now and then and that's fine for them. It's what they want. But I don't *want* to do that stuff. It is the absolute least appealing thing to me, and besides, I've made it this far. The Olympics will be over in three months, and whether I make it or not, I'll be able to catch up on everything I missed out on once they're over."

"I'll support your decisions, always, but just don't want you getting your hopes up and then getting disappointed. It's not that I don't believe you can do it, but there's just so many other girls with the same dream and it's going to be really hard. Ruby was a sure shot four years ago and look what happened to her. Nothing is certain in this life, Amalia, so don't put all of your eggs in one basket. That's all I'm saying."

We ride in silence the rest of the way to the gym, but before I get out of the car, my dad clears his throat.

"Mal, your mom and I have something to tell you. Remember before the Open when I told you I had a surprise?"

This sounds serious, not like "we're giving you a car." My mind immediately goes to a crazy place. In the two seconds it takes before my dad begins speaking again, I'm already picturing myself at divorce court or standing next to someone's deathbed.

"I got a job offer," he starts. "We've had funding problems in our district for years and I'm at a loss. There's nothing I can do to help as principal. I've been trying to reach beyond my role and do something on a greater scale for awhile now."

"Did you get a promotion?!"

"I did get a new job, yes. As a superintendent."

"Dad, that's amazing!"

He glances nervously at his hands on the wheel. "In Mabton."

"What's *Mabton*?"

"It's in South Central Washington. They're desperate, so I'll be transferring before the end of the month."

My heart stops. "That's the middle of *nowhere*, dad. It's like hours and hours away?! I can't just leave my gym!"

Dad clears his throat again, a nervous tell like my nail-biting before I compete. He gives my mom one of their shared looks where they somehow communicate telepathically and she continues speaking for him.

"We are staying in Seattle," she offers with a smile. "Just the two of us. Dad will visit on weekends, and after the summer, after the Olympics, we'll figure out something a little more permanent."

"This is so unfair," I pout. "Why can't you just stick it out at your school until I go to college and *then* have a midlife crisis?"

"Amalia, please, you're being melodramatic," he says firmly. "My entire career has revolved around your gymnastics. I've ignored too many opportunities, turned down jobs, made sacrifices no other parents make all for you and your sport and I've been more than happy to do it. But this is a once-in-a-lifetime job and I can't pass it up. It's about time you make a sacrifice for me."

I sit in silence for a minute, tears brimming in my eyes not so much because I'm upset about the news but more because I'm a crap sandwich of a person. The guilt I feel about my selfishness is blinding torture but I can't handle admitting this to my parents. Instead, I paste on a smile.

"I'm sorry. You're totally right. Congratulations! You're gonna be amazing. When do you leave?"

I'm only half-listening as he drones on about the specifics; instead, I work on shoving my feelings down because avoidance beats actually dealing with real life, am I right? I'll take it out on the vault or beam later, Natasha will praise me for how aggressive my skills look, and my perfectly happy family will stay perfectly happy. Why rock the boat?

Saturday, May 21, 2016
76 days left

I'm just one vault away from my "weekend," which is really just the rest of this afternoon and tomorrow, but I'll take it.

Sprint, round-off, back handspring, push, tighten, twist, land. It's over in a flash, I get a "yes!" from Natasha after sticking it, we listen to some post-practice notes, and then we get the go-ahead to leave. This week has been hell, mentally and physically, at home and in the gym. A non-stop suckfest of pretending everything is super duper when in reality I couldn't be more stressed.

Actually, aside from feeling like my body belongs to an 80-year-old with 30 broken bones, gym has been an escape, allowing me to take out every frustration and asking for nothing in return. I'm forcing myself to be happy for my dad, but the spoiled little brat inside me can't get over not seeing him every day. I know it's temporary, and that I'm lucky because at least my parents are still together and I'll see him on weekends and can FaceTime him whenever I want, so I'm trying to make myself be mature about it.

But at the same time, I can't get over how much this change in routine is already affecting me mentally. Logically I know in the grand scheme of things not much is going to be different, but the little things he does – turning off my bedside fan every morning to gently wake me up, the "just for fun" mid-week surprise gifts he leaves on my bed, cooking the worst meals ever together when my mom has to work late which is always – are going to be hard to forget.

I'm being a baby, and I know it, which is why I've kept my feelings a secret. Plenty of people have it way worse, and he's right. I've held him back long enough. Besides, if I can't survive not seeing my dad five days a week, how will I survive making it to the Olympics? I need to get my life together.

"You doing anything tonight, Mal?" Ruby asks, hopping in the shower.

"Dinner. Homework. Sleep. And I couldn't be happier. Minus the homework part."

"Wanna grab dinner in the city? My host family is out of town and I have car access."

"I have to check with my parents, but actually, as exhausted as I am, that sounds great. I need a change of scenery. Between gym, school, and my parents, I am going stir crazy."

"You were literally *just* in San Diego," Emerson chimes in.

"Yeah, *doing gymnastics*," Ruby retorts. "It's not like we were on a luxury vacation, or a vacation at all."

"Do you want to come with us, Em?" I ask once Ruby steps into the shower. Ruby's probably gonna be pissed but I feel bad, especially considering that she's new here, has literally no friends, and we're not generally known for treating her like a pal.

"Umm...I have to look into some things but sure, if Ruby doesn't mind."

"Look into some things," I repeat in my head with a pity eye roll. As if. But also, sad. Damn my conflicting emotions.

I shower, change into jeans and a t-shirt, call my mom, get the okay, and then as I'm blow drying my hair, Emerson heads out of the shower bank. "I can come!" she announces.

Ruby laughs. "With us?"

"I invited her," I hiss.

"I mean, the more the merrier and teammate bonding and all that good stuff, but I hope we don't bore you to death with our lameness and nerdery. Get ready for the least exciting night of your life."

We pile into Ruby's fake parents' car, Emerson in the passenger seat and me behind them like the child that I am, even though I'm sure most people would agree I'm more mature than the two of them combined. It's sometimes weird to remember that they're both older than me by three or four years. In the gym, you get used to being friends with people of all ages, but in real life the gap between 18 and 19 (them) and 15 (me) is pretty wide.

Ruby wants to go to the University of Washington area, so we drive off in that direction, talking about practice the whole way over because it's the one thing we all have in common.

"I'm so glad Natasha's letting you keep the Chow on bars," Ruby mentions. "You look a billion times better."

"Yeah, not having to worry about the stupid half twist is making it so much easier. Like, that one skill going away fully makes me more confident with that routine by a billion percent."

"It looks like it. Seriously, you wrap your mind around something like that and it becomes your sole focus and you ignore everything else. I've been there."

"I don't get why Natasha would have you keep it in all that time if you couldn't do it," Emerson remarks. "You'd think she would have taken it out if you were struggling all this time. My coach would have."

"It's more my fault than hers," I say quickly, before Ruby can yell at Emerson for questioning Natasha's coaching methods. "I wanted it in the routine, and I was too stubborn to ask to change it. Natasha always knows when I physically can't do a skill, so she lets me work at it until I either get it or give up. Besides, this wasn't an ability thing. It was a mental block."

"I mean, I could tell it was a problem the first time I saw you doing it, so that's the only reason I bring it up." She shrugs.

"Whatever," Ruby says. "Natasha's one of the best elite coaches in the country, but she also has a million J.O. kids who just finished nationals and regionals and states, so she's not going to catch every under-the-surface freak-out from Amalia. No offense, Mal."

"None taken." My inner crazy is infamous at our gym.

"Either way, it's fixed, and the routine does look much better now," Emerson concedes. "Even if bars aren't really your thing."

"Thanks?"

"What about you?" Ruby asks. "How are you liking it at MGMA?"

"It hasn't really made much of a difference aside from the few little collaborative drills Natasha and Sergei put together. I'm still Sergei's athlete, just at a different gym."

"Why *did* you and Sergei come here?" Ruby asks. "Especially this close to the Olympics. I still don't get it."

Emerson turns red. "The owners of my last gym..."

"Yeah, blah, blah, blah, they tried to make you sign a contract, they wanted you to earn money for them, that's what the press and everyone is saying. But it's weird because you've never turned down money-whoring schemes before. What's the real reason?" Ruby's pushing it now. But no one in the gym world has bought that story from day one, and honestly, I'd like to know the truth as well.

A moment of silence. Emerson crosses her arms and I watch her right fingers lace around her left elbow, squeezing tight. "It's none of your business," she finally hisses.

We're silent for the rest of the ride until Ruby parallel parks on University Way and cheerfully announces, "we're here!"

What a super fun team bonding night this will be!

***

Thankfully, dinner at Samir's Mediterranean is less stressful than the car ride. Now that we're face to face, daring Ruby is less apt to dig into Emerson's personal life and the atmosphere is much more chill.

We're all pretty limited in what we can order, so we each put in very particular requests. The wait staff is only slightly annoyed by we three preteen-sized gals with abnormally defined arm muscles picking apart each dish to get it Olympic-diet approved, but we're used to it. I automatically add in a "sorry" under my breath with each minor alteration.

"Realistically, at this point," Ruby says in between bites of her vegetarian plate (half the rice and hold the pita bread), "who do you think will make the Olympic team?"

Ugh. I glance at Emerson, my eyes begging her to answer first, mostly because I want to know if I'm included in her picture. She doesn't answer or even look at me, choosing instead to pretend the lemon in her tea is super interesting.

"Um," I start, not sure to include myself or not. Do I really have that little faith? I just think I'll sound absurd if I actually say my own name.

"Well, you guys, duh." I'm just gonna end there. Easy.

"No, you have to give all five members!"

I sigh audibly and Ruby's eyes twinkle. She loves to see others in pain and I hate her more than anyone else who has ever lived.

"There are like a billion other people who could fill those spots," I whine. "Like, so many injuries can happen between now and then, someone could come out looking amazing, someone else can come out looking like crap...it's impossible to say."

"Booooo, it's no fun being diplomatic. Name the first three off the top of your head. NOW."

"FINE, Maddy, Charlotte, and me."

Emerson wrinkles her nose.

"What, you disagree?" I huff, my nostrils flaring.

"No, it's a good team, and you went the safe route, picking the top three at the Open, so basically the top five all-arounders in the country right now. But that team isn't really balanced at all."

"I don't know," Ruby says slowly, plotting her perfect team in her head. "Vault, fine, we'd all have Amanars except Charlotte. Bars is fine, beam would have three of the best routines in the world, floor is great too. What's wrong with it?"

"Bars is grotesque. No offense, but neither of you are bar workers. You'd have me, and then two mediocre routines."

"My bars score at the Open was a 15.4!" Ruby says, slamming her fork down.

"Home scoring," Emerson scoffs. "You'll never get that internationally."

"Fine, then who would *you* include?" I ask.

"Sophia or Irina," Emerson says, folding her used napkin neatly instead of crumpling it up like a normal person.

"Instead of..." Ruby and I press on at simultaneously.

Emerson looks down at her controlled mess, inspects a nail though it's perfectly manicured, and "ahems" before responding. "Amalia."

My heart flips over.

"It's nothing against you. I'm just thinking about the team and my opinion is that we need someone more on bars, not beam. It would suck leaving you behind because your beam is like...like, you could win a gold medal for your beam. But you have to think about the team. Ruby and I have really great beams, and Maddy's is good when she hits *and* she can win a vault medal. She outranks you."

"That's crap," Ruby says. "What about Charlotte? Mal would make it over Charlotte."

"Charlotte has experience and is a better all-arounder."

"My silver to her bronze at the Open begs to differ."

Emerson shrugs. "By what, two tenths? You have two really high-scoring events and two, no offense, kind of pathetic ones. Hers average out to be the same so if the team needed someone in a pinch, she could go up anywhere and be reliable. If it was me in charge, I'd rather take a zero in qualifications than use your floor."

"You're just being a bitch for no reason," Ruby says. "Charlotte can't win individual gold on anything, and Mal can. My team would be me, you, Mal, Irina, and Maddy. Bars *and* beam are covered. Charlotte is useless."

"I respectfully disagree, but it's not like any of this matters anyway. We'll see what Vera says when the time comes."

I don't know if I want to cry or punch Emerson in the face. Like, she does have a point, I really only would be useful on one event in the team final, and it's an event we're already super good at. But *Charlotte*? For her *experience*? This girl totally bombed at worlds last year. I highly doubt Vera would trust her in Rio.

It honestly sounds like Emerson is threatened by me. No, I'm not a better gymnast than Emerson Bedford. I probably never will be. But I could very well beat her on beam and she knows it. Any bid to keep me off will open up one more medal spot for her.

"Would you ladies like the check?" the waitress asks. She has been standing there listening to us scream at each other for about five solid minutes.

We all cough up some money, Emerson and I both tense, Ruby just being Ruby, off in Rubyland where the state motto is *Schadenfreude*. Look it up.

As we're about to pile into Ruby's car, Ruby turns to us and waves. "See you Monday!"

Whoops, I didn't exactly plan how I was getting home. Perfect. I say goodnight back and debate between a million-dollar cab ride or calling my parents, who won't be thrilled about the twenty-minute drive each way.

"No ride?" Emerson asks, swiping through her phone, not looking at me.

"Nah, my mom's on the way...I mean, after I call her, she'll be on the way. It'll be awhile...do you need a ride home? We can probably take you."

"I'm just gonna Uber it."

We tap away on our iPhones in silence, and I'm about to call my mom when I realize she and my dad are at a dinner tonight. Fantastic. Is it possible to sigh aggressively?

"Hey, my car's gonna be here in like three minutes," Emerson says. "If you want I can get it to take you home after."

"Don't you live in the city? I live crazy far out of the way."

"I'm in Magnolia."

"Yeah, well I live like a half hour from there, so..."

"Hey, what if...I mean, do you think your parents would mind if I crashed at your place for the night?"

L-O-L. What the eff? I play it cool. "I doubt it, why?"

"I'm just so sick of being with my host family all the time, with like middle-aged adults and a bratty little kid, and I'm forced to either spend time with them or shut myself in my room for a hundred hours. It's not like I know anyone here."

"Um...yeah, it's fine."

"Cool, I'll just have Uber bring us to your place then. Address?"

I tell her, and then text my mom to let her know we'll have company. "Be prepared for the most awkward sleepover of my life," I type. Emerson grins at me, like this is the happiest day of her life. I hit send, smile back, and internally freak out when I realize there's still a magazine clipping of her on my dream board, embarrassing on top of embarrassing. If I have to burn the whole house down so she doesn't see it, I will.

***

"The bathroom is through that door, and I have shorts and a t-shirt you can borrow for pajamas." I motion to my dresser while making a ninja-esque move toward my desk, positioning myself in front of the bulletin board where I've kept various gymnastics-related clippings over the years for inspiration.

"Your room is really neat," she says, turning to face the window, allowing me to stealthily rip her photo from the board and crumple it into a tiny ball. Nailed it.

"Thanks? I guess it's not that bad...but still super babyish. I've been begging my parents to let me redecorate for like three years."

Emerson laughs. "No, like, *clean*. Do you really think I would use 'neat' meaning like, cool? Am I Greg Brady?"

"Solid *Brady Bunch* reference. You don't get too many of those any-more."

"We watched a lot of TV Land at my house."

"Same."

It's not late at all, but I start changing into pajamas anyway, because I'm 85 years old. My classmates are all grinding to Ke$ha at this very second and on a normal Saturday night I'd be getting ready for some ibuprofen and a bath right about now.

But not tonight, because Emerson Bedford is sleeping over.

"We don't have a guest room," I explain, slightly embarrassed. Queen Emerson definitely isn't used to such meager accommodations. "I can sleep on the couch, or we can share my bed, whatever."

"Sharing's fine." She rifles through my t-shirts, chooses an MGMA invitational shirt that's 900 sizes too big for both of us, changes, and sits cross-legged on my bed. "I wasn't just being a bitch when I didn't include you on my Rio team."

My face gets red. "I don't care. It was just hypothetical."

"I just picked who would go if I had to choose at this moment. Obviously things can change. Honestly, I'd rather have you on the team than Charlotte anyway. Or Maddy, really. They're both kind of jackasses. Worlds with the two of them was torture."

"I thought Maddy was your best friend."

Emerson rolls her eyes. "She was like my sidekick, as if we're thirteen and trying to become queens of the middle school cafeteria. She has no mind of her own and only likes me because of who I am. Like, not 'who I am' personality-wise, but 'who I am' in terms of like, celebrity or whatever."

"Yeah, I get it."

"She's a dick, and the second someone else on this team wins nationals or gets endorsements or goes on talk shows, she'll be all over them. She's the worst."

"That sucks."

"She's just so vapid. Everyone is. No one is a real genuine person." Emerson sighs, hugging her knees to her chest and resting her chin on top. "That's kind of why I love it here. You and Ruby are both actually chill. Don't ever tell her I said that."

I laugh, and recline back in my armchair by the window, curling my legs under my butt. "I won't."

"Do you ever wish gymnastics was just...gymnastics?" she asks suddenly, staring at her toes. "No press, no endorsements, no...I don't know, no Olympics even?"

"I wouldn't go as far as no Olympics, but yeah, the rest is kind of annoying."

"I love competing and everything, but like, I remember doing rec gym when I was four or five and it was just *fun*. There was no coach drilling you on skills or making you do pressure sets. If you wanted to do cartwheels for a full hour, fine. Wanna just jump up and down on the trampoline? No problem. I still love training, but it's not the same with so many expectations. It's too complicated."

"Yeah, well, look at school. You color in kindergarten, you play with blocks, you go to recess...and then in high school the only thing that matters is getting good grades so you can go to college. It's just growing up. Things are supposed to get more complicated."

"Mmmm. I guess. Doesn't mean I hate it any less. The business side, I mean. The Olympics, this whole journey, would be amazing if I could just do gymnastics and not have to deal with a single agent or manager or contract or reporter."

"Or gym owners?" Whoops, that slips out. "Sorry, I didn't mean to pry."

"Sure you didn't." She laughs, then pauses. "Promise not to tell?"

"Yes." My heart flutters, as if I'm about to have the identity of the Zodiac Killer revealed exclusively to me. "I promise."

A big sigh, and then she starts. "It was Vera's idea to move me, so that part is true. But the gym owners at Windy City were fine. I barely had anything to do with them since Sergei and I basically did our own thing. I don't like that the gym is getting a bad rap because of these rumors that have nothing to do with them."

She pauses and stares at me for a second. I clear my throat, trying to think of what to say, but before I can add my two cents, she sighs again and continues.

"Okay, so...my mother is the worst. It's your basic Lifetime drama with my father walking out and my mom working two jobs to raise me on her own. She put me in gymnastics so I'd have something to do after school, like a baby-sitter with benefits basically.

"But when I was seven, she started partying a lot, not really taking care of me at all, reliving her wild youth that came to a halt when she had me. Forgetting to pick me up from school and the gym became a regular occurrence, and because I was so embarrassed of her, I would beg friends for rides home with their parents.

"One day, I had no one and decided to walk, a truly solid plan until the cops saw me waiting to cross six lanes of traffic and picked me up. You can imagine the social services drama that followed, and in the end, my grandmother got custody. I saw my mom occasionally, but she clearly cared about other things more than me, so my grandma took over. She wanted nothing to do with me, so aside from giving me food and a bed, I was pretty much on my own.

"When I got older and started winning everything and getting into higher levels of the sport, suddenly there's my mom again, getting involved in my 'career' and moving into my grandma's house to 'manage' me. She became, like, the craziest gym mom ever even though she had no clue what she was talking about and she basically drove me out of my first gym. She made things worse no matter where I went, and then pushed me to go pro the second I made elite. When my coach at the time advised against it, she ripped me out of that gym and moved me somewhere new.

"I started earning money, first a little from EliteWear leo catalogue modeling, and then more each year when I became more well-known. But she was spending it faster than I could make it, so when I was 15 I had to get a restraining order. I also had to sue my grandma for emancipation so I could get away and live on my own.

"My mom is so manipulative, she had me convinced she was better and I let her back in again, stupid me. But when I got huge deals after winning worlds, she started asking for thousands of dollars. After win number two last year, she said I owed her because she spent the first half of my life raising me. She tried to guilt me into giving her a ridiculous amount, and it worked. I gave her a lot of money.

"As if that wasn't enough, this spring she started trying to blackmail me, saying she'd go to the press with 'incriminating evidence' if I got another restraining order or didn't give her more money. Like, she has nothing on me, she's just batshit crazy, but she lived so close and the threats were nonstop. I changed my phone number, email, whatever, ignored her, but nothing worked. Sergei was afraid it was destroying my focus, and then finally told Vera, who suggested – well, demanded – the move."

I'm stunned. I don't speak for a minute, letting her words settle before I can say anything, and even then, I have no idea what to say.

"Wow," is all I can muster. "That...sucks."

Emerson laughs, and dabs her eye. "Yeah, well...yeah. It sucks."

"You just always seem so...confident, or whatever, well-adjusted? I never would have guessed things were so crappy." I don't add that I wouldn't have been a monster bitch if I had known...not that I've been absolutely terrible to her, but I haven't exactly been welcoming either.

"It's called 'faking it,' my dear innocent Amalia. You'll get used to it when the media crawls up your ass this summer. God, you're so fresh and new, like a baby. At least your parents are sane. I'd kill for your family."

Suddenly my drama doesn't seem so massive. I won't get to see my dad five days a week but at least he didn't abandon me and makes major attempts to make our relationship great. And my mom might work late a lot but at least she has always provided for me and would never in a million years try to ruin my life. I feel like a genuine ass and am now actually *so* glad I didn't complain about this whole new job situation to anyone.

Emerson yawns. "Mind if I go to sleep? My brain is aching, I'm so tired."

"Yeah, I'm pretty wiped as well." We crawl under the covers, facing opposite one another, and within seconds I can hear her breathing, deep and even.

My mind is still going a million miles an hour after this chat, just in shock that Emerson is so much more complicated than the picture she shares with the world. Like, Ruby is Ruby – what you see is what you get. Sure, I guess even she has her secrets – like certain hot 20-something coaches sneaking out of her hotel room in the middle of the afternoon – but she says whatever is on her mind, every thought and emotion on the surface whether people like it or not.

Emerson is a billion percent more like me than I could have imagined, hiding her exhaustion and shame and drama behind expensive sunglasses and a fake smile. This is all making me more bummed out than I thought it would, and I can feel my anxiety rippling under the surface, my body's natural reaction to situations even the slightest bit uncomfortable.

I curl into the fetal position, hugging one of my throw pillows tight to my chest, breathing in through my nose and out through my mouth while slowly counting backward from a hundred. It doesn't fix anything but the yucky aura fuzzes slightly into the background of my mind and I'm able to drift into an only somewhat fitful sleep.

Monday, May 23, 2016
74 days left

When I woke up on Sunday, Emerson had already left, probably in an Uber back to the city. I almost don't believe any of last night happened, though when I check my phone there's a text thanking me for the night out and the t-shirt she wore is folded neatly on my desk chair.

I'm early for practice this morning, but I don't want to go straight to the locker room in case it ends up being just the two of us, which could be awkward. Why? I don't know. I'm an awkward person and even if the situation itself isn't, I can easily figure out a way to make it so. I don't know what else to say to her.

Thankfully Ruby saunters in shortly after me, and by the time Emerson gets there, we're already changed, making small talk by the water fountain.

"Hey," Emerson says, eyes down. Ruby and I respond "hey" in unison, neither of us looking up, though for Ruby it's because she's busy trying to pick out a warm-up playlist from Natasha's iPod, not because she is crippled by the memory of her teammate gushing extremely personal secrets in her bedroom 36 hours earlier.

I jog out to the floor and run the perimeter until I feel warm enough to abuse my muscles. Really, I wouldn't be able to live without my Sundays off, but it feels like the years and years of stretching that got me to my current levels of flexibility all completely disappear in the span of a single day. Mondays are always a killer.

The music starts, courtesy of Ruby, who has selected some old school NSYNC, which she blasts at full volume.

"This is terrible!" I yell when she barges through the door.

"Nope. You're wrong." She smiles, end of discussion.

Emerson walks in at the same time Natasha steps out of her office. "This brings me back to my early 20s," Natasha sighs. "God, our music was the worst. Okay, today marks one week until we leave for nationals. It's pressure sets all week. I want your brains in competition mode starting right this second, and honestly, I don't want them leaving competition mode until the closing ceremony in Rio."

"You all look like zombies today, so we're gonna do something a little fun to wake us up. Ruby's idea, actually," Sergei says, grinning at Ruby. Ruby squeals and claps. I projectile vomit. "When you finish warming up, head to beam. We'll start there today."

When we get to the beams, Sergei has a trunk with him. It's from the kiddy zone, full of costume pieces, beach balls, squirt guns, and various other objects that the baby rec kids use when they get bored, as if tumbling and jumping and climbing ropes isn't enough to occupy them.

"Emerson, your face is the grumpiest. You're up first. Get some warm-up work done and when you're ready for a full routine, stand in your mount position and close your eyes. Natasha will spot you." She rolls her eyes but listens dutifully, and there's a hint of a smile on her lips.

"Okay," he whispers to the rest of us. "Grab something from the bin. Your job during her routine is to annoy the crap out of her. Tickle her with a feather boa, bounce a beach ball at her face, squirt water at her...just be safe about it. I don't want you pelting her with a beach ball when she's in the middle of her flight series. The goal is to fight distraction, not kill your teammate. Oh, and scream a lot. This is a game where screaming is encouraged."

This is actually awesome. When Emerson's ready, she mounts the beam and we immediately begin our attack.

"Jesus!" she screams as a shot from Ruby's water gun blasts her in the face. She jumps off and wipes off on her jacket, which she angrily tosses back to the mat.

"One point for Emerson!" Ruby yells, gleefully entering the demerit on a little notepad.

"One point for *what*?" Emerson's still incredibly annoyed.

"You get a point every time you fall due to our merry antics. Whoever has the most points at the end loses. Just like golf."

"Not fair!" Emerson whines, despite the fact that she is 18 and not six. "If I knew what you were doing before you did it, I wouldn't have fallen."

"What's fun about that?" Ruby grins. "Get back on the horse, cowboy!"

Emerson pouts, but climbs back up and starts her routine again, her look of anger and consternation making it the most hilarious beam routine I've ever seen.

"In what world would this ever happen at a meet?!" Emerson says after dismounting, the rest of her routine fall-free. She was right – if she knew the game before she started, she definitely wouldn't have come off. "I'm going to demand security checks everyone for water guns at the arena in Boston."

"Obviously *this* won't happen, but plenty of other things are there to distract you, like the crowd gasping when someone falls on another event just as you're about to go into your dismount, or like a child randomly shrieking in the crowd, as small children are wont to do," Natasha explains. "Now that you know you can hit beam through *anything*, the normal distractions of a meet won't get to you."

"They never do," Emerson replies haughtily. "Now who do *I* get to *distract*?"

Ruby volunteers, happily. Emerson lightens up after giving Ruby a taste of her own medicine, but Ruby is as sturdy as ever, and actually laughs mid-pirouette as I tickle the heel of her foot that's in relevé.

By my turn I'm expecting the worst, but it's not so bad. The distractions clear out of my brain just as easily as an arena does. Ruby does manage to fire a line of water directly into my nose, but after a slight choking attack I'm fine and finish with no problems.

"Tie for gold!" Natasha announces. "Ruby and Amalia share it with perfect score. Emerson gets bronze with one point. This game was too easy for you."

"But fun," Emerson admits. "And a good way to psych us up for the rest of practice."

Ruby smiles, looking at me as if to say "we finally broke her."

"Yup," Sergei says. "Now it's time for the real work. Floor, all tumbling and then dance through. Vault, three apiece. Bars, first half, second half, then full routines. When we're done with each, we'll work problem areas. *Khorosho*?"

"*Khorosho*." Russian for okay.

Any weirdness that I felt toward Emerson less than 40 minutes ago is gone as the three of us laugh on our way to floor. Look at us. We're a team.

***

"Surprise!"

When I get home from practice two days later, my entire bedroom is littered with confetti and Jack pops out from behind my bed.

"What the hell?!" I shriek. Can 15-year-olds have heart attacks? Because I definitely just did.

"I should have known better," Jack laughs. "I forgot about your seventh birthday when your parents threw a surprise party and you..."

"*Don't say it.*"

"...threw up in front of every single kid in our second grade class when they screamed surprise."

Yep. That happened. I'll never live it down. Nearly a decade has passed, I haven't been in the Lynnwood public school system in years, and yet whenever I run into a former classmate, I am fondly remembered for vomiting out of fear.

"I cherish the memory," I moan, but grin. "Why the celebration? Thank you, by the way."

"Not really a celebration, I guess...just more of a good luck party for nationals. Tonight's the last time I'll see you before you fly out."

"But I don't leave until next week! What about our Sunday marathon TV day?"

"You don't leave until next week, but I leave tomorrow."

"For?"

"I told you, didn't I? I'm doing this Google weekend workshop thing for high school computer science engineering nerds. I'm leaving for San Francisco in the morning."

"Jack, that's amazing! I'm sorry, I must have fallen asleep when you told me, or blanked it out or something. I'm a dick. Sorry."

Jack smiles. "No biggie. I know how stressed you are. Believe me, the Olympics are much more of a big deal than my stupid workshop."

"Please, this is basically the equivalent of the Nerd Olympics for you," I joke. "Seriously, I'm super proud. I know how hard you've worked and how much you love what you do, even if I don't understand it even a little."

There's a moment of awkward silence between us, which is weird. I lean down to rifle through my gym bag, and then we both speak at once.

"I know you can't..."

"How long are you..."

We laugh. We pause again. I motion for him to speak.

"I was gonna say, I know you can't have cupcakes or anything that actually tastes good, so more for me. But I won't taunt you and will wait to eat them when I get home. Instead, I got you this."

He holds out a box wrapped in shiny purple paper. I carefully open it, using my short fingernails to peel the tape rather than ripping it open. I slide the box cover off and inside there's a framed newspaper article from when I won my first state title at the age of eight.

"Wow, that's really sweet, Jack. Where did you find this?"

"I saved it. I remember when my mom showed it to me in the paper I thought you were famous and were gonna have to move to Hollywood. I cried and cried...I cut it out so I could remember you, and I guess I could just never part with it even after I got older and realized that the

Lynnwood Today wasn't exactly *Page Six*."

I skim the article, just a tiny fluff piece describing the state champion-ships held in Everett almost a decade ago. I can feel tears well in my eyes, so I pinch the skin between my thumb and pointer finger to stop it, a handy trick Jack actually taught me years ago.

"Thanks. It means a lot."

"There's more." He lifts the frame from the box and underneath, there's a flash drive. "Put it in."

I slide the drive into my MacBook and open the video file. "Eye of the Tiger," my motivational music, starts to play and a second later, there's a video of me hanging upside down from a set of uneven bars at age four, my first time in a gym.

"Your parents gave me all the video footage," Jack blushes. "But I put it together."

It's a montage of videos from that first gym visit to me standing on the podium at the Open earlier this month. My eleven-year career reduced to four minutes of greatest hits set to the sweet sound of aggressive 80s rock.

I can't stop the tears this time. I wipe them with the back of my sleeve, keeping my face glued to the laptop screen so I don't have to look at Jack.

"I just thought...I mean, I wanted to get you this bracelet I saw at the mall but I'm broke, so I had to make you something. I hope you don't think it's lame."

"It's awesome. For real. No one's ever done anything like this for me before." I give him a hug, and he pulls me close, resting his chin on my head. The hug lasts about a second too long to be a friend hug, which feels awkward and bananas. When he lets go and walks away, he avoids my eyes.

"I need to pack," he says, swinging his leg over the windowsill. "I'll see you when you get back. I'll text you. Good luck."

"Have a good flight," I call as he shimmies down from the awning and drops into the grass. I don't know what else to say. I watch him slip into his window, as always, and then grab an old meet t-shirt. I wrap the framed article carefully and place it in the front pocket of my suitcase, for good luck in Boston next week.

My brain is soup right now. I've never considered Jack as anything but a friend, but then again I've never really looked at *any* boy as something more than a friend, at least until I met Max at the farm back when I thought he was cool.

I've known Jack since we were in diapers. Our parents used to joke that we'd get married someday. When we were five, we were forced to go as dates to our neighbor's wedding. Everyone thought it was adorable, but that's about where our love affair ended. With my obsession with gymnastics and his own obsession with technology, neither of us never really saw the other as anything more than a best friend.

But now I'm wondering if maybe he's had more-than-friend feelings for me that I've been completely oblivious to? Or am I just being a silly girl for assuming he's in love with me just because he did something nice? This gift is more than nice, though, no joke. Meanwhile, I didn't even have the common decency to listen to him about his Google thing when he first told me. Like, hello, could I be more self-involved?

I sigh, long and hard, and then curl up on top of my bed. After humiliating Max in New York and the asshat at school, I assumed I was a natural-born man-repeller, but now I can't help feeling my heart twitch when I picture Jack's shy smile, his lanky arms and legs, his bushy eye-brows. He's the exact opposite of frat boy Max and the assholes at school. He's perfect.

I position my laptop so it's inches from my face, open the video again, and press play. But while my eyes watch a younger me stick dismounts and show off my medals, my mind is only on Jack.

Saturday, May 28, 2016
69 days left

"Last practice before nationals!" Ruby announces when she bursts into the gym early Saturday morning while Emerson and I stretch. "Ooh, I just realized we get to see *Maaaaaaax* in Boston!"

Until this second, I'd completely forgotten that nationals and the Olympic Trials are mixed, unlike the Open, which is just for the gals. In Boston, the guys will compete on Friday and Sunday while we compete on Thursday and Saturday. We're so busy, we won't get to see much of them, but they'll be there and that's more than enough to get some of the boy-starved younger girls excited.

"Why do you care about seeing Max?" Emerson says on her way back to the locker room for her hoodie. "He's disgusting."

"I don't," Ruby shrugs. "But Mal might. She's totally in love with him."

"What?" It's now that I remember Ruby has no idea what happened between me and Max in New York. "Ew, no I'm not."

"I thought you were obsessed with him after you talked to him at the farm."

"Yeah, for five seconds."

"Please, I left you two alone for 20 minutes in New York and when I came back, there were *50 Shades of Grey* levels of sexual tension in that room," Ruby continues to tease.

"Shut up!" I laugh, trying to mask my annoyance. "I pretty much told him to go to hell, actually. The tension was more *American Psycho* than *50 Shades*. In that Max totally wanted to murder me."

"Yeah, right," she says, shaking her head. "I bet you a hundred bucks you'll be chasing him down at nationals. You *loooooooove* him!"

Her habit of saying whatever she wants is normally a frustrating, yet endearing quirk. Not today. Today is the last day my dad is home before moving to Mabton and my life stops being the same it's been for almost 16 years. Today is two days away from our flight to nationals. Today I am exhausted from staying up all night cramming for the final exams I'll have to take after nationals. Today, Ruby is on my last nerve.

"Not as much as you love Sergei," I whisper, so Emerson can't hear.

Oh. Fu...dge. Balls. Fudgeballs. Why, why, why.

Ruby reddens, coughs, and rage-whispers, "what are you talking about?"

"I'm talking about Sergei sneaking out of our hotel room in San Diego," I hiss. "And the obnoxious flirting every chance you get, which you think is adorable but is actually nauseating. He's like 30."

"He's 26, but thanks. And I'm almost 19. Not that there is anything going on," she's quick to add. "But if there was, it's not like it'd be gross."

"It's gross because he's a *coach* and works for our gym now, technically. There are rules about that."

"Fantastic. Where would I be without you constantly reminding me of the rules? Rules that have nothing to do with me because *nothing is going on between us.* We're friends. He gets me. We've been through similar shit. Jesus, Amalia."

"Jesus Amalia?" Sergei *would* happen to walk into the room right at this moment. "Is this an official name change?"

I look at Ruby, who gives me a "don't you dare" glare. "Yes," I say, standing up. "I'm on my way to the court right now."

"Let's get through routines first, okay?"

I toss him a super fake smile which turns into an eye roll as I glare back at Ruby, who is trying to look impassive. If there was nothing going on, wouldn't she – the girl who never misses an opportunity to make herself heard – say something like, "oh my *gawd*, Sergei, you'll never believe what Amalia just said!" The fact that she is silent makes it pretty clear that my accusation is legit.

Emerson bounds back out of the locker room and the two of us use a set of uneven bars to do some pull-ups and leg lifts. I'm huffing a bit more than usual, I guess, because in between sets she asks what's up.

"Nothing," I exhale as I breathe out.

"Sure," is her response. "Ruby looks like she wants to kill you, by the way. Trouble in paradise?"

"It's nothing, really. I just…assumed something. I was wrong, I guess. According to her. It's not a big deal."

Emerson hops off the high bar and claps her hands, leaving a cloud of chalk dust behind her. "Sure."

Natasha calls us over to begin our actual training. We found out our rotation group will start on beam in Boston, so that's where we've been starting in training all week. We do our regular pre-meet warm-ups on each event, just working various skills and slowly putting the pieces together, and then we move on to pressure sets.

Lots of full routines, lots of hard landings, lots of being exhausted. If we fall, we have to start over until we get it right, which really smacks the importance of hitting into our heads.

"Some business before we start," Natasha says, eyes glued to her phone. "We fly out Monday at 9:10 a.m., should be in around 5:30 p.m. So tomorrow, on your day off, you need to keep your muscles happy. Get a massage...that's an order. Do some stretching. When we get to the city, we'll use the hotel gym to get in a mini-workout on the treadmills and bikes just to get our bodies moving after the trip."

"No *gym*-gym?" Ruby asks.

"Just say *gymnastics*," Emerson retorts.

"We don't have access to the training facility until Tuesday morning. Two practices on Tuesday, two on Wednesday – one with the media watching – and then a morning practice on Thursday before the juniors compete. Competition is Thursday and Saturday nights. Friday is a rest and recovery day. Sunday morning we'll have a national team meeting – I assume all three of you will make the national team – and then we fly home in the afternoon."

I stress-exhale and it's ridiculously loud. The others laugh.

"Yes, and let's not forget this is Amalia's first nationals, and it's an important one. Set a good example," she adds, eyeing Emerson and Ruby. Especially Ruby. Ruby responds with a double thumbs up.

"All right! Let's have an awesome last practice so we can have an awesome day off and then an awesome meet. Sound good?"

"Sounds *awesome*," Ruby answers. Sergei stifles a laugh. I grit my teeth and breathe out through my nose. Emerson watches this series of events closely and raises an eyebrow at me, her eyes growing big. I gesture that I'm going to slit her throat if she opens her mouth; she understands.

"Great, let's go!" Natasha smiles, oblivious to the drama unfolding before her.

***

"All packed, I see?" my dad remarks, entering my room bright and early Sunday morning. He inspects my two suitcases, backpack, and duffel bag, all stacked neatly by desk.

"Of course." I'm doing homework and trying to get as much studying as possible out of my system so I can focus on nothing but gym this week. "I'm assuming you are as well?"

He smiles sadly. "I'm the one moving out but I think you have me beat, kiddo. I only have one suitcase."

"Is your apartment all set?"

"Yup. They set me up in a residential suite at some local motel. The glamorous life."

"And you start work tomorrow?"

"I'll be shadowing tomorrow and for the rest of the school year, yes."

I sigh. "I'll miss you so much."

"Hey, it'll be nothing, at least this first week. You wouldn't have seen me this week anyway, you being in Boston like the big-time superstar you are. And I'm taking the red-eye out to you on Friday night," he adds, eyeing the American Open silver medal hanging from my bedpost. "So I won't see you compete on Thursday, but I'll watch on TV and will be there live and in person for the big finale on Saturday."

"I know, you've told me a thousand times," I mumble, not looking up.

"Everything good?"

"*Yes*, everything is fine. I'm just super busy."

"Sorry, I don't mean to annoy you."

I close my book. "I'm sorry. You're not annoying me. I just have a million things to do before I go. School things. Thought you might appreciate my commitment."

He laughs. "You know me so well. How did practice go yesterday?"

"Fine. Nothing went wrong, anyway. I'm doing a new skill on bars instead of that tricky one I was telling you about, the one I changed in San Diego. It's actually looking really good, really clean. And my floor feels better. I think I can hit everything, no problem."

"That's all you can ask for, right?"

"Well, I mean, hitting no problem is one thing but a lot of girls can hit with no problem. I need to hit *and* show that I have something to offer the team. I need to make Vera see how important I am, how badly she needs me in August."

"I have no doubt you can do just that," he says, petting my head. "I'm heading out in about ten minutes, so it's about that time we say goodbye."

I choke back tears and reluctantly climb off my bed, staring down at the floor as he reaches in for a hug.

"I'll miss you like crazy, kiddo. Kill it this week. I know you have it in you. Be the best you can be."

I pull away and nod, trying to avoid his eyes. "Drive safe," I whisper.

"I will. I love you, Amalia."

"I love you more."

He leaves and I sit cross-legged on my bed until I hear the front door shut and then I bolt into the bathroom with the window facing our front yard. He and my mom talk for a few minutes before hugging, and then he climbs into the driver's seat, backs out of the driveway, and is gone. I grab my teddy bear, hug it tight, and finally cry.

"Amalia, anything special you want for lunch today?" I hear my mom bellow from downstairs after I've been wallowing for a full five minutes. She's handling this way better than I am.

"Whatever you want," I yell back, retreating to my room to check my phone. A message from Emerson sent last night reading "tell me everything," I'm assuming about the Ruby drama, sits with no response. But there's nothing from Ruby since our little spat, and she's the only one I want to hear from in my current melodramatic mood.

I curl up and debate what I should say to her. We were perfectly cordial to one another at practice yesterday after "the incident" but "cordial" isn't me and Ruby.

"Sorry," I text, adding the emoji with the tears streaming. I hate emojis but everyone I know practically communicates solely via this wordless language. Gotta keep up. "I was being a [poop emoji]." Perfect.

I wait a minute, pick up the phone, put it back down, read five words in *Crime & Punishment*, look again, and my heart leaps at the three little dots that signal Ruby's typing on her end. Seconds later, a message pops through.

"cant talk now, busy with my russki lover slash coach, gymnastics is way more fun OUTSIDE the gym"

She finishes with the winking face and heart eyes emojis, and then I see her typing again. The phone buzzes a nanosecond later.

"8===D"

A dick. I think I'm forgiven.

I do a few lunges to get out some nervous energy, and then stretch, Natasha's orders. My massage is later this afternoon, at the place near the gym we frequent at some sort of MGMA discount. I suddenly get an idea, and call Ruby, who picks up instantly.

"I'm not kidding, Mal, Sergei is here and we're putting on quite a show for my host family."

"You're an actual pervert."

She laughs, a big belly laugh. "Did you really think he was over?"

"Not even for an instant, perv."

"Cool. You're an idiot for thinking anything's going on. Seriously. I've never had a boyfriend in my life. It's pathetic, really. You think I'd start going after dudes now, with two months before the Games? The only D I chase is my difficulty score."

"Well, you're an idiot for thinking I'm into Max, and honestly, yeah, that's what I thought you were doing. I didn't want you to miss out...again. Over a guy, of all things. I didn't think you were dumb enough to do it, but..." I trail off.

"Yeah, whatever, it's over. I'm sorry I got on your ass about Max. Let's forget about all of this because it's time for *nationals*, baby. We should *party*. That was a joke, in case you thought I'd also throw my career away for a can of beer."

"Very funny. Actually, I was wondering if you want to get massages together today? Team bonding?"

"Yeah, I hadn't scheduled yet, so that's perf. Lemme give them a call. Did you call Emerson?"

"Not yet...but I was going to..."

"I'll call her now. What time is your appointment?"

"Uh, four."

"Great, consider it done. I'll meet you there. You got a ride?"

"My mom said she can bring me."

"Awesome, see ya."

She hangs up before I can say bye. My nerves settle. That's the best thing about having Ruby as a best friend – you can monumentally screw up, but she's so fiercely loyal, she very easily forgives. If I were her and someone accused me of getting it on with a national team coach, I'd be rewriting my enemy list.

I roll onto my stomach to get back to Raskolnikov, whose problems seem so annoyingly stupid to me right now. "Just confess, moron," I yell after five pages of his rambling. "Free your conscience."

It feels freaking great to get things off your chest.

Monday, May 30, 2016
67 days left

"Emerson, room 612. Amalia and Ruby, room 614. Polina and I are in 616, Sergei's in 618." Natasha hands out our electronic keycards, which feature glossy photos of Emerson doing a switch ring at last year's nationals on the front. She's already Instagramming.

"What, no penthouse suite?" Ruby asks, only half kidding.

"I make so many sacrifices in the name of this team," Emerson pouts, sarcastically. I hope. "First I sit in coach on a plane, and now I'm slumming it on the sixth floor? I don't know how you survive. Also, this place doesn't have a suite. Trust me, I looked."

We're at the host hotel, where rooms are set aside for national team members and their coaches. The Open was child's play. Nationals are a huge deal with sponsors everywhere, and we represent them in everything from what we wear to the food we eat right down to where we sleep at night. I'm not on the national team – ahem, yet – but MGMA is a national team gym thanks to Ruby, so we get the national team treatment.

The trip to Boston was long and uneventful, though I did marathon five episodes of *Toddlers and Tiaras* on my iPad. So much for getting ahead on school work. Now I'm super sleepy and would love to go right to bed, but my legs need the treadmill...six hours on a plane and no gym for two days makes them feel atrophied.

"What's the rest of the night like?" Ruby asks. "My bed is calling my name."

"Meet in the gym for a mini-workout at 7, and then how about we do a team dinner at 8? Unless you wanna be lazy and get room service."

"Team dinner sounds good," I pipe up. I have an aversion to room service ever since I ordered it on a cruise when I was 13. My parents were out of the room, I felt like a badass ordering on my own, everything was going smoothly, and then the delivery guy reached across the door to close it and I thought he was leaning in for a hug. Naturally, I hugged him right back. Whenever I feel confident about anything, my brain loves reminding me that I can't function as a human.

"All right, Amalia wants team dinner, and she's the boss," Sergei smiles. "Go freshen up or whatever you need to do."

Ruby pushes into our room, which is nice but basic as far as hotel rooms go. We're in a generic brand hotel, nothing fancy like our digs in San Diego. She claims the bed by the window by flopping onto it and curling up. "Freshen up, my balls," she moans. "I'm napping."

I laugh, fully knowing that five minutes before we leave, she'll run to the bathroom and come out looking like a supermodel. She has this whole Beyoncé thing going on, making it scientifically impossible for her to ever look bad.

Me, I'm the opposite. I have hair that is flat and dumb and yet whenever I fly it gains some static power that makes it stand out in 800 different directions. Despite showering this morning, my face also feels gross and slimy. A pre-workout shower it is.

Before heading to the bathroom, I check my phone and *yes*, finally, a text from Jack. I texted him when we landed, letting him know I was safe and sound, but stupidly forgot to ask how his thing was going because I'm obviously too obsessed with myself to care. Stupid, stupid Mal.

"Cool, have fun in Boston. Your mom just called mine and asked if I want to come over to watch on Thursday...we're gonna have a mini party. Can't wait. Good luck!"

"How was your trip?" I type back. "When did you get home? Can't wait to hear all about it."

There. At least I don't come across as a total jerk. I want to tell him I miss him, that being away for over a week is unbearable, that I want him to be the first person I see when I fly home next week, but it's much easier to think these words than to actually say them.

"Got back last night," he responds. "Workshop was awesome. My brain multiplied itself by 80%. Head physically expanded. Had to check it on the flight home because it was too big for a carry-on."

I laugh, toss my phone on my bed, see Ruby is already snoring, grab my things for the shower, and jump in. The water pressure is amazing. I let it beat down on my back and shoulders, soothing muscles that had stiffened from the long flight. I feel random excited nerves jolt through my body so I try to breathe and just *be*. My biggest goal this week is to not let the experience of being at nationals get to me, but I know it's impossible to keep from freaking out entirely. The shower is the best place to let it happen.

I wake Ruby just before it's time to go. She throws on a tank top and shorts, looks like a million bucks, and we make our way to the gym.

"Feeling good?" she asks.

"Yeah, actually." I tug at the baggy t-shirt I decided to wear. I look the opposite of cute but whatever. "I feel great."

"You're gonna be awesome this week, Mal," Ruby says as we wait for the elevator. "Ever since the Open, you've been this unstoppable force in practice. Really, super impressive."

"Thanks, Rube."

"For real, I know this is a huge week for you and you're always a great competitor so I doubt it'll bother you but I know the press and everyone makes this a big deal which can take away from your focus. So just don't listen to anyone who makes it bigger than it is and you'll be fine."

"Why are you so worried about me losing focus all of the sudden?"

"I'm not, and I don't think you will lose it. But I've been there. You can tell yourself 'it's just like practice' a thousand times but then you get to the arena and you lose it. It's not like the Open or any competition you've done before. No matter what you do or how you approach it, there are always those outside factors that come in and mess with your game. You've done a crap ton of work, so just remember that, and you'll be fine."

"I know I will," I respond. "Thanks. But I promise I'm not letting anything psych me out. Actually, you getting all concerned about my mental well-being is what's really psyching me out, so *staaaaahp*."

"Sorry, Mal. I just know how nervous you get, even if you hide it well. I just wanted to make sure you're prepared for how much of an insane event nationals can be. Especially in an Olympic year. Whatever you're thinking, in reality it's a lot crazier. It's good to know that going in."

The elevator comes and we step on to see Maddy and her coach. Maddy doesn't look up from her phone.

"Earth to Maddy," Ruby sings. Maddy looks up and basically glares at us, goes back to her phone, clicks it off, and finally says hi.

"Where are you guys going?" she asks.

"Gym. Then team dinner. No idea where."

"Is Emerson going?"

"Why do you need to know the whereabouts of Emerson? Are you her keeper or just obsessed?"

Maddy scoffs. "I don't. Actually, she's been kind of a bitch to me ever since she moved gyms. But I saw her mom at the airport. Emerson wasn't expecting her mom to make it to any of her meets this summer." She smiles and I want to slap her face. "That should be an awesome surprise! I can't wait to tell Emerson. She'll be so...thrilled."

"If you even think about telling Emerson her mom's here, I'll..." Crap, I don't have a way to end this and Maddy's lingering grin is just frustrating me even further.

Ruby steps in. "She'll tell everyone about the time at the Venice meet when you had a stomachache but were afraid to tell your coach and then had a very public and very explosive case of diarrhea."

Maddy turns white. I try to stifle a laugh but can't. "Is that true?!"

"Yep," Ruby smiles. "Back when we were both juniors. You know, when I was Maddy's obsession before Emerson came along. They had to pull her from the meet and gave some BS injury reason but nope, she crapped her pants."

"Ladies, behave," Maddy's coach finally steps in as Ruby and I laugh. The doors open and we spot the rest of our group by the gym doors.

"What about Emerson's mom?" Ruby whispers as we step into the lobby.

"I'll tell you later," I hiss back.

"Took you long enough," Natasha shouts. "We're going for tacos at this healthy gourmet Mexican place after the gym, by the way. Hey, Maddy, wanna join us?"

Ruby and I look at each other and burst out laughing again. I don't think she'll be saying anything to Emerson anytime soon.

***

"Okay, right now, biggest goals for this weekend, one big and one small," Natasha says at dinner. "And go."

"Win the all-around," Ruby says. "That's the small goal. Big goal is to make Emerson cry while doing it."

The whole table, including Emerson, laughs. It's been super weird watching their relationship go from mutual hatred to mutual respect. I don't know if you can call them friends, really, but seeing Ruby defend Emerson against Maddy and then joke about her here, it's like she has this new "I can make fun of her all I want but if you do it, I will mess you up" attitude, which is better than finding ways to torment her.

"Very funny," Emerson responds, sipping water. "Because my small goal is to win the all-around and my big goal is to find something to keep me busy while doing it. Seeing as how easy it'll be."

"Mine was better," Ruby smirks.

"Okay, enough from the lunatic brigade," Natasha groans. "Let's hear from Amalia."

"Um, well, the big goal is to finish on the podium." I blush a bit with the attention turned toward me. "And the small goal...I guess I just want to have fun while doing it."

"Here, here!" Sergei cheers, raising his glass. "To having fun while kicking ass." We all raise our glasses in response, clinking them together in the middle of the table.

"Now, and serious answers only...what are your biggest doubts coming into this week? Or obstacles? Might as well tackle 'em now."

As usual, Ruby goes first. "I don't have any doubts. Or obstacles, really. I feel like this is my year. But I do have a chip on my shoulder, and that's the press. So my obstacle is going to be kicking ass in front of them but not gloating too much or shoving it in their faces when the time comes."

"Good one," Sergei raises his glass again.

"My biggest obstacle will be, um..." I can tell Emerson doesn't have a single obstacle in her mind but is trying really hard to come off sincere, which makes me smile. "I guess showing Vera and everyone that I can do even more than what everyone has seen already. That I'm not boring just because I've won it before."

"Hashtag humblebrag," Ruby laughs. Emerson rolls her eyes.

My turn. "Bars and floor are my concrete obstacles," I begin. "I want to hit both and show that I can be trusted in a team final. My biggest *mental* obstacle is not letting the size and importance of this meet psych me out. I keep telling myself it won't, and I thought I was fine, but then people tell me not to freak out and it's making me freak out more. So not letting that get to me, I guess."

"You'll be fine, Mal," Polina offers. "You know every trick in the book for keeping the pressure from getting to you. Just treat it..."

"...like practice?" I finish, smiling.

"Easier than it sounds," Emerson says. "But you have a whole team of people here who will kick your ass into gear if we see you falter."

"Yeah," Ruby adds. "Pep talks galore. And if that doesn't work, I'll just dump water on you until you chill."

"See?" Natasha smiles. "Everyone here has your back. If the press or other athletes or anyone brings up pressure or anything like that, stay iron on the outside. Half the battle is *looking* confident. If you can do that, you'll trick yourself into *being* confident. You know your routines cold, your skills are fine, your landings have been looking great...all you have to do this week is hit eight routines."

"Thanks, guys." Ugh, why am I being so needy and annoying all of the sudden? I've never needed people to talk me down before. At my J.O. meets I was the one talking people down.

"Enough of this," Natasha says, as if she can read my mind. "No more being silly about how you'll compete this week. You're all rock stars and everyone else here knows it. They're crazy afraid of the three of you and don't forget it."

"To being the best and being super cocky about it!" Ruby cheers, glass of water high in the air.

"Not to be a party pooper, but it's almost 10," Polina says, clearing her throat. "We need to be in the arena at 8:30."

"Polina's right," Sergei says, slamming down his water, which I'm pretty sure is actually vodka with the way he's been aggressively cheering and reacting to everything. Good for him. It's a tense week. Someone here should be drinking.

"Ladies, you should head back," he continues. "I'll wait for the check. I have old teammates in town I'm supposed to meet up with in a bit."

"Thanks. I knew this coaching partnership would benefit me." Natasha stands up and brushes taco shell crumbs from her shirt. "God, I'm a pig. Thanks, Sergei. I'll get it next time. Come on, ladies."

We all say our goodbyes to Sergei, who I still don't fully trust in this whole Ruby situation, even though I believe her when she says there's nothing happening. That doesn't mean he's not interested.

The walk back to the hotel is long but a great way to end the day. It's a muggy night but the breeze coming off of the Charles River feels perfect. We make small talk as we digest our food, but don't breathe a word about gymnastics. Sometimes it's just nice to be humans first, gymnasts second.

Because for the next week, nothing but who we are as gymnasts will matter. A normal night talking about normal things like normal people takes the edge off and soothes my brain, which will enter overdrive in less than 12 hours.

But I'm ready, I tell myself. I'm a rock star. My teammates have my back. Everyone else here hates me cuz they ain't me. Bring it on, nationals. Bring. It. On.

Tuesday, May 31, 2016
66 days left

The morning is one big dream. From checking in to pick up our credentials to walking through the ginormous backstage area of the TD Garden, I'm basically just along for the ride, following everyone else and trying to remember how everything looks, feels, smells.

This isn't a college arena. This is where the Boston Bruins play. The Boston Celtics. Taylor Swift did a concert here once. This is a huge deal.

When we walk out onto the floor, I lose my breath at the view. Thousands and thousands of yellow seats as far as the eye can see. Hanging from the ceiling are all of the hockey and basketball banners, a visual reminder that this is where champions play.

It's 8 a.m. Warm-ups start in a half hour with general stretch. We have the arena until 11 and then we'll get time for lunch and a nap before hitting the practice gym at 2.

"Blowing your mind?" Ruby asks.

"Uh, yeah." I'm seriously speechless. I know from my Wikipedia research that this place holds about 19,000 people. I don't know if 19,000 people will actually turn up to watch us but the city has turned itself upside down for gymnasts and fans. Hotels are sold out, banners and posters are everywhere you look, restaurants have discounts for people with gymnastics ticket stubs or credentials, and Causeway Street in front of the arena has been renamed Cartwheel Avenue for the week.

It's absolutely nuts.

But nothing I can't handle. Once I get over the overwhelming sense of enormity in the arena, I start to cool down a bit. The U.S. Gymnastics

Association setup is the same at every single meet. When I turn my focus to the floor instead of up in the stands, I feel like I'm back in San Diego.

We're the first ones here and find prime real estate on the floor podium. There's half hour until general stretch, so until then we'll just get limber. Emerson pulls out her iPod and I follow suit. It's a great way to get in the zone.

Plus, it also makes us look like we're super focused when other gymnasts walk in. There are only 22 of us this time around, so there's definitely more of an intensity than there was at the Open. With the exception of a few of us newbies, it's mostly veterans who have been on the scene since they were juniors. Everyone knows each other from years of national team camps and competitions, and yet no one is talking.

"Any other year and we'd all be in the middle of the floor right now, laughing and joking around," Ruby whispers, yanking one of my earbuds out. "This year it's like...if someone drowned in front of us now, we wouldn't look up."

"Good thing there's no pool in here," I laugh.

"Ice bucket." Ruby grins. "It'll happen. Before the end of the evening practice. I'll bet on it."

One of the other first-year elites, Leah Manning, shyly makes her way over to us. She's 16, tiny, with heaps of curly red hair.

"Hey, I'm in your rotation group...I don't know if I'm supposed to sit with you now or whatever," she blushes.

"Leah, right?" I want to exude confidence so I take the reins with this newbie. "I'm Amalia. We don't have to warm-up in our rotation groups but you're more than welcome to join us! This is Ruby and Emerson."

"I really loved your floor at the Open," Ruby says, though I highly doubt she saw it. Leah only just made it to nationals, earning exactly a tenth above the qualification score. She won't be more than background noise here, which is harsh but true.

"Wow, thanks, your floor is like, my dream floor, seriously."

I nudge Emerson, who removes an earbud to say hi but immediately goes back to her zone.

"Forgive her," Ruby smiles. "She was raised by a pack of wild gorillas. Didn't get human interaction until she was 12, but explains why she's so good at bars."

I laugh. Leah looks like she's mentally questioning whether she's allowed to laugh.

"Where are you from?" I ask, trying to make small talk before general stretch begins.

"Florida. I go to South Florida Gymnastics Academy."

I've never heard of it, but I respond eagerly with "oh, cool!" so it sounds like maybe I have. "Do you know who else is in our group?"

"Ummm, yeah. Kaitlin and Caroline."

Nice. They're also pretty much non-contenders and would be lucky to make it to Olympic Trials. But they're sweet girls and wouldn't bring the drama that some of the others here would bring. Namely Maddy.

"Oh," Leah adds. "You know how we're starting on beam? I saw the start list draw for qualifications at the Olympics and the United States is gonna start on beam! Hopefully an omen."

I smile, partly because I'm thinking "what a nerd" but also because I'm also a nerd and knew that already.

A few more minutes of chit chat and there's an announcement over the loudspeakers.

"General stretch for all senior women's competitors officially begins in two minutes and lasts until 9. If you finish early, you may move to your first event for the timed warm-up but you must wait until 9 a.m. to begin."

"Here we go!" Leah squeals. I feel ya, girl.

I toss my iPod into my bag, hop off the podium, and drop it off on a chair by the beam podium before getting ready to "officially" warm-up. On my own in the corner of the arena, I breathe in deeply. Close my eyes. Exhale.

I shed my yoga pants and jacket and then run back to the floor podium just in time to jog the perimeter with the other 21 girls here. Let's go, Mal. Confidence. Strength. Awesomeness. Steady breathing. I've got this. Just have fun.

***

"Now that we're all fed and rested, let's go over this morning's practice," Natasha says as we hustle back to the TD Garden to use the practice gym, nestled deep in the belly of the arena. The guys have the actual competition floor for the afternoon.

It was a great practice for all of us. We didn't do full routines, just worked on slowly getting a feel for the podium, which was nice. "I don't want you doing too much too soon this week," Natasha had cautioned. "Just get used to the equipment and we'll come back for harder landings in the afternoon."

That's exactly what we did. We used about half of our allotted time for each event, spending the rest of it stretching or working on dance elements, things that wouldn't tire us out too much.

"Ruby, fantastic accuracy," Natasha starts. "That's what I noticed most of all. You're usually so good with the attack but sometimes a few details get lost. Not at all the case today. Keep it up. I think my biggest concern for you was the Ray half to straddle-back half on bars, which looks awesome, but as your coach I can sense the hesitation a bit. It's a super ballsy combination, but now you have to make it look as easy as the rest of your skills look, otherwise it comes off as labored, too much of a challenge. But your dismount was awesome. Good job."

There's a smile from Ruby but I can tell that one criticism was getting to her. Ruby's death-defying combo is basically the coolest skill done on bars in the world, but "cool" means nothing to the judges if you mess it up.

"Emerson...power, power, power," Sergei sighs. "I know it was just practice, I know we were taking it easy, but I just need to see that you have *some* power in you, especially on vault. You can't rely on twisting speed alone. Your block today was really rough, so we'll try to pay attention to that tonight. Bars and beam were lovely, but again, even on beam you're not getting quite the punch you need for your dismount. Even just five percent more strength here and there will do wonders. But your work on floor looked great."

Like Ruby, Emerson's not happy with her critique, but also smiles to show respect for the man giving it to her.

"Amalia, I was really impressed," Natasha continues. "You were hitting every mark, you showed a ton of confidence out there, and you were also an excellent motivator. Really nice touch giving some love to your teammates and the other girls in the rotation when you noticed they needed a bit of encouragement. If I had to be nit-picky, I'd say your swing on bars was looking a little labored, but even then you were hitting handstands. A few landing deductions but nothing like at the Open. The big things are easy for you. Just stay focused and make sure the little things are always in your mind."

I'm beaming so hard I have to bite my cheek to keep my face from looking like the sun is shining out of it. That whole "fake it 'til you make it" confidence trick ended up being my saving grace. But it's too early to get a big head about it — I still have three practices and two days of competition to get through.

We walk into the practice gym, prepare to train, go through the national team warm-up and the general stretch shenanigans, and then move to beam to start the second workout of the day.

"Did you have a good lunch?" Leah asks in between turns. She's like my shadow now I guess. I'm right behind her in the rotation order so we're around each other a lot and it's only a *tad* annoying so far.

"Yep," I respond. "We ate at the hotel and then I had the most amazing nap ever."

"What did you eat?"

Good God, this girl is going to drain me of every last drop of energy by the end of the week. "Grilled chicken and red peppers. It came with fries on the menu, but obviously those were a no-no, so we got salad instead. Heartbreaking," I joke.

"Oh, that sounds amazing, I'll totally get that for dinner."

She's blabbing so much she almost misses her turn. We're supposed to be ready to go when the girl ahead of us jumps off, and she's not concentrating on that at all. I have to nudge her when I see Ruby jump off after working her flight series.

I have to bust out a full routine by the time this session is over, but for now I'm working the more difficult combinations...first, the side aerial to Onodi, and then the sheep jump to front tuck to switch ring.

Combinations on beam are tricky because if you don't connect each skill quickly, you're not awarded the extra tenths in difficulty, which really blows if your routine relies on connection bonuses for your high start value. Mine does.

I'm usually pretty seamless with everything, but I like getting as many reps in as possible because you never know what will trip you up when the time comes. The endless repetition makes the combinations feel more natural, as if they're skills on their own. Like, I want to feel like I'm *supposed* to do an Onodi straight out of my side aerial, as if that's how I was taught from day one and as if the two skills don't even exist as two separate entities.

"Good, Mal!" Polina calls out after I hit each series. "Just make sure your back leg position is more accurate in your Yang Bo."

I do the skill on its own and then try it again in combination.

"Much, much better!"

Natasha, grinning, signals for me to hop off. I go to the side of the beam to work the Yang Bo on its own a few times off the beam, partly to work on the leg position but also so Leah will be less likely to continue her quest of becoming my new BFF.

A few more turns with working single skills and combinations, and then I run through the whole routine, including the hard landing on the arabian double front dismount. After I salute, some of the coaches in my rotation group actually clap.

"My God," Natasha melts when I run over for notes. "That was perfect.

Olympic gold perfection. Combos were on point, dance elements were beautiful, acro was big and clean, dismount had power, the form was good, and you were like, one tiny step from sticking."

She gives me a high five and lets me take the rest of this rotation time to work on dance elements for floor. I can't help smiling the whole time, even when Leah starts asking me how I thought her routine looked while I'm in the middle of a triple pirouette.

"You were fantastic," I say, too happy to be annoyed. A small lie, considering I didn't see it at all, but she looks thrilled with my praise and if those three words help her get through the rest of this grueling week, so be it. I get back to work feeling like I'm conquering the world.

Wednesday, June 1, 2016
65 days left

"Sharp, Amalia! Sharp!"

I slow my swing down to regroup, kip cast into a handstand, and then work the toe full to Gienger again, making sure I hit every position correctly instead of breezing through them as I've been accused of doing on my last attempt. I point my toes extra hard for brownie points.

"Better! And excellent toe point! See, Ruby, she's extending through the whole foot, not just bending her toes. That's what I need from you."

I do the combination one more time to make sure Polina's corrections sink in and then hop off and re-chalk.

Our morning training session is in the practice gym and then in the afternoon we'll be in the arena, flip-flopped from yesterday. The media is in the arena today, so they'll see what we do in the afternoon and we want to be totally polished, though I think we're going to skimp on full difficulty since that worked at the Open. We'll see. It'll be interviews again after we finish training, and that's it until the competition. Yikes.

My next time up on bars will be a full routine. At the chalk bowl I make sure to get my grips exactly the way I like them, and then when I see Ruby dismounting and Leah getting ready to mount, I run over and take my place.

Leah's routine isn't bad. Bars are probably her best event, but it's such an easy routine, it's not like it'll matter much. Her dismount is just a giant full to double tuck, which is something you never see in elite. Too easy.

I mount the low bar the second she walks away and I float through my first transitions, the Maloney to pak and then the Chow. A million percent different from the Open. Not a single concern here, and I'm basically on autopilot at this point.

The toe full to Gienger is as sharp as it can possibly be, I catch my other release – the Markelov – no problem, and stick the double front.

"*Yes*, Amalia!" Natasha screams, pumping her fist into the air. I run over for a hug. "Seriously, best I've seen you do it."

Polina reaches in for a hug of her own. "Good job with corrections. Keep them in mind for tonight and tomorrow, okay? Your execution there was definitely above a 9.0, by the way...no way judges could have deducted more than a point. That would be a 14.9 in competition, which would be huge for you."

I can't stop smiling. First practice of the day, check. I grab a towel and wrap it around my neck while watching Emerson's routine. She's about as perfect as she can be as well. Has been all day.

"Come on, Em, you got this!" I yell as she winds up before the dismount, and she nails her double-twisting double layout – new for her this year, and easily the most difficult bars dismount in the country – with just a small step. Sergei throws her a celebration similar to Natasha's for me, and I high five her once she's off the podium.

We gather our things and walk back to the hotel for lunch and a nap. I could get used to this shortened day. Five hours of training is nothing compared to my usual seven hours in the gym and five hours in school.

Practice notes are boring. We all did fine today, Natasha and Sergei aren't worried, keep the focus, blah blah blah. I just want to eat lunch and nap at this point.

"Oh yeah, interviews," Natasha remembers right before letting us go.

Uuuugggghhhh. "The press will watch you practice and then interview you, same as the Open. Be professional and diplomatic. Try not to look bored," she grins at Ruby. "If you get a question about other athletes and aren't sure how to answer it without being a jerk, try to swing it around to make it about you." Again, a look at Ruby, who smiles sweetly as if to say "who, me?"

We stick to the deli in our hotel for lunch. They have chicken Caesar salads that don't look super appetizing but are preferable to doing a grand search for something yummier.

"Ooh, *grapes*!" Ruby shouts when we get to the deli. "New development in our diet this week! Old apples need not apply."

Everyone grabs a pre-made salad, some form of fruit (grapes for Ruby, obviously), and yogurt with some granola, minus Sergei, who goes straight for a slice of cold pizza.

"I hate you," Ruby pouts.

"Win an Olympic medal and you can have all the pizza you want," he retorts.

Polina finds an empty table off to the side of the lobby and we cram around it. The mere smell of Sergei's gross pizza is taking me way back to a happier, carbier time. If a reporter asks me "pizza or the Olympics?" during interviews they might be a bit surprised to hear my answer has more to do with sauce and cheese than Rio.

"I have to say," Natasha starts between bites of salad, "as a team, you guys are the best out there, hands down. Windy City might have a larger group but you guys could easily finish top three this weekend. I don't think Windy City could get three in the top 12."

Sergei clears his throat. "Irina and Charlotte are pretty solid. So is

Bailey on vault, and Olivia does great work on bars and beam. They're collectively not quite at our level but I could see one or two making the team depending on how things pan out. Let's not forget that half of last year's worlds team came from Windy City, which is almost impossible. They could definitely have a few surprises."

"Charlotte's crap," Ruby argues. "She's just pretty to watch. Doesn't mean she's good."

"I don't know," he muses. "I watched her train a lot back in Chicago. She could surprise us, and she looked fantastic in training. I think out of anyone, she could have a really nice peak this summer...really start hitting her best routines ever and make a name for herself."

I play with my straw paper, pretending I don't hear the discussion at all. I just want one afternoon without speculation or hypotheticals. All I need to know who my competition is and how I measure up, and I've definitely done my research. I have a pretty firm grasp as to where I stand. Some gymnasts live with their heads completely in the clouds, thinking they're a lock for a major team and then they cry themselves to sleep for weeks after not making it, as if finishing 15th at nationals didn't clue them in.

But incessantly chattering day in and day out about things that haven't happened – who might peak, who might falter, who might take the world by surprise – does nothing more than take my relatively calm nerves and completely snap them around until I'm panicking about the "what ifs."

Natasha recognizes my frustration, thankfully, and sees I've finished my lunch. "All right, if you're done eating, how about a 45-minute nap? I'd give you guys a full hour but with interviews right after practice you're gonna need an extra 15 minutes of hairspray so you don't look like monsters on camera."

I thank her under my breath as I gather my trash and she gives me a half-smile and a nod. Ruby, Emerson, and I make our way toward the elevator, yawning a bit. Who knew salad and fruit could put you in a post-Thanksgiving dinner haze?

Ruby shuts the blackout curtains, making it midnight in the middle of our day. I drop onto the bed, pop in my earbuds, set my thunderstorm white noise relaxation app for 45 minutes, and try to get comfortable. My body shuts down right away, though as usual, my mind takes a bit longer to chill.

I can't help thinking of Sergei's comments about Charlotte "surprising" everyone. How can he tell? It's not like he magically knows the future. A year ago not one person could have guessed I'd be in the running for the Olympic team, and yet here we are. Literally anyone could be a surprise this week. Including me.

I yawn and flip onto my stomach, stretching my legs out so they take up the full length of the bed – not easy if you're five-foot-nothing. Eventually the fake thunderstorms lull me to sleep, but my brain rambled on for so long I'm wide awake again minutes later when the alarm goes off. Great.

Whatever. I stretch, yawn, and sit on the edge of the bed, rolling my neck and gathering my thoughts. I'll be the one surprising everyone this week, I decide. I've been kickass so far and before getting up, I repeat my little "just have fun" mantra. I've gotten this far. There's no way I'm slowing down now.

***

"What was the skill you were having problems with this afternoon?" a faceless reporter asks. It's the fourth time I'm hearing this question.

"My bars dismount," I sigh loudly. I can't help it. "Uh, it's called a double front."

"Any reason why, you think? Do you usually struggle there?"

"No, actually. Never." Ha, I sound like Emerson. "Probably a fluke. Sometimes the bars on the podium feel different than the bars we're used to and it was my first time on the podium today. I was hitting just fine yesterday. Better to get it out of the way today."

"You were having problems on bars at the Open, right?" another reporter asks.

"Just in training, and it was with a skill we were just playing around with," I lie, not wanting to let them know it was a skill we took out of my routine and replaced. "I don't compete it."

I don't have a damn clue as to why I couldn't hit my double front today, to be honest. My "fluke" response makes the most sense because everything was on point. Polina was watching closely and my swing was just right as I released the bar. My rotation was probably off or something.

Either way, it wasn't drastic. I sat it once when I first warmed it up, it looked fine when I tried it again on its own, and then took two steps forward when I did it with the full routine. It's not the end of the world. Those were the only two mistakes I've made on the dismount all season. It's not like I'm worried.

Except I am, a tiny bit. I wouldn't be me if I wasn't worried.

I try to keep a smile on my face for some of the lame questions, like "how do you think you did today" and "tell us about your day." I've only taken high school journalism as a requirement to write for the school paper but even I know not to ask "tell me about..." questions. Because *they're not questions*. See, Mr. Drucker? I was totally paying attention. Finally, I recognize Anna Young, the *Seattle Times* reporter who has been doing really nice human interest pieces about me, Ruby, Emerson, Natasha, and everything MGMA. She smiles warmly when she walks over to me after other straggling journalists wander away.

"Amalia. How are you?"

"Good," I exhale. "Great. You?"

"Fine, thank you for asking. I know you're short on time, so what's the one thing today you're taking with you as you go into the competition tomorrow?"

"Uh, between both practices, if I had to pick just one, it's probably to remember details. I think the big things are all solid at this point, so now it's fine-tuning, which I worked on a little bit on bars this morning, though kinda got side-tracked this afternoon with the dismount fall."

"Any insight there?"

"It could be anything," I say, giving her a little more credit than the others. At least this question came from a natural segue and wasn't just bloodhounds sniffing for their next meal. "I had kind of a crappy nap today between practices, and maybe the focus on the little things took away from the big." I shrug. "It'll all come together tomorrow."

"Good girl. How about your teammates? Did you see any of their warm-up? Do you think they're ready?"

"I didn't see much, honestly. I always try to watch some of their bigger skills and cheer them on a bit but we're so busy with our own distractions, it's hard to watch anything they do with like, any sort of critical eye. But they've been looking great with what I have seen, and no complaints from the coaches, so..."

"That's great. Any goal this weekend for how you'd like to place?"

I want to be bold and say top three. I want to be even bolder and say first place, but I've accepted that I'm not topping Ruby or Emerson anytime soon. I play it safe.

"Top five," I smile.

"Really, just top five? Even after silver at the Open?"

"That was without my teammates in the all-around," I remind her. "Had they competed and hit, I would have been fourth, off the podium. I think I can make top three if I really go after every detail, but even then I'd probably still need to rely on some mistakes from others. I don't think anyone can beat Ruby and Emerson for gold and silver, but the race for bronze here is going to be super close."

"Would you be happy with bronze?"

"Absolutely. It's my first nationals. I'd be happy with tenth," I admit. "I know I can reach the podium, but honestly even if I have a bad week and end up in tenth place, I'd just be happy to have made it this far."

"Tenth place still comes with an Olympic Trials spot," she smiles knowingly. "They're taking the top 12 from what I hear. I'd have to guess you wouldn't be quite as happy with 13th?"

"Well, no," I blush. "But I don't think that's gonna happen. I know my scoring potential well enough relative to the other girls that I could fall, like, three or maybe even four times and still not be in 13th."

"Doing the math, I like that. Do you do the math while you compete? Checking your score and seeing how you fit as you go along?"

"Nope. Actually, I made that mistake at the Open. I looked at my score after the third rotation and saw I was in the lead. I thought I'd totally won it. Got my hopes up and then Maddy had an amazing floor, like...her best ever. So it ended up being kind of a bummer. I don't usually do that."

"So you were unhappy with silver at the Open?"

"No." Good Lord these reporters know how to twist words. "I was just saying that it's not the best feeling to think you're in first place and then at the last second, get the silver medal. I was very happy with silver at my first senior elite meet ever."

So suck it, I want to add.

"I think most would be disappointed in coming within a tenth of gold and not getting it."

"Obviously gold was my goal but it didn't happen and I can't change the past. I also didn't have my best meet, and I knew that. It's not like I was perfect and still missed out. Getting that close to gold with the mistakes I made is actually awesome."

"Are you nervous for tomorrow?"

"No? Not really. I'm fully prepared."

"You seem a little tense."

This woman has quickly gone from my favorite journalist to someone I want to punch in the neck.

"I'm not tense," I smile. "Just tired. It's a long week and I've had four big training sessions in the past, like, 36 hours. But we're getting massages tonight and then have tomorrow off right up to the meet starts, so it gives us 24 hours to unwind and get into gear."

"Okay. Back to the competition, then. Who would you say you're most afraid of this week besides your own teammates? There are definitely a few who can beat you in that race for bronze."

"Absolutely no one," I smile again, bigger and brighter than before. Kill 'em with kindness. I'm over giving polite and honest answers.

"All right." She taps the stop button on her recorder app, types in my last name and the date, and then clicks her phone off. "I can tell you're mentally done for today."

She begins packing up, having already spoken to Ruby and Emerson, who are still surrounded by a gaggle of journalists.

"Thanks again," she adds before leaving. "And sorry if I came off as pushy. But a good story doesn't come from sunshine and bubbles. I like getting at the truth. The grit. That's what my readers want to hear and it's my job to give it to them."

"With all due respect," I say, hopping off of my chair, "your job is to report on what we're doing, which is trying to make the Olympic team. You want the truth for your *story*, but your *story* is my *life*. Maybe I'm not comfortable giving you the 'grit' because drudging up every little doubt and insecurity could affect how I compete and thus my chances at making the team. And no matter how much you push, I don't have to give it to you."

I pick up my bag and storm out of the mixed zone. Outside I seem pissed off but inside I'm fighting to keep a smile from forming. That felt amazing.

***

"I still can't believe it. Move over Ruby and Emerson," Natasha smirks after I finally tell everyone the interview story. "MGMA has a new diva."
"Oh, *man*, I wish I'd seen it," Ruby laughs, wiping tears from her eyes.

"It's my dream to make a reporter cry and you came *so close*."

I grin. "I wouldn't say I made her *cry*. But it was worth it to see the look on her face. She's definitely traumatized."

"There goes your America's sweetheart image," Emerson chimes in. "Good job."

"Nah, it's not like they'll publish anything about her being a bitch," Ruby reasons. "Then it gives Amalia license to bring up what a dick the reporter was being. They'll probably say something like 'the *strong-willed* Amalia Blanchard' or some nonsense."

"Yeah, it could've been worse," Natasha agrees. "This is nothing. Just apologize during the post-meet interviews tomorrow night. It'll blow over."

Ruby gives me a high five and I definitely feel a little proud still, even though I feel slightly bad about freaking out.

"All right, I hate to break up this little party but it's after 10," Natasha says, stretching and climbing off of Ruby's bed. "I want lights out by 11, and up by 7. Gotta keep the routine. We'll meet for breakfast at 8, lunch will be at 1, and then you need to start getting in hair, makeup, and practice leos at 4. We want to be at the gym by 5:30. The rest of the time is yours, but your 'freedom' is limited. Stay in the hotel. Rest. Think about the meet."

She, Polina, and Emerson head back to their rooms, leaving me and Ruby to get ready for bed.

"I know you probably don't wanna hear it anymore, but how's it going? Feeling good about tomorrow?"

"Yep, and for what it's worth, it sounds better coming from you than from some jerk journalist. At least you actually care."

"Yeah, journalists usually hate covering gymnastics because it's all teenage girls and we're boring, apparently," she shrugs. "You know, the standard 'I just wanna go out there and hit four-for-four' nonsense that everyone says. So they try to force more out of us by being rude."

"I never give lame answers. Like, I was giving her some actual insightful crap."

"Whatever, she's a bitch. Just forget about it. She'll be up your ass again tomorrow night after you compete."

I yawn and get out of bed, change into pajamas, brush my teeth, and crawl under the covers.

"I'm doing great, by the way," I offer once settled. "Like, I've been all over the place between anxious and confident this week, but after being here and getting in a routine, I feel great."

"Good," Ruby responds, scrolling through her iPad. I think she's reading. After a minute, she looks up. "The article's online, by the way."

Oh, crap. I get up, hating to leave the snuggly down comforter I've nested myself in, and jump over to her bed.

Seattle locals set for Olympic-sized test

by Anna Young, Seattle Times

This weekend marks the first major test for the top elite gymnasts in the United States on their way to securing spots on the 2016 Olympic team.

After surviving a massive cut at the American Open in San

Diego, Calif., this May, 22 gymnasts remain in contention for the chance to compete in Rio. Following Saturday night's results, this number will be whittled down to 12 who will compete at Olympic Trials, from which the selection committee will select the five who best represent the U.S. team's needs.

Three of these prospects traveled to Boston this weekend from the greater Seattle area, including Lynnwood native Amalia Blanchard, a first-year elite who captured the silver medal at the Open, Ruby Spencer, who relocated to Seattle from Iowa when she was 13 to train at the esteemed Malkina Gold Medal Academy but missed out on the 2012 Olympic squad due to injury, and Emerson Bedford, the two-time national and world champion who recently left her gym in Chicago due to contract disputes.

"The move was the best thing for my career," Bedford, 18, told the press after a training session on Wednesday night. "My coach [Sergei Vanyushkin, a 2008 Olympic gold medalist for the U.S. men's team] thought it would help if I kept my distance from the drama in Chicago, and it has. The facilities at MGMA are incredible and my teammates push me to be the best."

Though she and Vanyushkin maintain their own training plan, Vanyushkin and gym owner Natasha Malkina, the record-holding seven-time Olympic gold medalist and daughter of U.S. national team director Vera Malkina (who won some Olympic gold of her own for the Soviet Union in the 1960s), work together to ensure the best possible outcome for their elites.

"It's been great having Natasha in the gym. Two heads are definitely better than one, so when I'm struggling with a skill and get frustrated with Sergei, sometimes Natasha's perspective can be a better fit," Bedford explains.

Spencer, whose 20th birthday next month makes her one of the oldest gymnasts competing, says she's enjoyed the break in routine with a new teammate joining the mix.

"Everything's gone on as usual, nothing has been a distraction, but there's definitely more of a competitive spirit," she notes. "Having Emerson around has kicked me into high gear. I see her training, I see her routines, and it makes me want to work harder so I can stay ahead."

Both are ready and eager to compete this weekend, and if all goes according to plan, they're the favorites for the gold and silver medals in the all-around.

"It'll all depend on who has the better week," Spencer shrugs when asked who she thinks will win. "We're on equal ground. One day it could be me, another day it could be her."

The third gymnast in the mix, 15-year-old Blanchard, is a spirited late-bloomer. She's not as naturally gifted as her older teammates, and missed out on nationals a year ago, placing just 26th at the qualifier. But she's a hard worker with an especially strong beam routine, and has a shot at making the podium this weekend.

"My goal is top five," she said shyly, slightly underestimating her ability. "I think I can make the top three if I go after every detail."

Like everyone else, she doesn't believe any other U.S. gymnast has what it takes to defeat Spencer or Bedford, but thinks third place is anyone's game.

"The race for bronze is going to be super close, though it's my first senior elite nationals. I'd be happy with anything. As long as I make it to Olympic Trials."

All three of Seattle's hopefuls will have no problem qualifying to trials, which begin in Atlanta next month. The site holds a special significance, as it's where the U.S. women won their first Olympic team gold medal 20 years ago.

"Competing in the same arena as legends like Dominique Dawes and Shannon Miller? It's like a fantasy," Bedford gushed. "I've always admired and respected the 1996 team. They've inspired greatness for generations, and it's an honor knowing part of my own Olympic journey will include a nod to their history-making achievement."

"Well, she didn't quote me exactly, but it's a billion times better than I could have imagined," I say after a pause.

"15-year-old Blanchard, a bitch with a capital B, told the press that no one has a chance against her," Ruby mocks. "'Everyone else should quit now,' the star said, downing shots. 'Imma whip their asses.'"

I burst out laughing. "That's almost word-for-word what I said, actually. But I added 'so suck it, nerds' at the end."

"Oh, of course, my bad. I love Emerson kissing the 1996 team's asses. You know in her head she was like, what does this have to do with me, I'm better than anyone who has ever competed, shut your mouth and never speak of such peasants again."

"Accurate," I giggle. Then yawn. I'm exhausted.

"Okay, bed, sleepyhead," Ruby yawns back. "Sweet dreams of kicking everyone's ass tomorrow."

"Thanks, you too."

I burrow back under the covers, thinking of one line in the article that especially stood out to me – that I "underestimated" my ability. It's true, I was being modest, but the fact that this reporter with whom I have a love-hate relationship thinks I was selling myself short is nice to hear. It means she thinks I have a shot. I fall asleep with a smile on my face.

Thursday, June 2, 2016
64 days left

This whole day has been spent trying to stay calm and focused for the meet tonight. No one's talking about pressure, or who we think will qualify to nationals, or any of that nonsense. It's all light and airy and fun.

Between breakfast and lunch, Emerson joins us in our room for movies. We watch *Stepbrothers* and *Superbad*, both of which I've never been allowed to see before but which I found hilarious.

We don't really talk, aside from the occasional reaction to what's on TV. After lunch we nap, I take a hot bath with my favorite Lush bath bomb while reading a Sarah Dessen novel, we paint our nails, and I play games on my phone, which I have on airplane mode so I'm not tempted to text anyone or google myself.

The meet is in the back of my head the whole time, of course. I'll randomly think about it, but just as quickly as it pops into my mind, I shove it back out. I'm trying to make myself believe I'm nonchalant, and it's actually working. The power of suggestion. Or distraction.

That's really what I'm doing. Everything today is a distraction. The more I distract my mind during the day, the better I'll be able to focus tonight. It's preferable to sitting around worrying all day. I don't need to go over my routines in my head. I know them. I won't forget them. It's impossible. If I make it a big deal, by the time I get to the arena my brain will explode.

No, better to go in with a clear mind. Nothing can be done in my head, anyway. So the distractions are welcome.

Around four, Ruby and I commence our meet prep. Gymnastics-ready hair is a sport on its own, especially when Vera requires us to look polished and presentable, preferably with ballerina buns. This requires a gallon of hairspray, roughly 800 bobby pins, and endless patience. The last thing you want to think about in the middle of a meet is your hair spilling down around your face as you tumble. More than being annoying as balls, the strands whipping into your eyes as you spin or flip or swing hurt like hell.

Luckily I have it down to a science, and it doesn't take more than 15 minutes to achieve perfection, so I have time to help Ruby, who always gets frustrated with her own attempt. We put on makeup, nothing fancy, but enough to make sure we don't look washed out on television. Then we tug on our practice gear, sleeveless cerulean Adidas leos with the white stripes down our sides. Yoga pants and team jackets are next, then sneakers, and we're off.

After a last-minute bag check – tape, pre-wrap, grips, lip gloss, iPods, earbuds, water, granola bars, energy chews, bananas, competition leos, the essentials – we head downstairs.

"I hope you had a perfect day," Natasha greets us. "Feeling good?"

"Great, actually," I respond.

"Amazing," Ruby grins. "I could get used to this. Relaxing all day and then gym for a few hours at night."

Emerson joins us a few moments later. Her hair is a bit snazzier than ours, with a braid wrapping back into her blonde bun, but otherwise we – even Natasha and Polina, minus the leos underneath – look identical in our uniforms.

Finally, Sergei – in a dude version of our warm-ups – emerges from the elevator bank and we're off. The walk to the TD Garden is as light as the rest of the day. We chat about how pretty Boston is in the spring, how we can't wait to try clam chowdah, and how hilarious these accents are.

When we get to the arena, we flash our credentials at the athlete entrance, walk the long hallway to the elevator, and Natasha surprises us by pushing the button for the top floor. Emerson raises an eyebrow. "Just trust me," Natasha smiles.

She leads us to the last row of seats in the steep upper balcony. It's almost completely empty, aside from a handful of USGA staff and a few photographers bustling around on the floor, claiming their spots. It looks so pristine and holy like this, before the screaming kids and the smell of nachos and hot dogs sully it.

The TD Garden is like a church in its silent stillness and in our reverie. We take it all in. I imagine the seats full, the crowd cheering as I hit my landings, standing atop the podium with a medal around my neck. A chill runs down my spine and I can't keep a smile from spreading across my face.

Without a word, Natasha leads us back onto the elevator. The doors close and we begin our descent back down into reality.

"I know you all know how important this meet is," she says once we've found our spots on the floor. "I'm not going to remind you. And I didn't bring you up there to make a silly metaphor about this big arena representing your big dreams or whatever."

Ruby laughs. Emerson's eyes are closed, still taking it all in. I curl my knees up to my chest and hug them tight.

"I brought you up there to center you. To give you some perspective. You've all done big things in this sport, but this is different. It feels different. I've been there. It doesn't matter if you've won national or world titles. No one outside the gymnastics world cares about either. But the Olympics, they're life-changing. You all have this in mind whether you like it or not. It can make you lose perspective. You can lose focus. It's enough to make even the calmest competitors fall apart. But think about what you felt from way up top. Remember that. Whatever went through your mind up there in the calm before the storm, that's where you need to be when you compete this weekend."

We're quiet for a minute, breathing in her words like they're gospel. But eventually, as always, Ruby has something to say.

"I just hope no one was thinking about their debilitating fear of heights."

***

Warm-ups go smoothly for all of us. I hit all of my landings, and just as I thought, yesterday's issues with the double front bars dismount were nothing more than a fluke. Even warming up the full routine, I have no problems. Everything's as it should be.

There's less than a half hour between the end of training and the start of the meet. Ruby, Emerson, and I lug our bags back to the bathrooms and change into our competition leos, also a shade of intense blue but prettier, with matching mesh shoulders and sleeves, a silver and white pattern swirling around our bodies, and a sprinkle of gemstones meant to look like the stars.

I grab an energy chew right before we head to the tunnel to line up. My group will be called out third, so we hang near the back, leaving room in front of us for the girls who will start on vault and bars.

"I'm gonna pee my paaaaaants!" Leah is squealing in front of me. Ruby, earbuds in, doesn't turn around so Leah swings back to face me. "Are you freaking out yet?! Did you see the crowd?"

I try to play it cool, even if my feelings are closer to matching hers than

I'd like to admit. "It's not so different from the Open," I lie. It's like, the opposite of the Open.

"Well, I'm freaking out. I'm officially losing my mind."

"Can you please freak out in your head like a normal person?" Emerson hisses behind me. "Or I'm going to freak out. In a different way."

Leah turns ashen. "Sorry," she whispers, like a kid getting a warning from the teacher. She looks at me, but I stare straight ahead. I feel bad for the little weirdo but I have my own internal freak-out to keep under control.

Confidence, I think. Have fun. I close my eyes, picturing the view from the top of the arena and it really does work to center me. I meditate on this for a moment, recalling how I imagined the meet from the top, me finishing on the podium.

Of course, no medals will be determined tonight. It's just the first of two nights of competition. We'll get scores tonight, and then a second set of scores after Saturday's meet. The final ranking is determined by the two scores added together, so consistency is the name of the game. It's not enough to have one really superb night and then show up looking rough for night two. A gymnast with a 60 one day but a 57 the next night will come out with a decent two-day score of 117, but which single day score do you trust? Was the low 57 a fluke after a bad day? Or was the high 60 a one-time thing?

Vera's more likely to consider a girl with back-to-back 58.5s than a single 60, Natasha has explained over and over again, stressing the importance of making our routines look close to identical on both nights. "That's who she'll want at the Olympics," she hammered into us. "Someone she can trust to hit the same exact routine every single time."

I fidget a bit in line, shuffling back and forth from foot to foot. My iPod's in my bag and I don't feel like taking it out now, just minutes before we walk out, but I wish I had the music to distract me from the announcer's lame jokes.

Finally, I see the lights dim and then fade to black. Neon lights and billowing smoke turn the arena into a rave, and the walk-out music starts. I jump up and down to get pumped for the crowd, something that actually helps with how I compete, and then before I know it, my group is marching up to the floor podium.

"Starting on beam is Ruby Spencer from Malkina Gold Medal Academy!"

The crowd roars. Everyone's dying for her big all-around comeback after coming up short last year.

"Leah Manning from South Florida Gymnastics Academy! Amalia Blanchard from Malkina Gold Medal Academy!"

I get cheers. They're more than just the polite applause Leah got, but nowhere near Ruby's, of course. I step forward, wave, turn around, wave, and step back into line.

"Emerson Bedford from Vanyushkin Gymnastics!"

The crowd straight up goes out of their minds for Emerson. Definitely the biggest welcome thus far. I mean, once you win two world titles in a row, that's kind of what you can expect.

"Kaitlin Abrams from Sawyer Burke Athletics! And Caroline Lockwood from the Gymnastics Academy of Houston!"

More appreciative applause for Caroline, but Kaitlin's reaction is thunderous. She's a local kid and has been hyped pretty heavily leading up to nationals even though she's not really Olympic caliber. Still, any recognition is good recognition. With the crowd that intense for her every move, she's bound to have one of her best meets ever.

The last group to come out is the Windy City club. With five athletes at nationals, they take up the whole lineup and look like a small army with everyone in matching warm-ups.

A local high school a cappella group does the national anthem, and we stand with our right hands on our hearts, the left behind us, fists clenched at the smalls of our backs. The second it ends, we get the signal to go to our first events for the touch warm-up and my heart flutters.

"This is it," Emerson whispers behind me as we march over. Even she sounds like a healthy mix of excited and jittery, instead of her usual unfazed blasé cool kid mode.

I reach behind me and squeeze her hand. "Kick ass," I whisper back.

***

"Eye of the Tiger" blares in my ears the second I finish my touch warm-up. I'm in the corner of the arena, facing the wall and jogging in place to the world's best fight song, trying to keep my energy where it needs to be. I can't help letting this music remind me of the montage Jack made, which helps in my motivation. Look what I already fought for and accomplished! Now it's time to do more.

Ruby's up on beam now. I can't watch, but I'll know how she does based on the crowd's collective reaction. So far it's all cheers and applause and then I know she's hit her dismount when they go wild.

When Leah mounts, I make my way back to my bag, toss my iPod in, and close my eyes. Now is the time for visualizing my routine, going over every skill and body position and hand motion so I can see the routine, be the routine before actually doing it. Sounds silly, but it helps me more than anything.

I gather from the crowd's groans that Leah has fallen, and then I wait for the applause that tells me she's finished. I climb the podium and stand perfectly still, not wanting to give away a hint of nervous energy while I wait for her score to come up. Even though I'm full of it. I just take deep breaths instead, going back to a couple hours earlier, standing at the top of the Garden with the whole world at my feet.

Finally. Her score flashes above, the judges take a moment to gather themselves, and I finally get the green light. I smile, I salute, I pause. The two seconds I use before mounting beam are crucial to my success. Inhale, exhale, beat, and then I give myself a bounce on the springboard before pushing up into my press mount.

It's an intricate mount, though not worth much at all, so some call it a waste of time. Most girls just hop onto the beam, taking a split second before moving onto their more difficult skills, but I love it. It's slow and elegant, giving me brownie points with the judges, who love seeing a bit of artistry. It also gives me time to ease into the routine, getting a feel for the beam before doing anything more difficult.

I press up into a handstand, finishing with my legs in a split, and then rotate my torso 90 degrees so I'm facing the length of the beam. Staying in the split, I touch my front foot to the beam and give my back leg a bit of a push so that my split becomes an over-split, my legs now at about 210 degrees instead of 180. I then do a forward roll onto my back, cross my right leg over the left, bring the right back into a split again – at this point I'm just showing off my hard-earned flexibility – and then bring the right leg forward again so I'm straddling the beam. The crowd gasps and applauds.

Now for the hard part.

The required flight series is something I get out of the way at the very beginning. I do a back handspring, another back handspring, and then a layout landed on two feet, one of the more difficult series, so I'm rewarded well with bonus points. I cross my right hand over the left and exhale sharply before springing backwards, and it's smooth sailing. My legs are straight, I'm perfectly aligned with the beam, I'm quick, and I hit the final skill with a clean body position and a satisfying smack of my feet against the equipment, not moving a centimeter. I smile.

My switch ring leap is about as good as it's ever going to be; I can practically feel my back foot grazing my forehead, the leg is so perfectly extended. After that comes the easy sissone to split jump, which one day I'll hope to connect to the switch ring just for fun, but for now they're fine on their own.

A little bit of arm choreography helps me get back to an end of the beam, and now it's time for the side aerial to Onodi, the latter skill also known as a back handspring with a half twist. It's super clean and the connection is so fluid, there's no way the judges can argue their way out of crediting it. For the required turn, I compete a double spin with my leg held out in front of me horizontally, one of the hardest turns one can do on beam, and I make it look as effortless as a basic pirouette.

More little choreo bits, and then another killer connection. I first do a sheep jump, where my body bends backwards, making the letter C in the air. The skill is made especially difficult by the fact that I can't see the beam for my landing considering my head is arched all the way back, but it's never a problem for me. As soon as I land, I rebound right up into what's called a Yang Bo, basically a fancy split jump but with my back once again arched back and my head dropping behind me so I can't spot the beam and have to land blindly. Even so, I hit it expertly.

Lots of pieces of my routine get oohs and applause from the crowd, but it's the big standing arabian right into a Korbut, where I flip backwards but grab the beam with my hands and then straddle it, that makes them actually gasp. I bounce right back up on two feet, hands still on the beam, and then raise one leg into a split just to show off my flexibility once again.

There's one final series of choreo as I make my way to the end of the beam again, and then it's the pièce de resistance. The dismount. The most difficult beam dismount in the world.

Again, my right hand goes over the left, and I put my right foot forward to prepare for the roundoff. I hear the ding of the timer signaling that I only have ten seconds left, but that doesn't faze me. I visualize for a moment, exhale sharply, and then hit the round-off back handspring into the arabian double front.

I hit the mat hard and try to steady myself without moving. I don't hop or take a large step, thankfully, but I do have a little small step over to the side to steady myself. A tenth off, max. No big deal.

The crowd erupts with my landing, and I can tell I've impressed a lot of people. It's one of my better efforts, and if I hit all of the connections to the judges' liking, I should get somewhere between a 7.0 and a 7.3 start value. It's an impossibly difficult routine, and no one in the country comes close to matching it.

A smile overtakes my face, I salute to the judges, and hop off of the podium into Natasha's outstretched arms. She has tears in her eyes.

It takes everything in me to not look at my score, but I don't want to jinx myself. Like tapping my fingers for the first 180 seconds on an airplane, I now firmly believe that I hold the power to my success by following my own made-up rules, especially after what happened at the Open. Maybe it's silly, but if someone's ahead of me or if I get a low score, I'd rather be blissfully unaware so I can finish the competition in peace rather than with a chip on my shoulder or with an over-inflated ego. Neither is a good thing in this sport.

Ruby gives me a hug and a double high-five when I return to the chairs. "Unbelievable, Mal," she gushes. "I want to be you when I grow up. You are a national beam savior."

I thank her, still a little out of breath. Ruby hands me the cup of Gatorade she poured for me mid-routine, and I gulp it down, grateful for the electrolytes. When I see the judges hand the score runner the sheet of paper with my outcome, I close my eyes and put my head down. And I keep it down for the rest of the rotation, not wanting a single distraction to break my flow.

I know I got off to a tremendous start, and if I can just hit the rest of my routines with no problems, I can finish this meet the way I began it – on fire.

***

Sometimes I feel like I'm in another world. This is never more pronounced than when I'm at a competition surrounded by thousands of people and still manage to retreat into the zone. Earbuds in, eyes closed, and I could be anywhere – school, my bed, Antarctica – all I have to do is picture it and reality disappears.

I hit floor with no major stumbles, and going up first on vault was great for me. I had no wait time at all between warm-ups and actually competing, which meant no opportunity to let the anxiety build. Everything happened so fast, and then when I was done, I had a million hours to get my grips on for bars. Bonus.

Now I'm in the opposite predicament. I'm the last to go up for bars, which means a huge stretch of time between warm-ups and competing, and plenty of time to get fidgety. Which is why I shut out the world completely.

With the volume on my iPod at its maximum level, I can't hear a thing beyond my music. With my eyes closed, I don't see anything in front of me.

When I was eight and visiting family in Alabama, we went to a speedway to watch some kind of race, a demolition derby, which is where a bunch of drivers bring their cars onto the track with the sole purpose of smashing them.

Being the obnoxiously anxious person I am, I somehow got it in my head that people were going to die doing this. In front of me. I screamed over the noise that I wanted to go home, but everyone else was having so much fun. My dad turned to me and said, "pretend you're not here."

It was the best advice I ever received. He gave me his iPod and his giant noise-cancelling headphones and then told me to close my eyes. "Pretend you're on the beach," he said, putting on my favorite Beatles album. "Everything will be fine."

I thought it was magic. I had to open my eyes a few seconds after closing them because I figured my dad really found a way to transport people through thin air, like in *Harry Potter* or something. I was almost shocked to see the cars crashing in front of me, like I really expected to find myself actually sitting on a towel surrounded by water and sand.

Half a lifetime later I still believe in the magic. Okay, maybe not *literally*, but it still totally works.

Five girls compete before me. Natasha promised she'd tap my shoulder when I'm on deck so I can do a bit of warming up before it's my turn. Everything goes pretty quickly, even with judging, so I know I'll only have about 15 minutes or so of peace.

I'm not even thinking when I'm in this zone. I don't know how to meditate but I'm assuming this is the stage of enlightenment any Buddhist would die to reach.

Eventually I feel Natasha's hand gently rest on my back. I open my eyes and push back the headphones.

"Ready?" she asks.

I nod, put my iPod away, tug off my jacket, and stretch my shoulders before following her to the corner of the arena for a brief pep talk.

"You got this, Mal," she starts, her hands on my shoulders while she looks directly into my eyes. "Everything to this point has been some of your best work. All you have to do now is finish it. That's it. Just one clean routine, nothing fancy, and you're home free."

"Okay," I whisper. "Got it."

"Just remember to keep your legs tight and toes pointed. The little things are what will set you apart. Hit your handstands. That's all."

I nod again, loosen and then tighten my grips, and look over at the bars, where Leah is finishing up.

"Go get 'em," Natasha says, lifting her hands from my shoulders for high fives. I grin, slap them, and jog over to the podium. As soon as Leah salutes, I run up and begin chalking up while I wait for her score. I only have a minute or so, maybe two if there's something questionable and the judges need to deliberate, but I have my process down to a science and am ready to go no matter what.

I get into position to mount and wait for the green light. When it flashes, I smile, salute, and then stare down the low bar as if I'm about to enter a boxing ring, just me against the apparatus.

A single deep breath, a clap of my hands, and then we're off.

***

I hear the crowd roar before my feet even plant firmly on the mat and it's hard not to smile.

I wait a half second in my position to gauge whether I'll need to take a step for balance, but it's totally unnecessary. I stuck the double front.

After holding the position for a moment, really feeling what it's like to stick your dismount on your final event at national championships, a grin spreads from ear to ear before I turn to my right to salute the judges. I turn back toward the crowd, give them a wave, and then jump from the podium into Natasha's arms.

"You did it!" she screams. "You totally freaking did it."

Emerson, Ruby, Polina, and Sergei are all waiting to congratulate me as I reach our little sitting area. Two cameras are in my face as I give them all hugs. They want my reaction to my score, but I won't give it to them. I won't look until everyone in the arena is done.

The excitement dies down and I get back to routine, neatly wrapping my grips and storing them in my grip bag, putting my warm-ups back on, and then leaning back in one of the padded folding chairs to enjoy a much-deserved granola bar and Gatorade.

We still have a few routines left on beam and floor before all scores will be in. Natasha comes over and gives me a few little corrections on bars, but I can barely pay attention. I try to remember, but it's stuff she always tells me anyway...don't rush, hold the handstand before moving to the next skill, extend your toe point through your whole foot...someday I'll make all of this happen at once.

Ruby sits by me after the camera crew disappears, moving on to torment others who actually are looking at the scoreboard.

"How do you feel?" she asks. "I watched pretty much all of your routines and you were awesome, no joke."

"I feel amazing." It's not an exaggeration in the slightest. "I didn't think it was possible for a meet to go as smoothly as today went."

"I've seen your scores. I think you'll be *very* happy with things."

I playfully punch her arm. "Don't tell me anything else! Not everyone's done yet."

"The people who matter are done," she shrugs. "No one left to go can change the outcome. I've done the math."

"Still, I want to wait. I'm superstitious."

"Nerd," she laughs.

I finally allow myself to check my phone, anxious to see what my parents have to say, and see about a million texts from everyone I've ever spoken to in my life. My parents are in there, but so is a former teacher, every aunt and uncle, various kids at school I've never spoken to...

My mom's texts read like a live blog of everything I did tonight. All of my routines were on TV, which is kind of surprising...I assumed beam would be shown but totally didn't expect the rest to be of interest.

There are a few texts from unknown numbers, and then the one I'm dying to see. Jack.

Like my mom, he's sending me his live reactions, though his are funnier and include random comments on my actions (like "you just side-eyed a girl so hard for tripping over a mat" and "your resting bitchface should be a meme"), screenshots of my face looking contorted as I grit my teeth during a skill, and snaps of me sitting on the sidelines totally zoned out, edited with thought bubbles that have me contemplating philosophical conundrums and mysteries of the universe.

"You're brilliant," is his last text. I grin from ear to ear.

"Someone sexting you?" Ruby asks, eyebrow raised. I toss my phone in my bag, shake my head, and smile.

"Just reading my mom's play-by-play," I lie. "She should take over as one of the NBC commentators."

Ruby laughs and thankfully doesn't ask to read it. "Your mom's nuts." We sit in silence for a minute, and then the rotation fanfare plays, meaning everyone has finished competing. Day one is done.

We reach for our bags and march toward the tunnel where we'll be interviewed before heading back to the hotel. I see the final floor score flash on the LED screen alongside the edge of the arena and prepare myself to look up at the rankings.

Top 8 After 4 Rotations

1. Ruby Spencer, Malkina Gold Medal Academy, 61.300
2. Emerson Bedford, Vanyushkin Gymnastics, 60.900
3. Amalia Blanchard, Malkina Gold Medal Academy, 60.400
4. Maddy Zhang, Texas Tornadoes, 59.600
5. Zara Morgan, Reynolds Gymnastics and Cheer, 59.300
6. Charlotte Kessler, Windy City Gymnastics Club, 58.900
7. Bailey Dawson, Windy City Gymnastics Club, 58.600
8. Amaya Logan, Waimea Sports Center, 58.300

My hand flies to my mouth and I look at Ruby.

"Told ya so," she smiles.

Third place. Only my own teammates, the best gymnasts in the country, are ahead of me. Oh, and by the way, I got a 15.8 on beam with a 7.1 start value. Holy. Crap.

***

"Thanks so much," I say for the billionth time tonight, this time to a junior gymnast and her family before leaving the elevator at the hotel.

We get off and head down the long hallway to our rooms, takeout salads in hand. I'm basically floating. Ever since I saw my score, life has been magical.

At interviews, I heard more compliments than questions. We were only in the mixed zone for about five minutes, and all the journalists asked was how we thought our performances went, if we were happy, and what we wanted to work on before Saturday.

We went out the main arena doors instead of through the athlete entrance because of the huge crowds that had gathered. Of course, we were still recognized, but by the time we left, the main doors were mostly clear so it was only a few kids who stopped us for autographs and pictures.

The whole experience was so surreal. There were a few fans waiting at the Open, though most got to me as part of a package deal with Emerson and Ruby, the main attractions. But tonight I was on their level. I felt like a rock star.

Sergei went out and bought dinner while we finished up with fans. When we met up with him at the hotel, there were more people in the lobby waiting to meet us and the other gymnasts staying there. After about 20 minutes, Natasha finally led us to the elevators, apologizing to the crowds.

"They're starving, guys," she yelled over the noise. "And so am I."

By the time Ruby and I make our way into our room, it's almost 11. We invite Emerson in, and the three of us sit cross-legged on my bed going over the events of the day.

"I honestly can't believe it," I admit, referring to my ranking.

"Almost a point ahead of Maddy," Ruby laughs. "I wish I could've seen the look on her face when she saw. I bet it looked a bit like Emerson's face when she saw she was four tenths behind me. I *did* see that."

"Very funny," Emerson rolls her eyes. "Just remember it was only one day. We still have Saturday."

"I'm *so ready* for Saturday," I announce. "It's crazy how much of a motivator this was. Now all I care about is beating my score from today."

"Just do what you did today and you'll kick ass," Ruby smiles.

"Yeah, you got over the hump," Emerson adds. "Going down the mountain is way easier than going up."

We eat in silence for a few minutes, Ruby flipping through channels. Emerson's phone vibrates and she taps out what sounds like the world's longest response.

"Anyone interesting?" Ruby asks.

"No."

"Come on, spill," Ruby presses. "Secret lover? Long lost sister with a Lifetime movie background story? Drug dealer threatening to share your addiction with the world?"

"How do I shut her up without punching her in the throat?" Emerson looks at me, pleading for help.

"Yep, she's frustrating," I sigh, and then turn to Ruby, motioning for her to shut up.

"If you must know, it's my mom." She fake yawns. "I should go. I can't stay awake a second longer."

"Night, Em," I say, watching her disappear into the hallway and quietly close our door behind her. I get up and deadbolt it just to be safe.

"What was that all about?" Ruby laughs. "The best thing about Emerson is that she usually fights back. This Emerson is no fun."

"Come on, leave her alone," I warn. "Not everyone has it in them to match your levels of personality at all times."

"For real, do you know what's going on?"

"Yes," I finally say after a long pause. No use keeping this from Ruby. I mean, Maddy knows, and wants to use the info against her...at least this way, Ruby will at least understand that she has to be somewhat sensitive to what's going on.

I tell her what Emerson told me at our weird sleepover a couple weeks back, about her mom trying to make a buck off of her daughter and the subsequent threats that forced Emerson to change all of her contact info and move halfway across the country.

"Wow," Ruby exhales once I'm done. "No wonder Maddy was so excited to share the news of her mom being here. Emerson must know now, huh?"

"Yeah, I'd imagine if her mom is texting her, she probably has a clue."

"We should set her phone on fire or something so she can't text." Ruby stands up and angrily slams her copy of *People* on the desk. "Like, how dare her mother show up and mess with her head and try to ruin this for her? What a bitch."

"I didn't think you'd care this much about protecting Emerson."

"It's more about not wanting her to go through what I went through. To go into an Olympic year as the best in the country and then blow it because you're injured or there's something mentally messing with you? It's literally the worst thing that can happen as a gymnast. We may not get along and I wouldn't necessarily choose to hang out with her, but I wouldn't want anyone dealing with that heartbreak."

I can't think of anything to say. "I get it," I finally respond, and head to the bathroom to start unpinning my hair, which is one big mess of hair-spray, sticking out at every angle once out of the bun. "I'm taking a shower," I yell over the sound of the TV and the running water.

"Cool," Ruby yells back. "I'll probably be asleep when you come out. Awesome job again today, for cereal."

I smile to myself, and wait for the water to get hot. "Thanks, Rube. You too."

Right as I'm about to climb into the tub, my phone dings. I grab it with my dry hand and take a look, my heartbeat quickening. Somehow I know it's from Jack.

"You're probably getting ready for bed," it reads, "but you were serious-ly incredible today. I'm so proud of you. Just wanted to tell you that. FaceTime tomorrow?"

I stare at my phone until I feel bad for the amount of water I'm wasting. Every part of me wants to respond with my every feeling for him, feelings that have multiplied times a billion since the night he gave me his gifts, but I would feel so awkward. Like, especially over text. I think for a second and just type "Sure and omg you are the BEST, thank you!" I add a toothy smiley face emoji and then toss my phone to the counter before finally getting in the shower.

The pulsating stream feels amazing on my muscles, still tense from the meet, and I try to scrub Jack from my mind, instead focusing on the great *gymnastics* things that happened today. Hitting my routines. Killing it on beam. Finishing third. Kicking butt. And I'm gonna keep kicking butt all the way to Rio.

Friday, June 3, 2016
63 days left

"Vera would kill us all if she found out I was letting you go to the guys' meet, so once and for all, it's a no," Natasha says. "Sorry."

Ruby groans. "So we're locked up for the night, then?"

"Yes. Just chill out and enjoy it. Tomorrow's a big day. You'll be able to watch everything on TV anyway. I'll even get you some popcorn."

"Cool, no salt, no butter, no taste. That totally makes up for being imprisoned."

Natasha rolls her eyes and turns back to the margarita she's enjoying with dinner. The day has been low key and boring, with our meals, a workout in the hotel gym, and a brief walk around the river our only release. Otherwise we've been stuck in our room, though I have to admit I enjoyed the time off. It's basically how I spend my Sundays, lazy and relaxed.

I got to FaceTime with Jack for like ten minutes when he was up and getting ready for school, but it's not easy to carry on a conversation when Ruby, ahem, is screaming in the background, making herself laugh with her newly adopted Boston accent.

We finish eating dinner and I'm excited to get back to the room for a hot bath during the senior meet, which I'll watch from the tub with the door open. Yes, I am so excited about this bath. Bubbles, a cup of tea...I'm secretly 90 years old.

Emerson joins us in the deli where we buy a couple bags of fat-free no-butter popcorn and microwave them there. Ruby starts eating from her bag while Emerson and I wait for our shared bag to pop, causing

Emerson to stick up her nose.

"Don't be so disgusted," Ruby says, her mouth full. "It's a 100 calorie bag. It's like eating air."

"It's not *what* you're eating, but *how* you're eating. You're like a cartoon character."

"Whatever," Ruby retorts.

"There she is!" we suddenly hear a woman scream.

Emerson whips around to face the bar. "Oh, shit."

"What?" Ruby asks between bites, though Emerson doesn't respond. Her eyes are glued on this woman seated at the bar, surrounded by a flock of people. I know instantly. Her mother.

"Emerson, baby!" The very large and very Midwestern woman comes barreling toward us, Emerson stuck in stunned silence, Ruby continuing to munch popcorn.

"Mom. I thought you said you weren't gonna stop by until *after* the meet."

"I did! I didn't know you'd be here. Small world." Mrs. Bedford leans in for a hug.

"It's the host hotel, mom. What, were you just hanging out in the lobby hoping to catch me going past?

"Come on, Emerson, I'm just here having a drink with some friends."

"Yeah, I can smell it. Your breath is atrocious. And what friends? You don't know these people."

"We just met," her mom snaps. "You're being awfully rude. This is no way to talk to your mother, especially after disappearing and not even telling me."

"You know why I left," Emerson hisses. "I don't have time for this. I'll see you after the meet tomorrow. If you want to mooch more money from me, I actually need to win. Goodnight, *mother*."

Emerson storms off to the elevator. Her mother laughs, calling out, "what a diva!" I watch her run back to her "friends," none of whom heard the hushed conversation but are clamoring for details about the future Olympian.

"She had to go off and get her beauty rest," Mrs. Bedford says a little too loudly. "As if she needs it! She's a natural beauty. Pretty obvious she gets it from me!"

Ruby rolls her eyes. "Come on."

We run toward the elevator and storm down the hallway to her room.

"You okay, Em?" Ruby knocks but she doesn't respond. "Come on, it's just me and Mal."

The door opens and there's Emerson, her face tear-streaked. She's biting her thumbnail, the first sign of weakness I've ever seen her show in public.

"She wants to ruin my life," Emerson says after a minute of pacing back and forth.

"It's not that bad," Ruby tries to calm her. "So what, she brags about you to a bunch of random fans. I thought you wanted everyone to think you had the perfect life and the perfect family? What's more perfect than like, the most over-enthusiastic mom ever?"

"Believe me, a mother trying to steal money from you while getting drunk and saying God knows what to a bunch of random people isn't perfect."

"You're an adult. How does she have any control over your money?"

"She doesn't have control over my *money*, she has control over *me*. If I don't give her money, she threatens to go to the press. Empty threats, at least I think they're all empty, but I can't escape her. I move to Seattle, and she follows me to nationals. I can't deal with her now, not with finals tomorrow."

"So don't deal with her. Ignore her. Forget about today, do your job tomorrow, say hi to her after, and be done with it."

"It's not that simple!"

"I don't know what to tell you. I don't understand why this is stressing you out as much as it is."

Emerson sighs and starts rage-tidying her room. "All my mother has to do is tell the press one little detail about how my perfect existence isn't actually as perfect as people think, and bam, that's what the press focuses on. I just don't need it. Just having her here makes me stressed. I feel like I'm going to lose it. It's too distracting."

We're all silent for a minute, and then Emerson's phone starts to buzz.

"My mom," she says, staring at the many messages piling up on the screen. She swipes her screen and reads to herself. "She said she met a fan who can't believe Ruby beat me and said it's a bad omen and that my peak was last fall. See?! Who says that to someone the day before a competition?"

"*Ignore her*," I finally say. "Turn your phone off and push her out of your head. You can't let someone who clearly doesn't care about you, no offense, ruin what you've worked for from day one."

Emerson continues staring at her phone, trying to decide whether to respond. Ruby finally snatches it from her, throws it on the floor, and stomps on it. "Sorry, Emerson," she says. "I'll buy you a new one."

"Part of me wants to slap you but weirdly, I also want to hug you. And don't worry, that was the 6. I wanted to upgrade to the 6S anyway."

Ruby smiles. "We got your back, Em. Now take a bath, watch a terrible Lifetime movie, and go to bed. Remember, I was leading yesterday. You have a lot of tenths to make up if you want to beat me tomorrow."

"Just chill," I agree. "Remember when you forced me to do hot yoga against my will? Center yourself. Tomorrow's too important to throw away."

"Thanks guys, for real. I promise, I'll be fine by morning."

I follow Ruby out into the hallway and to our room. "Still wanna watch the men's meet?" she asks, turning the TV on once we're inside.

"Nah. I think I just wanna take a bath. Let me know if Max falls a lot. I think that'll boost my mood."

"You really don't like him, do you?" she asks with a smirk.

"Nope. Aside from his cuteness, he's kind of the worst."

"Well, I'm glad you realized it before you did something stupid, unlike every other girl who has ever met him."

I laugh. "I know there are guys out there who are both cute *and* sweet." I start to blush, and though I want to tell her about my newfound feelings for Jack, I decide it's not worth adding even more insanity to our already messy scenario. One distraction at a time.

I make a cup of chamomile tea, climb into the bath, and slide down into the bubbly water until I'm covered up to my chin. I do some deep breathing, feel my muscles melt, and try to clear my mind of absolutely everything but tomorrow.

Saturday, June 4, 2016
62 days left

Ruby and I opt for breakfast in our room the next morning, aiming to make this day as low-key as humanly possible, and that unfortunately means avoiding Emerson. We do meet up with her and our coaches at lunch, though, and she tells us straight out that she doesn't want Sergei to know.

"I'm fine," she whispers before we sit down. "I know Sergei will just stress me out more than I already am, asking me about how I feel and blah, blah, blah."

"Sorry again about your phone," Ruby says.

"No, really, I needed that. I kept getting texts from her but would have cut my thumb if I tried to swipe. I did get the sim card out...I'll just wait to get a new one when we get back to Seattle."

"Did you read any of the texts?" I ask.

"No. I told myself I'm not letting this mess with my gymnastics. If any-thing, I'll be better than ever. I'm going to absolutely destroy everyone tonight. Even you, Ruby. Sorry in advance."

"We'll see about that," Ruby laughs. "Don't think I'm gonna take it easy on you and let you win. And what about you, Miss 7.0 beam start value?"

"7.1, actually, and same. I'll be unstoppable."

"People are assholes," Ruby mutters. "Seriously. It's not like my own mother is trying to sabotage me, I can't imagine what special hell that is, but remember the press last year when I had a bad first day at nationals and they basically stalked me around the hotel trying to get me to snap?"

"Seriously," Emerson echoes. "But please, I don't even wanna talk about it. It's just gonna mess with my head, and I don't want the coaches asking questions."

"Coaches asking questions about what?" Natasha butts in, practically on cue.

"My phone," Emerson blurts. "I was taking picture of my view and dropped it out the window. It shattered into a billion pieces." Emerson is a fantastic liar. Even I believe her and I was there when Ruby smashed it.

"Yikes," Natasha says, totally oblivious. "At least it was the phone and not you!"

"She could have tumbled her way down and probably stuck the landing," Ruby laughs.

"Actually, some Dutch guy did that," Sergei adds. "We were at a party after a friendly meet back when I was competing, he was drunk, and he fell out of our hotel window three stories up. Did a couple of front tucks and landed on his feet. Walked away with a sprained ankle."

"Not surprising," Ruby shrugs. "Gymnasts are ninjas."

After Emerson's successful deflection of the conversation, Natasha gets serious. "I wanted to chat with you all a bit before you start getting ready to compete. Today's a big day."

"Most obvious statement ever made by a human being," Ruby grins.

"Shush. All three of you are going to make Olympic Trials no matter what," Natasha starts. "It's nice to have a national title but don't push yourselves past your breaking point. If something goes wrong, run with it. Don't stress. Move on and have fun. That's the best way to keep a small problem from turning into a catastrophe. I've been there. I've lost my mind in front of a huge crowd. It happens, and the more frustrated you get, the more you continue to implode. But if something happens, just think, like, 'I won't win the title or won't make the podium, but this competition isn't the big picture.' Because it's not. In five years, no one will remember who the medalists were at nationals. I'm sure we all know what the big picture *actually* is, what people will *actually* remember. I know you know this. I know you understand how to compete. But I also know that once you get this close to the Olympics, it becomes super easy to forget everything you know, no matter how good you are and no matter how many times you've competed before. So don't forget it."

We sit in silence for a moment, trying to fully absorb the power of Natasha's words.

"Thanks, coach," Ruby finally says. She gets up and gives her a hug. Emerson and I follow suit.

"You still have a couple of hours to chill before you need to start getting ready, so I'll leave you to it. But for what it's worth, I think you're all gonna be brilliant. Don't let anything make you think otherwise."

She doesn't know a thing about our hidden little drama, and yet her words are exactly what all three of us need to hear.

***

Our rotation group begins on floor tonight. Personally, I'm thrilled to get it out of the way early. The arena has this crazy tense energy, and it's making things weird. Normally during warm-ups there's a sense of camaraderie among the athletes; even though we know we're each other's competition, even with how tense it's been all week, we've still behaved like normal people.

Tonight it's way different. No one spoke above a whisper during general stretch. When a newbie fell out of a pirouette and stepped within two feet of Maddy practicing leaps, she totally lost it. Even the coaches were on edge, angrily yelling corrections across the floor instead of taking their gymnasts aside.

Thankfully, Ruby, Emerson, and I have had zero issues all afternoon. Our warm-up session is excellent, and I'm really thriving on the momentum from day one. Especially in terms of my confidence levels. I feel like an upperclassman walking the halls in a school full of freshmen, despite being a freshman myself.

I sit back with my iPod, eyes closed, when the rotation gets started. I'm fifth to go on floor, and with each exercise and judging period lasting about three or four minutes, I have at least 15 minutes to kill before I go. I'll just transport myself to another world until Natasha taps me to go on deck.

But I feel a tap only about ten seconds after the bell rings. I open my eyes and take out my earbuds. It's Leah.

"*What?*" I hiss, annoyed.

She looks visibly shaken. "Bailey. On vault."

I notice the arena is dead silent. I stand up and turn to face toward the end of the vault runway, on the opposite side of the arena. A gymnast in hot pink is on her back, one leg elevated, with several coaches and medical staff crowded around her.

It's Bailey Dawson. She does an Amanar and is usually great at it. It's the sole reason why she was on last year's worlds team.

"What happened?" I ask, my face pale.

"She tried a triple," Leah answers. "A triple freaking Yurchenko. She landed short and was still twisting as she hit the ground."

I put my earbuds back in and close my eyes, trying to drown out the deafening silence that comes with such a devastating injury. That'll be it for Bailey. She'll have a dislocation, a meniscus injury, an ACL or MCL tear...or some combination of these that will end her season, and probably her Olympic dream entirely. Years of back-breaking work and everything's over in a flash.

It's the same thing that happened to Ruby four years earlier, though it was the Achilles for her. I glance over to see how she's doing, and she's just shaking her head. She's up third on floor and is trying to stay warm as she waits. I don't think this will mess with her own performance, but I know I won't be able to watch.

Eventually Bailey is wheeled out of the arena, and I retreat back to my world to try to forget. I can still hear the floor music slightly over my own music, so I know when Ruby's up and I also know that she finishes when I hear the insane applause. I smile. Good. Nothing will faze her.

Leah's music starts, so I get up and start jumping up and down to get my muscles ready. I give Ruby a big hug, congratulate her even though I didn't see anything she did, and wait my turn, standing by the steps that lead up to the podium, head down, hands on my hips.

Finally, it's my turn. And because the human brain loves nothing more than sabotaging the person in which it lives, I have a flash of me on my back clutching my own knee on floor. Seriously, brain? While I wait for the green light, I imagine myself sticking everything, and mentally give the finger to my mind.

Green light, music starts, salute and smile. This is it.

My first pass, the double arabian, soars. I feel my legs glued together as I tumble forward, my hands grasping the backs of my knees. The landing on this skill is blind, meaning I don't have a view of the floor and have to rely on muscle memory to ensure I stick, but I do. And because my landing is so clean, I'm able to rebound back up into a wolf jump for the bonus tenth. I typically miss that connection, so I'm already doing better than usual.

The triple full is a tiny bit under-rotated and I have to take a step out to the side so I can steady the landing, but my leaps are superb, my triple pirouette gets applause, and I hit the double pike and double tuck with only the most minor of form issues. I still have a bit of choreography after the last pass, but I can't help grinning ear to ear as I finish up.

I not only hit, but had one of my best elite floor routines and I know the score will be great.

Natasha waits for me on the edge of the podium and gives me a big pat on the back. "Good job with that quick thinking on the wolf jump connection," she praises. "I knew you'd eventually get that. Now you'll never miss it. Your rotation on the triple was obviously off, as I'm sure you know. It looked like you were relying more on twisting quickly than on power, which can work but I'd rather you come in strong as well. Get a bit more punch out of the back handspring *and* twist fast. But overall, a solid routine. Keep doing it like this."

I run back to my seat Ruby's waiting for a high five. "Awesome. Just awesome. You are becoming fierce before our eyes."

This is just what I need to hear. I gulp some water and then bring up Bailey. "Did you hear any news?"

"No," she sighs. "A shame. No idea why they'd push the triple on her now. It's not like it would make her win. And now she'll never get to the Olympics, never get the chance to have it named for her. That's the kind of vault you save for event finals when you have nothing to lose but an individual medal."

I agree.

"Just try not to think about it, okay? It *will not happen to you.* I promise. Your skills are too solid for something like that to happen."

"No, I'm weirdly okay. Bummed for Bailey, obviously, but I know I'll be fine. I was more worried about you, because...well, you know."

"Ahhh yes, the Fall That Shall Not Be Named. Don't worry about that. That is the past, this is the now."

We hear Emerson's music start and turn to the podium to watch her routine. She's luminescent, performing her dramatic music with fire in her eyes. Her tumbling is perfect, and she's sharper than I've ever seen her.

"Jesus Christ," Ruby whispers.

"She needs mama drama at every meet," I whisper back and Ruby laughs. Emerson finishes to a standing ovation and waves to the crowd while descending the stairs to an insanely happy Sergei.

"Great, now I need to up my game," Ruby moans. "I thought this would be smooth sailing."

The change of rotation fanfare starts and we wait for Emerson before marching over to vault. We quickly hug and congratulate her, and then the three of us line up, looking like a badass team of champions. Because that's exactly what we are. Squad goals.

***

I spoke too soon. Of course bars would be my downfall.

It's not my downfall, really. It's just a minor, fixable mistake. I could feel myself starting to rush skills in the middle of the routine and after I caught my Gienger, I knew that if I kept going into the next segment I'd run into problems.

An extra swing isn't the end of the world. If anything, it kept me from making a big error, or worse, falling. But it is going to be a sizable deduction, and I can't help but get mad at myself.

The rest of the routine goes smoothly. I catch the Markelov and land the double front with just a tiny step, nothing more than a tenth, which won't matter at this point. Unless I lose out on a medal by a tenth, in which case I'll regret that step for a very long time.

"I know you think I'm annoyed with you right now, but I'm actually proud," Natasha says. "Quick thinking for the second time today! A few months ago you would have continued on at that horrific pace and spontaneously combusted. Are you otherwise happy with how you did?"

"Yes. I finished strong."

"You sure did. Now just go over your beam leaps and choreo on the sidelines before this rotation ends. You're so close, Mal. One routine closer to Olympic Trials."

Before this event, I stuck my Amanar on vault, and with beam left I know I'm still in the running for a medal. Bars isn't totally going to destroy me. Though I can't help hoping that Maddy makes mistakes, just to give me a bit of security.

I go over my beam routine in the space between the bars podium and the wall twice instead of once, figuring the last-minute extra practice can't hurt. We march over, go through the touch warm-up, and then since I'm second up, I take my spot on the side of the podium while Leah goes, keeping my eyes down because I just know she's going to fall and I don't want that in my head when I go up.

When it's my turn, Natasha comes up for a pep talk. "Have fun," is all she says, and I smile before climbing the stairs.

For such a difficult routine, I'm barely nervous. I can do this in my sleep, and sometimes dream about the sequences and connections. The first big test is the flight series, and I can feel that the layout is probably a bit piked, but I try not to let that rattle me. Bad form is bad form, but wobbles and falls show a lack of confidence and I'm reeling with self-esteem for once.

I pause for a split second longer than usual between my side aerial and Onodi, and don't think that'll be credited as a connection worthy of a bonus. And I don't get the punch I need off the end of the beam to get the tucks in the double arabian all the way around without cowboying my legs, pulling the knees apart to flatten my body so that it rotates faster in the air even though the leg form is incorrect.

Mistakes on my best event, but they're minor, and I'm still able to walk away from the podium with a smile on my face. I wave to every corner of the arena, trying not to cry from happiness. Without a doubt, I've made it to the Olympic Trials, just one competition away from the Olympic Games. I am so alive, and never want this feeling to go away.

Natasha doesn't even give me notes or corrections when we leave. "I'm so proud of you," she says, tears in her eyes, as we walk back to the seating area. She pats me on the back and then I get hugs from the rest of the girls in my rotation and a few from other rotations who have meandered over.

Because I'm done, I can watch Emerson go up next and Ruby finish things off. They've both been brilliant today, fighting with every particle of their minds, bodies, and souls. I don't think it's as much about the national champion title as it is about proving to themselves that they're the undisputed best.

For Emerson, it's knowing she's never lost a title and isn't about to start now. Winning titles in 2014 and 2015 wasn't easy, but the competition was definitely not as tough, so adding a third title when her rival is someone like Ruby would be a major win.

With Ruby, it's the thrill of returning from a major injury, a subsequent depression, and a rough comeback a year earlier. It's showing everyone – the press, the fans, her teammates, herself – that she didn't peak four years ago, and it's the realization that doing it all over again was worth it.

As Emerson waits to mount the beam, a woman screams, "that's my baby girl!" from the crowd. I look up and see her mother, standing in the very front row of the section facing the beam, only about 20 feet from Emerson.

"Now's the time, Emmy! This is it! Are you gonna be a winner or a loser? Are you gonna let the girl who didn't even make worlds last year beat you today?"

Ruby, trying to focus on her own routine coming up, shakes her head and puts in her earbuds. Elsewhere in the arena, floor music is playing and people are cheering for other routines so the outburst is at least somewhat contained, though Emerson in her silent preparation can certainly hear every word. Tuning out an entire arena is easy; we get so used competing with background noise, we actually need it to compete the way some people need to fall asleep with fans on.

But when someone screams out like that, making noise above the din, it stands out like a screaming baby on a red-eye flight, jolting you from your zone back into the real world. Basically, there's no way Emerson is tuning her mom out. I see pain in her eyes, her top teeth clamped down on her lower lip, her cheeks flushing slightly as she's given the green light.

When she mounts, I can see her breathing deeply, trying to forget the obnoxious cheering behind her. And she's mostly fine, but she's definitely shaky. Not good. Usually on beam, if I feel shaky I tend to bobble on every skill, which not only racks up deductions, but the more you bobble, the bigger of a chance you'll fall.

I hold my breath during her flight series, a tricky yet required combination of skills where we flip from one end of the beam to the next. Emerson's is especially tough – a first back handspring, a second back handspring, and a layout with a full twist. That layout full is one of the most difficult beam skills, and she has to do it after an already shaky routine under crazy pressure.

The first two skills are easy, she stays in line, and she gets nice air going into the layout full, keeping her body straight in the air as she twists. I see it coming apart a bit at the end, though...she's not twisting fast enough and has to really pull to get the last bit around, and by then, she's not in a good landing position.

The crowd gasps as one foot touches the beam before the other. I see her leg wobble as her back foot comes into join the front, and she's too far over to the side to grab on with her toes. She's a fighter, though. She tries throwing her weight over the beam, tries locking her back foot in place, tries flailing her arms to hold her balance...the struggle is interminable, like I'm watching in slow motion, until she finally has to give in.

Emerson simply drops to the mat, landing on her feet, no big overdramatic collapse for her. She puts both hands on the beam, leans forward like she's stretching her back, puts her head down, and breathes. Only the dismount is left after she re-mounts to supportive applause, and it's perfect. The crowd goes wild at her triumphant comeback, but Emerson storms off of the apparatus and out the arena door.

When Ruby goes up, she knows the title is hers. There's no way Emerson's going to win this thing with a fall. The crowd also knows, and they give her a standing ovation before she even mounts. They love Emerson, love what she's done in the sport over her career thus far, but Ruby came in as the underdog and crowds love underdogs. She's who they're pulling for.

Her whole routine is utter perfection, and before she even dismounts, the crowd is collectively on their feet once again. The cheers turn into an uproar when she sticks the full-in, and she responds the way any comeback queen would – a fist pump, a wave to the crowd, a leap from the podium into Natasha's arms, and tears streaming down her face for all of it.

I'm sobbing, too. What Ruby has just done is almost impossible in our sport, returning from major injury at 19 to win a national title and what will likely be a spot on the U.S. Olympic team. I feel gutted for Emerson, who worked her ass off only for her mother to ruin her night in her final routine, but like, she'll still probably go home with silver, so I feel justified in rooting for my best friend.

Ruby and Natasha run over to let me and Polina into the group hug.

"I actually frigging nailed everything," she gasps between huge, choking sobs. "I'm back, bitches!"

We wait until her score flashes for her win to be confirmed, holding hands and nervously jumping up and down.

"15.4 for Ruby Spencer on balance beam," the announcer says. "Ruby Spencer is the 2016 U.S. national champion with a total two-day score of 122.1."

Again, the crowd erupts, we continue our screaming and crying, and though I'm still celebrating with my team, I let my eyes roam to the big screen with the top eight in the rankings to see my own fate.

Top 8 After 8 Rotations

1. Ruby Spencer, Malkina Gold Medal Academy, 122.100
2. Emerson Bedford, Vanyushkin Gymnastics, 121.200
3. Maddy Zhang, Texas Tornadoes, 119.300
4. Charlotte Kessler, Windy City Gymnastics Club, 119.200
5. Amalia Blanchard, Malkina Gold Medal Academy, 119.000
6. Zara Morgan, Reynolds Gymnastics and Cheer, 118.300
7. Olivia Nguyen, Windy City Gymnastics Club, 117.100
8. Amaya Logan, Waimea Sports Center, 115.100

Fifth overall. I gulp, blinking back tears. Talk about an emotional roller-coaster.

There are no single day scores listed from today, just the overall total, but knowing my day one score, I'm able to subtract and see that I got a 58.7 for my all-around performance tonight. It's over a point less than Thursday's score, and without the mistakes I probably would have broken 60 and won bronze. Damn.

Maddy ahead of me isn't a surprise, and I don't think I would have been as upset with her getting the bronze medal had I placed fourth. But Charlotte in fourth? That's a blow.

I have no idea how she crept ahead of me. She was sixth on day one! She must have had an absolutely perfect day today, possibly her best ever.

"You okay?" Polina asks quietly. Natasha is now up on the beam podium celebrating with her superstar, Ruby Spencer, the 2016 U.S. national champion.

I wipe my eyes with the back of my hand and smile. "Yep. Totally fine. And happy. I did what I could. Other people just had a better meet."

"You were great. Don't even get it into your head that you weren't." She gives me a hug. "Now go congratulate everyone. You don't want the press calling you a sore loser, even though I know you're not."

I take a moment to gather my things, putting everything neatly in my bag, and then I put on my warm-ups, which we're required to wear for the medal ceremony. I push myself to think about the good in the situation. Like the national team. The top six all-arounders get automatic berths on the national team, meaning I've made it, no questions asked. I've also qualified to Olympic Trials. A year ago I didn't even qualify to nationals, so both of these things are huge deals and I really am thrilled, even with the sting of fifth place.

When I feel a bit better, I run up to the beam podium. Emerson has also joined in, celebrating her silver though I know she feels the same biting agony that I'm feeling. Nah, hers is much worse. She fell on one of her best events, she didn't defend her title, she ended her four-year winning streak, *and* there's that whole "my mother is a raving lunatic bitch" thing. But she's smiling, and if she can put on a happy face, so can I.

"Congrats, Ruby," she says, reaching out for a handshake though Ruby quickly pulls her in for a hug. "Before you get too cocky, you should know that I *would* have won without the fall, so technically this is a draw."

Ruby stares at her for a second with one eyebrow raised, and then breaks into spirited laughter, hugging Emerson tighter. "You're so much fun to beat," she yells over the crowd. "I can't wait to battle to the death with you again in Atlanta."

She turns to me and I open my arms wide for a hug. "I did it," she whispers, tears poised in her eyes and ready to fall. "I'm the best in the country again."

In that moment I forget about my own defeat. This is Ruby's day and nothing else matters.

***

The award ceremony takes forever. The top eight on each event and in the all-around are called up to the floor podium where we hug everyone a thousand times, receive flowers and medals from important-looking people, and have our photo taken by what looks like every photographer who has ever lived.

Aside from my national team spot and Olympic Trials qualification, the best part of my day is finding out I've won beam. I'm shocked, but Natasha isn't. "You have the highest start value by a mile," she says. "What do you expect?! Mistakes barely matter for you."

Winning the beam title is definitely an important achievement in terms of the Olympics, if only because now Vera knows for a fact that I'm the best on the event. It'll be hard to justify leaving me at home, even if my floor is weak and my bars aren't exactly cute.

After the final award is handed out, a voice over the loudspeaker tells everyone to stay put, as the national team and Olympic Trials qualifiers will be announced shortly.

Next to the floor podium are two large cardboard boxes. "Team USA tracksuits," Ruby whispers. "They do the official national team photo with us wearing these while holding our plaques and wearing our medals."

The girls who placed in the last all-around spots don't bother waiting around, Leah included. They know there's no hope, but a few in the middle of the pack stick around just in case. Vera hasn't left her perch at the USGA table by the media seating, but she's sent the athlete rep, a former gymnast who competed back in 2004, to read off the list of those of us who've made it.

"Spencer, Bedford, Zhang, Kessler, Blanchard, Morgan, Nguyen, Logan, Farrow, Kerr, Abrams, Turner, Borovskaya, Harper," she reads off. "Grab a set of warm-ups, put them on, and line up to go back up on the podium."

"Excuse me." One of the Logan twins, Nalani, sidles up to the athlete rep, looking a bit pale. "You said Logan, but were there two Logans? Or just one."

"Just one," the rep says, a bit softly as if it'll make it hurt less. "Amaya. Sorry."

Nalani nods, and starts to sob. Awkward. Her sister, also crying, gives her a hug though you can tell she's battling her emotions there, having placed eighth to make the team. Her sister, meanwhile, was borderline...the top 12 made the cutoff, and Nalani was 14th.

Top 12 all-arounders, that is, plus two more. Sophia Harper doesn't compete all-around, just bars and beam. But she's so good on both, she has a legit chance to make it as a specialist, so they couldn't leave her off. The only other specialist, Kara Lennon, went to the Olympics in 2012 but her two events are vault and floor, which just happen to be the best events for pretty much everyone on this team rendering her pretty much useless, so she doesn't make it.

Irina Borovskaya is the other one Vera names...she's more of a surprise addition, but not really, I guess. She fell four times on bars today, earning a 9.1 on the event. A pretty far fall, considering she won the gold medal at worlds last year. Because of her bars score, she only placed 17th, so Vera must have included her knowing the low ranking was a fluke, especially considering she was in the top eight on day one.

With our brand-new red, white, and blue uniforms on, we line up and are announced one by one back up on the podium, the first seven standing and the second seven kneeling in front of them. This will be the team photo. I used to print out the team photos each year when a new national team was named. I don't think I have to explain how surreal it feels to be in one.

"Ladies and gentlemen, the 2016-2017 U.S. women's national team!" the announcer's voice booms. "All members of the national team have been invited to attend the Olympic Trials in Atlanta at the end of this month."

Those remaining in the crowd cheer one final time, and then begin to disperse. We take a few more group photos, and then we're rushed off to interviews in the mixed zone once again.

"Congratulations, Amalia. You said before the meet you'd be happy with tenth. Do you think you'd still say that now that you've placed fifth?"

I know without looking that it's Anna Young, my nemesis. But I'm on such a high from the events of the evening, I'm not fazed by her. "I'm *thrilled*," I grin. "I achieved all of my goals this week. Top five, national team, Olympic Trials. Nothing could feel better."

"Not even a medal around your neck?"

I hold up my beam gold as a response, smirk, and then turn to face someone else, effectively shutting down Ms. Bitch.

The rest of the questions are broad and easy...how does it feel to make the national team for the first time, what was the most memorable part of the meet, what are your goals for Olympic Trials, are you doing anything to celebrate? Some are repeated when people I haven't yet spoken to wander over to me, but I answer everyone happily and without sass.

After ten minutes, the media coordinator cuts everyone off and lets us head back to the floor where we take selfies and gather up all of our things while a tech crew takes down the bars and beam to put up some of the men's apparatuses for tomorrow.

The whole post-meet process is more exhausting than the meet itself, so I'm thrilled when we get the go-ahead to leave the arena. By now, pretty much everyone has cleared away from the main doors, so we're free to escape without too much of a bombardment.

"Who wants froyo?" Sergei asks as we're halfway back to the hotel.

"You're serious?!" Ruby squeals. "We get to have a frozen treat that isn't a popsicle or *ice*?"

"You earned it. All of you. Cups, though. No cones."

"We didn't earn the cones," Emerson pouts. I *think* it's fake, but you never know with her.

The delicious, creamy frozen yogurt is mind-blowingly good, and we scarf it down like we're newly-released prisoners enjoying our first taste of freedom in 20 years. Heaven.

"Tomorrow we'll meet for ten minutes before the team meeting," Natasha decides. "I'll go over performances and notes and future goals then. Enjoy tonight, but don't stay up too late. Watch a movie or something and try to chill out. Remember, this wasn't it. You still have trials. But we *will* have a celebratory dinner next weekend, because what you guys did was awesome."

Ruby, Emerson, and I decide to hang out in our room for a bit before bed. We're all exhausted but we're also mentally jacked up from the whole experience and won't be sleeping anytime soon. Our coaches head upstairs while we sign for a few people in the lobby, and then we finally reach the elevator, thrilled to finally change from leos into pajamas.

When the elevator door slides open on the sixth floor, there are a couple of people standing near our doors, including a guy. I assume it's Sergei, checking to see if we made it back safely after facing the lobby mob, but when he turns toward us I stop dead.

Because it's not Sergei. It's Jack.

***

"*Jack!*" I scream, running up and giving him an overzealous hug. He looks a bit taken aback. I never greet him like this, but I'm just so shocked and thrilled to see him, I don't think I can hold back even if I tried.

"Hi kiddo," my dad says, clearing his throat. I run to hug him and my mom, who is holding flowers for me. "Fifth best in the country!"

"We were going to see if you wanted to get something to eat tonight, but we understand if you want to celebrate with *friends*," my mom says with a knowing wink. "We'll just do breakfast in the morning."

"Yeah, anything sounds good, breakfast is good," I respond, flustered. My parents congratulate Emerson and Ruby while Jack gives me another hug.

"I can't believe you're here," I say shyly, not wanting to pull away. "I wanna know all about San Francisco."

Jack laughs. "Please, tonight is all about you. But I did win a prize at the workshop...a thousand bucks for a programming contest. The second I got home I had my parents book a flight."

"Wow. That's...no one's ever done anything like that for me. Congrats on the contest."

"Thanks."

We stand awkwardly for a minute, watching my parents and teammates continue with the formalities. Ruby turns to say hi to Jack, I introduce him to Emerson, and we all stand in a little huddle until Ruby decides it's time to break things up.

"I know this hallway is a magical place, but I'm gonna change," Ruby announces. "As much as I love wearing a leotard for hours on end, if I don't change soon I'm going to need it surgically removed from my butt."

"Lovely," Emerson groans. "I'm going too. Nice meeting you, Jack. Goodnight, everyone."

"Tell me all about this whole Jack thing later," Ruby whispers as she walks to our room, winking.

"We'll leave you kids to it," my dad says, leading my mom down toward the elevator. "I'm so proud of you, Mal. See you for breakfast in the morning?" I nod, and they leave.

"So," Jack starts. "It's so weird talking to you right now."

"Yeah," I agree. "*Why*?"

"I don't know," he laughs nervously. "Maybe because we're having a conversation in the middle of a hotel hallway."

"Whenever I watch movies where the characters are being awkward and stupid because they have feelings for each other, I always get so annoyed. Like, wouldn't the world be a better place if everyone could just say how they felt and didn't drag things out? 90 percent of movies wouldn't exist if people were just honest from the start. I like you, you like me, bam, let's get married, or I like you, you don't like me, too bad, onto the next one, you know?"

"We're being weird because we are afraid to say we like each other?" he asks, his eyes meeting mine for a split second before darting away.

"I mean, in general, not like…" I am hardcore blushing, trying to get myself out of this until I realize there's no point. I'd just be going against everything I literally just said. "No, screw it. I'm sick of skirting around everything and being shy and not saying what's on my mind. I think the video you made was one of the best things anyone has ever done for me and maybe I never saw you as anything more than a friend until that moment because I'm oblivious and blind because you're like one of the only good guys in the world, but the fact is I like you a lot and please say something because I'm babbling and don't know what else to say."

Jack bites his lip. "It's about time."

"About time what?"

"I've only had a crush on you since kindergarten."

"You did not."

"Remember when we were five and in your backyard with that kid who used to live down the street?"

"No?"

"Well, a gigantic bee was swarming around all of us. You and that kid, I can't even remember his name, were trying to be really tough saying you weren't afraid of bees but I was terrified and wanted to get the hell out of there. The other kid kept trying to impress you by going near the hive. He even told you he was friends with them and he had pet bees at home. Seriously, what a douche. Eventually a million bees started swarming, and I pulled you away and pushed you to the ground and covered you and I ended up getting stung but you were fine and you kept saying I saved your life."

"*How* do you remember this?!"

"It's the first time I felt, like, wow, here's someone not in my family and I love her," he kind of mumbles. "Obviously *love* back then had a different meaning, but I can't remember ever not having a crush on you."

My mind feels like it's been put through a blender. How is it possible I've missed ten years of signs and signals and clues into his affection? Gymnastics, that's how. I've been so obsessed with this sport and my career, my training, my competitions, my preparation...when I look at where I am right now, two months away from the Olympics with a realistic chance at making the team, I don't regret any of the sacrifices or choices I've made. But I do feel tremendous guilt for ignoring the people in my life who matter.

"Jack..."

"Listen," he exhales. "I don't know a lot about sports but I know how important it is for you to make it to the Olympics. I know how hard you've worked. I'm not like that asshole Max who thinks girls should drop what they love for a guy. But I do like you a lot, so...do what you want with that info."

"Jack," I start again. "I like *you* a lot, and it's super new for me. And yeah, I'm trying to make it to Rio and I have finals next week and there's so much to think about and I can't handle it all at once. You're like the only constant in my life and I need you to be my friend, the way we've always been friends."

"I get it," he sighs. "I'm sorry, I didn't want to make you feel like..."

"You didn't make me feel like anything. I like you all on my own. And even though I'm not ready for a relationship or dating or anything right now, I want 'someday' to be a possibility."

"Yeah," he smiles. "Someday. Take your time. I've waited ten years. I think I can wait two more months."

We're silent for a minute, watching a couple walk arm in arm back to their room, so in love they're oblivious to everyone around them.

"I better go," Jack bites his lip. "I gotta get back to my roommates. Your parents."

"That sounds creepy."

"They're treating me like a son. So, yeah, if we do become something *someday*, I guess it is pretty creepy."

I giggle, we share another quiet moment, and I take out my key to swipe into my room. "Goodnight, Jack."

"Bye, Mal. Congrats again." He disappears down the hallway, and I wait until he's gone before I push into my room. Ruby's sprawled on her bed in jeans and a white tank top, a giant grin on her face.

"You guys lovebirds yet? I've been waiting years for this day."

"How is it that even you knew before me? You, my parents, Jack, obviously..."

"You may seem mature in many ways, young Mal, but in other ways you're ten years old," she smiles. "No offense. But yeah, you're pretty clueless. It's okay. It's cute. You're getting there. So what happened?"

"Nothing, really. Just...we talked. I'm tired," I yawn, trying to emphasize my point, even though I know I probably won't get much sleep tonight. Silly brain. "Can we talk about it tomorrow? I need to go to bed. Who schedules a national team meeting at 8 a.m.?!"

"Chill. We'll talk tomorrow. I'm gonna go get a snack or something...you want something before bed?"

I shake my head. "I'm gonna start packing."

"K, I'll be back in a bit."

She leaves, so naturally, that's when I realize I'm hella thirsty. I grab a few stray dollar bills, run to the door, and look toward the elevator hoping to catch her, but she's not there and I'm too lazy to go downstairs. I'll drink from the sink.

When I turn around to go back in, I spot her standing outside of another hotel room. I hold my breath, 99% certain of what I'm about to see, but a tiny part of me still holds out for the hope that I'm wrong.

The door opens, and what I fear is confirmed. It's Sergei.

He reaches down to hug her and she begins speaking animatedly, though I can't hear what she's saying because they head into his room. I quietly shut the door behind me, climb into bed, and angrily hug a pillow. Today was a mess of emotions and I've been everywhere from crushed to elated in the span of seconds. I've dealt with it all, some on national television, and made it through with only minimal scarring...but this is the final nail in the coffin. My best friend is lying to me.

Sunday, June 5, 2016
61 days left

"Congratulations again, ladies," Vera says, her lips in a tight smile, looking more like she's addressing guests at a funeral than a room full of potential Olympians. "This is a great accomplishment, and whether you make the Olympic team or not, you should be proud of getting this far. The Opening Ceremonies are exactly two months from today, and though we have a lot of work to do, I'm confident that anyone in this room would be able to represent the United States on a high level."

The meeting was all business, mostly for parents and coaches. We received national team handbooks, discussed everything related to the Olympic Trials, and got instructions for setting up direct deposit for our national team stipends. $2000 a month to cover training, travel, and other related expenses makes me feel like I've hit the lottery, but I know it's a small consolation after the enormous funds my parents have funneled into my career over the years.

"I still can't believe this," my dad sighs, shaking his head as he signs document after document. "I don't think college acceptance packages have a paper trail this insane. Remind me again why we put you in this sport?"

This is the only time I've been able to spend with my parents since they got here, aside from brief hugs and congratulations at the hotel last night. They're totally overwhelmed by the whole ordeal.

"There," he says, signing the last form with a flourish. "Go turn this in so we can *eat*."

I gather everything, slip it back into the file, and turn it into Miriana Sundstrom, the woman who runs the administrative side of the national team. She gives me a smile, congratulates me, and we're free.

"Enjoy lunch!" Natasha gives me a hug. Ruby's already out the door with her parents, off to wake up her brothers so she can get her celebration started. I haven't said a word to her about Sergei. When she came in two hours after "going to get something at the deli" last night, I pretended like it was a normal amount of time for an errand like that and kept my mouth shut.

I spot Emerson on my way out, legs curled under her and balancing a clipboard on her knees. She's there with her agent, who meticulously scrutinizes every piece of paper before allowing her to sign it. No idea why. It's mostly like "I agree to not post stupid things on social media." And yet someone will inevitably post something stupid on social media.

I feel bad she has no family here, and want to ask if she wants to join us for breakfast when she's done, but I chicken out at the last minute and I don't know why.

"Bye," I utter meekly as we walk past. "See you at the airport."

She gives me a little wave but doesn't take her eyes from her paperwork.

"So, how's your new life?" I grin at my dad once we're outside. After seeing Emerson's nonsense family situation up close and personal, I'm almost too thankful for my normalsauce parents.

"Oh, you know. I already have a secret family," he laughs. "Come on, it's boring. This is about you, Miss National Beam Champion. Where do you want to eat? Your choice, but preferably somewhere in a one-minute radius. I can't function a second longer without bacon.

"I tried texting Jack, by the way," my mom adds. "I think he's still asleep. Teenagers."

I'm relieved, to be honest. I'm happy I spoke from the heart last night, but now I'm in one of those hangovers of awkwardness, regretting everything I said and wishing I just kept my mouth shut so everything would be normal.

I find a nearby diner on my phone and we start walking over, my parents chattering excitedly about everything they've been dying to say since the meet.

"I knew this was serious, I knew you wouldn't have been invited to such a big meet if you weren't the real deal, but I had no idea you were...well, one of the best in the country! The Olympics, Amalia! It feels like a dream." My dad pulls me into a side hug and I can't help the smile that spreads over my face.

"I didn't either," I admit. "Not until recently, anyway."

"Do you know many gymnasts train in this country? I googled it. It's like, a hundred thousand. And you're in the top five. That's almost impossible. We're so proud of all of the work you've done to make it happen. The top *five*."

"Dad, stop before my ego explodes. You're gonna really regret it if I go full-out diva on you."

My parents laugh. "Don't worry, we've already hired a full-time limo driver and from now on, school is optional," my mom says.

"Please, there are actually girls here who have that as their reality. One girl's dad flew her and her coaches here on a private jet. She's not even that good!"

"Well, she might have a private jet, but you have the gold medal," my dad responds. "That, and you're a great kid, and I know you won't make any bad decisions or turn into a nightmare when you make it big." He gives my mom a glance, and she nods.

"Amalia," she starts. She pulls a business card out of her purse, but hesitates before handing it over. "An agent approached your coach after the meet. Natasha gave us her card, along with some advice about going pro. We know how hard you worked to get an NCAA scholarship, so we don't want to see you just throw those offers out the window. But we also know how many incredible opportunities exist for gymnasts at this level."

She hands it to me, and I stare while my dad continues. Tania Tolino. ProSport Talent. New York.

"We trust you. It will be your decision in the end. But Natasha also told us some horror stories – girls giving away their NCAA eligibility the second an agent approaches them, but then not making it to the Olympics and never hearing another word about endorsements."

"Look at Ruby," my dad adds. "Everyone thought she was going to be a star, she signed with an agent when she was 15, and then she got hurt and nothing more came out of it. Well, until now, I'd guess. I don't want to talk you out of it, but I do want you to use common sense. Maybe wait a bit and see where you end up before you decide. Talk to your friends who have had to make the decision before."

"I don't even wanna go pro," I whisper after a moment. And I didn't, until about five seconds ago. Now that this little card is making it real, my mind is racing with the possibility.

"Don't think about it right now," my mom says, taking the card away. "Enjoy the rest of the day. But know that you've done something big here, and now things are going to be very different. Natasha warned us. Whether we want things to change or not, we need to be prepared."

"You're a big deal now, kiddo," my dad pats me on the back.

We're seated at a booth in the diner and the whole world is bustling around me, forks clanking against dishes, waitresses yelling orders, my parents going over their every thought about last night's meet, but as usual, I'm lost in my own brain.

I've worked so hard for this and now here comes the payoff. Literally. Agents knocking on the door, endorsement deals worth hundreds of thousands of dollars at my fingertips, living in the limelight...if I make the Olympic team, life as I know it will cease to exist.

This is my first time truly letting it sink in that the Olympic Games aren't like a competition you finish and then life goes back to normal. Gymnasts turn from nobodies to superstars overnight after competing at that level. Everything changes in an instant. I really have no idea what I'm getting myself into, and I'm absolutely terrified at the thought of facing this great new unknown.

But underneath my fear, there's a spark of excitement. I'm ready for whatever's going to happen, even if I feel like I have no clue. I'll just keep doing what I know how to do. Train. Compete. Win. Everything else is just background noise. That includes Jack, sadly, but he'll be there when it's all over.

"You ready?" I look up. It's our waitress, asking if I'm ready to decide between waffles or eggs, not whether I'm ready to take on the big and scary world, but either way, I have an answer. I push aside the menu I haven't touched, smile, and reply.

"I'm ready."

Results

National Team Camp Verification – April 15, 2016

Rank	Athlete	VT	UB	BB	FX	AA
1	Ruby Spencer	15.9	14.8	15.3	15.1	61.1
2	Maddy Zhang	16.0	14.2	14.6	15.5	60.3
3	Emerson Bedford	15.8	13.9	15.1	15.4	60.2
4	Amalia Blanchard	15.8	14.7	15.6	13.9	60.0
5	Irina Borovskaya	14.8	15.6	15.4	14.0	59.8
6	Zara Morgan	16.1	14.4	13.6	15.2	59.3
7	Charlotte Kessler	15.1	14.7	14.4	14.5	58.7
8	Bailey Dawson	15.7	14.5	14.1	14.1	58.4
9	Olivia Nguyen	14.3	15.0	14.4	14.2	57.9
10	Amaya Logan	14.3	13.6	14.1	14.6	56.6
11	Brooklyn Farrow	15.4	12.9	14.7	13.1	56.1
12	Nalani Logan	13.8	13.3	14.4	14.3	55.8
13	Kaitlin Abrams	13.5	14.1	14.5	13.6	55.7
14	Sophia Harper	-----	15.5	15.3	-----	30.8

American Open – May 14, 2016

Rank	Athlete	VT	UB	BB	FX	AA
1	Maddy Zhang	15.6	13.7	14.1	15.6	59.0
2	Amalia Blanchard	15.4	14.6	15.4	13.5	58.9
3	Charlotte Kessler	14.9	15.1	13.9	14.8	58.7
4	Zara Morgan	15.9	14.9	12.9	14.9	58.6
5	Bailey Dawson	15.6	14.1	14.1	14.6	58.4
6	Irina Borovskaya	14.6	15.3	14.4	14.0	58.3
7	Olivia Nguyen	14.4	14.9	14.7	14.1	58.1
8	Nalani Logan	15.1	13.4	14.4	14.7	57.6
9	Amaya Logan	14.4	13.9	14.1	14.7	57.1

10	Kaitlin Abrams	13.7	14.6	14.4	14.2	56.9
11	Beatrice Turner	13.9	14.2	14.3	13.9	56.3
12t	Madison Kerr	14.8	12.7	13.9	14.7	56.1
12t	Brooklyn Farrow	15.6	13.1	14.4	13.0	56.1
14	Caroline Lockwood	14.7	14.3	12.3	14.5	55.8
15	Carly Weinstein	14.1	14.2	13.8	13.5	55.6
16	Laura Siegel	13.3	14.8	13.6	13.2	54.9
17	Hannah Portman	13.7	12.1	14.1	14.3	54.2
18	Leah Manning	13.9	14.1	13.0	13.1	54.1
19	Danielle McIntyre	14.0	12.9	13.5	13.5	53.9
20	Joanna Price	14.9	13.7	11.4	13.3	53.3
21	Kate Lindley	14.2	13.3	12.0	13.1	52.6
22	Addison Webster	13.3	12.6	13.4	13.0	52.3
23	Elise Connor	13.6	13.1	11.8	13.4	51.9
24	Mackenzie Graham	13.9	12.9	12.7	12.3	51.8
25	Sophie Zeman	13.4	13.0	12.1	12.6	51.1
26	Nora Isherwood	12.7	13.5	11.8	12.4	50.4
27	Olivia Fischer	14.1	10.6	11.9	13.1	49.7
28	Emerson Bedford	15.9	-----	-----	14.8	30.7
29	Ruby Spencer	-----	15.4	15.1	-----	30.5
30	Sophia Harper	-----	15.6	14.8	-----	30.4
31	Kara Lennon	14.8	-----	-----	14.4	29.2

U.S. National Championships Day 1 – June 2, 2016

Rank	Athlete	VT	UB	BB	FX	AA
1	Ruby Spencer	15.8	15.3	14.9	15.3	61.3
2	Emerson Bedford	15.7	15.6	15.0	14.6	60.9
3	Amalia Blanchard	15.7	14.6	15.8	14.2	60.3

4	Maddy Zhang	15.9	14.3	14.3	15.1	59.6
5	Zara Morgan	16.0	15.1	13.5	14.7	59.3
6	Charlotte Kessler	14.9	14.6	14.3	15.1	58.9
7	Bailey Dawson	15.6	14.3	14.4	14.3	58.6
8	Amaya Logan	14.5	14.1	14.5	15.2	58.3
9	Irina Borovskaya	14.9	15.3	13.7	14.2	58.1
10	Olivia Nguyen	14.1	14.7	14.3	14.5	57.6
11	Madison Kerr	15.1	13.1	14.2	13.9	56.3
12t	Beatrice Turner	13.7	13.6	14.1	14.3	55.7
12t	Brooklyn Farrow	15.4	12.1	14.2	14.0	55.7
14	Caroline Lockwood	14.9	14.6	13.5	12.1	55.1
15	Kaitlin Abrams	13.8	14.2	13.5	13.2	54.7
16	Hannah Portman	13.5	13.9	12.7	14.2	54.3
17	Leah Manning	14.1	13.4	12.9	13.3	53.7
18	Nalani Logan	14.8	12.2	13.7	12.9	53.6
19	Carly Weinstein	13.9	11.4	14.2	13.3	52.8
20	Laura Siegel	13.6	13.4	12.4	13.1	52.5
21	Sophia Harper	-----	14.4	14.6	-----	29.0
22	Kara Lennon	15.0	-----	-----	13.4	28.4

U.S. National Championships Day 2 – June 4, 2016

Rank	Athlete	VT	UB	BB	FX	AA	Total
1	Ruby Spencer	15.7	14.8	15.4	14.8	60.7	122.1
2	Emerson Bedford	15.9	15.4	13.7	15.3	60.3	121.2
3	Maddy Zhang	15.9	14.5	13.9	15.4	59.7	119.3
4	Charlotte Kessler	15.1	15.1	14.8	15.3	60.3	119.2
5	Amalia Blanchard	15.7	13.6	15.1	14.3	58.7	119.0
6	Zara Morgan	16.1	14.9	12.8	15.2	59.0	118.3
7	Olivia Nguyen	14.9	15.1	14.8	14.7	59.5	117.1
8	Amaya Logan	14.7	13.4	14.3	14.4	56.8	115.1

9	Brooklyn Farrow	15.6	13.7	13.3	14.3	56.9	112.6
10	Madison Kerr	15.0	13.9	12.2	13.8	54.9	111.2
11	Kaitlin Abrams	13.9	14.1	13.8	14.4	56.2	110.9
12	Beatrice Turner	13.9	13.8	14.5	12.7	54.9	110.6
13	Caroline Lockwood	15.0	13.1	13.7	13.4	55.2	110.3
14	Nalani Logan	14.9	14.3	13.5	13.9	56.6	110.2
15	Hannah Portman	13.6	13.9	14.1	13.9	55.5	109.8
16	Carly Weinstein	14.1	13.7	13.4	13.6	54.8	107.6
17	Irina Borovskaya	14.7	9.1	11.5	13.9	49.2	107.3
18	Laura Siegel	13.8	13.2	13.1	13.0	53.1	105.6
19	Leah Manning	14.0	12.5	12.4	12.5	51.4	105.1
20	Sophia Harper	-----	15.3	14.5	-----	29.8	58.8
21	Bailey Dawson	0.0	-----	-----	-----	0.0	58.6
22	Kara Lennon	14.9	-----	-----	14.1	29.0	57.4

Key: VT – vault, UB – uneven bars, BB – balance beam, FX – floor exercise, AA – all-around

Please note that the total score listed under the day two national championships results combines the day one and day two all-around scores.

The Elite Gymnasts and Their Gyms

Ann Arbor Aerials – Ann Arbor, Michigan

Danielle McIntyre

California Dreaming – San Diego, California

Olivia Fischer
Kate Lindley

Dallas All-Star Gymnastics – Dallas, Texas

Addison Webster
Sophie Zeman

Great Plains Gymnastics Club – Kimball, Nebraska

Elise Connor
Madison Kerr

Gym Starz – Palo Alto, California

Mackenzie Graham
Kara Lennon
Joanna Price

Gymnastics Academy of Houston – Houston, Texas

Caroline Lockwood

Los Angeles Elite – Los Angeles, California

Hannah Portman
Carly Weinstein

Malkina Gold Medal Academy – Seattle, Washington

Amalia Blanchard
Ruby Spencer

Nashville Gymnastics Academy – Nashville, Tennessee

Sophia Harper
Laura Siegel

Reynolds Gymnastics & Cheer – Norman, Oklahoma

Zara Morgan
Beatrice Turner

Sawyer-Burke Athletics – Newton, Massachusetts

Kaitlin Abrams

South Florida Gymnastics Academy – Jupiter, Florida

Leah Manning

Texas Tornadoes – Lubbock, Texas

Brooklyn Farrow
Nora Isherwood

Vanyushkin Gymnastics – Seattle, Washington

Emerson Bedford

Waimea Sports Center – Waimea, Hawaii

Amaya Logan
Nalani Logan

Windy City Gymnastics Club

Irina Borovskaya
Bailey Dawson
Charlotte Kessler
Olivia Nguyen
Maddy Zhang

Acknowledgments

When I was a kid, a woman at my piano studio asked me what I wanted to be when I grew up. Like most kids, I said something crazy – "an actor and a writer." This woman laughed in my face and said "dream on" before telling me to find something more realistic.

Thankfully, my parents brought me up to love books, and bought me tons of books featuring badass girls who go after what they want. Kristy Thomas, Laura Ingalls, Francie Nolan, Sally Freedman, Jo March, Harriet M. Welsh, Matilda Wormwood...from a very early age, they taught me to be fearless. Instead of listening to that stranger's "advice" I became infuriated and she only made me want the impossible even more. Almost 20 years later, I've done both of my dream jobs professionally, and I may not be the greatest or most successful at either but nothing feels better than doing what you love. So thank you, fictional people, for making me confident and scrappy and bossy and passionate, and thank *you*, stranger lady, for adding fuel to my fire with your doubt instead of putting it out. If I can give one piece of advice, it's to always spend your life doing what *you* love, not what you think you *should* be doing.

An immense thank you goes to everyone on the gymternet for believing in this project from day one. The past 18 months of planning and writing and creating have been intense but whenever I wanted to toss everything in the trash, your support and interest and excitement has meant the world in helping me continue going.

My fabulous friends who read early incarnations and rough drafts, your input, advice, and problem-solving ideas have been invaluable. Jennifer Iacopelli was the first to take a look and though I was thrilled to hear she *loved* it, her critique was even more valuable. Thanks also to Carrie Wasserman who gave her "non-gym fan" perspective, Joe Rinaldi who helped catch errors at the last minute and of course, my multi-tasking agent/editor/lawyer/pal Holly Glymour who red-penned it up like a champion. Also, all four of these early readers caught the personal anecdote I slipped into these pages and fully called me out on it despite never having heard the story, so thanks being correct in your assumption that I am a disaster of a human being.

I wouldn't have made it through this book (or this life, let's be honest) without Bekah Harbison, Sarah Keegan, Jackie Klein, and Emily Marver entertaining and inspiring me every day (and Joe Rinaldi, you get another mention, four for you, Glen Coco). Whether we're ranting about gymnastics or debating global politics or making fun of literally everyone or just sending ridiculous gifs, our epic group text is #squadgoals. No one is more passionate or knowledgeable about gymnastics than these fine humans and I am blessed to know you all.

Jessica O'Beirne, Mark Bajus, Dvora Meyers, Cordelia Price, Lauren Collins, Emily Logan, Christy Linder, Elizabeth Grimsley, Brigid McCarthy, Izzi Baskin, Sara Dorrien-Christians, Beatrice Gheorghisor, Wendy Bruce Martins, Anne Josephson, Valeria Violi, Kensley Behel, Blythe Lawrence, Rick McCharles, and probably a thousand more of you inspire me with your own talent and passion and friendship. Every gymnast, coach, and parent I've had the pleasure of interacting with over the years, you were the inspiration for this book and frankly I want to be all of you when I grow up.

Finally, to my family...mom and dad for supporting me in whatever I wanted even if they didn't always agree, for encouraging me to do the things I loved, for driving me to rehearsals and performances and auditions and ballet and tap and voice lessons and piano and flute and karate and every sport I was terrible at (really, *basketball*?), for sacrificing evenings and weekends, I was the luckiest. My brother Ricky and my sister Sarah (who did the fabulous cover design) have also been incredibly supportive and I love you all so much!

About the Author

Lauren Hopkins began writing about gymnastics for *The Couch Gymnast* in July 2010, and spent four years there as the U.S. expert while also contributing to *International Gymnast* magazine, GymCastic, and as a guest on several blogs. In 2014, she created her own website, *The Gymternet*, now one of the most popular gymnastics sites providing exclusive coverage for the most enthusiastic gym nerds. A New England native, Lauren is a 2014 graduate of Columbia University. She currently lives in New York City and she loves the Red Sox unconditionally.

www.laurenhopkinsbooks.com

FINDING OUR BALANCE